Praise for *Malicious Intent*

'Comparisons with Patricia Cornwell and Kathy Reichs are inevitable . . . *Malicious Intent* is the most exciting crime fiction from Australia for a long time.'

The Times

'Patricia Cornwell's forensic fantasies may have cooled, but Fox's morgue-talk promises to plug the gap with a crime debut that nicely marries the personal life of the sleuth with that of the murder victim' *Independent*

'*Malicious Intent* will keep you gripped from start to finish. Author Fox displays the deft hand of a natural writer, whether she's weaving her break-neck plots, imparting fascinating medical and police procedural details or breathing life into her characters – both good and bad. What a compelling new talent!' Jeffery Deaver

'Kathryn Fox has created a forensic physician who readers of Patricia Cornwell will adore.' James Patterson

'Fox is stomach-churningly good.' *Mail on Sunday*

'If you like a tale written like a violent film, this fast-paced novel will do the job' *Washington Post*

'Meticulously researched and seamlessly plotted, *Malicious Intent* marks out Kathryn Fox as a name to watch.'

Crime Time

'Fox forgoes conventional plot twists for far darker ones that are genuinely surprising.' *Baltimore Sun*

'It is a wonderful moment when you track down something that's really worth reading. And Kathryn Fox's first novel, *Malicious Intent*, is just that. A forensic thriller, it has just the right balance of pathological detail and tight plotting. Think *ER* meets *CSI: Crime Scene Investigation* . . . Gripping from its very first page, it carries you breathlessly through its deftly plotted twists and turns'
Vogue (Australia)

'Forensically speaking, *Malicious Intent* is top-notch in its genre'
Sunday Telegraph (Sydney)

'A finely crafted novel.'
Sydney Morning Herald

'Watch out Patricia Cornwell. Kathryn Fox's experience in forensic medicine gives authenticity to *Malicious Intent* without making it too drily scientific . . . an assured literary debut.'
Gold Coast Bulletin

'The plot is original and engaging . . . has obviously been well researched. Fox has created an appealing character, whose personal life and family background set a good basis for any future novels in a series . . . I look forward to reading the next one.'
Goodreading

'*Malicious Intent* is . . . much better than anything Cornwell has written lately, and much superior to anything Reichs has ever written. Fox may be a medical practitioner, but she knows how to write decent prose, create sympathetic characters and pace a thriller, and she keeps the reader turning the pages. It's all very unsettling and deeply satisfying.'
Australian Book Review

'Highly recommended reading.'
Daily Telegraph (Australia)

Also by Kathryn Fox

Malicious Intent
Without Consent

About the author

Kathryn Fox is a medical practitioner with a special interest in forensic medicine. She is the author of the internationally bestselling and critically-acclaimed thrillers, *Malicious Intent* and *Without Consent*.

Her debut novel, *Malicious Intent,* won the 2005 Davitt award for adult fiction and her books have been translated into over a dozen languages.

Kathryn lives in Sydney and combines her passion for books and medicine by being the patron of a reading programme for remote and indigenous communities that promotes the links between literacy and health.

KATHRYN FOX

Skin and Bone

HODDER

First published in 2007 by Pan Macmillan Australia Pty Ltd.

First published in Great Britain in 2008 by Hodder & Stoughton
An Hachette Livre UK company

8

A CIP catalogue record for this title is available from the British Library

ISBN 978 0 340 93308 4

Typeset in Plantin by Hewer Text UK Ltd, Edinburgh
Printed and bound by Clays Ltd, St Ives plc

Hodder & Stoughton policy is to use papers that are natural, renewable
and recyclable products and made from wood grown in sustainable
forests. The logging and manufacturing processes are expected to
conform to the environmental regulations of the country of origin.

Hodder & Stoughton Ltd
338 Euston Road
London NW1 3BH

www.hodder.co.uk

For Kerrie and Pip

1

Kate Farrer struggled to open the car door. The muscles in her chest had tightened like a vice. If only she could get more air. Her cramped fingers clawed at the contents of the glove-box, spilling a map and interstate guidebook onto the floor.

Pulse erratic, and struggling to stay focused, she located the bag. Burying her mouth and nose in the open end, she breathed in, then out, counting two, three, four. The paper crackled with each deflation. The flow was slow but reassuring. The lightheadedness began to recede as Kate's chest muscles loosened their grip on her ribcage.

Pull it together! Her body now coursed with anger, and her fist paid the price with a jarring thump on the steering wheel. Despite three months off work, the trauma remained raw. She had two choices – one was to stay a victim, the other, to become a survivor. Until today she had worked hard – damned hard – to be a survivor.

A fireman passing the passenger window startled her. She shoved the bag into the glove-box and closed the lid, rubbing the heel of her hand. For twelve weeks she had tried to come to terms with her emotions. At this moment, her stomach felt like a spin dryer with a cat trapped inside. The worst part was feeling out of control, not knowing when the panic symptoms would take over – again.

She knew it was now or never. Taking two deep breaths, Detective Sergeant Kate Farrer yanked on the door handle and stepped out of the sedan. Residual smoke stung her nostrils, and the smell of wet burnt wood was heavy in the air. The fibro cottage at the end of the tree-lined Moat Place bore little resemblance to other dwellings in the street. The left section of the house had been decimated and only a shell of the rooms remained. Black soot stained the outside walls, having escaped through shattered windows. The sound of glass smashing caused a flurry of firefighters to rush to the side of the house. Flames poured through the window in a plume and ignited the external overhang and the roof.

Kate stayed well back, talking into a hand-held recorder as teams hosed water from inside and out to extinguish the fire. Despite being at least fifty feet from the flames, her face tingled with the intensity of the heat.

She thought of her psychologist. He had made her scoff the first time he described linking thoughts and feelings as 'detective thinking'. The irony of his analogy was completely lost on him; so much for professionals having insight.

'Think of a stressful situation and ask yourself, "What's the worst that can happen?" Then ask yourself, "How likely is it?"'

2

The trouble was, Kate knew exactly what could happen on the job and how probable it was. She had seen hell, locked away by a psychopath for days, and she continued to suffer nightmares and flashbacks. A phrase, smell or noise that reminded her of her captor could reduce her to a sobbing mess in seconds. Now, her leave was almost up and she had been asked to return early because of a staff shortage. Police work was what she had always done best, until the abduction.

She imagined how a firefighter would deal with the psychologist's questions, designed to trivialise the causes of anxiety. The worst that could happen to any of them was that one day they'd go to work, attend a fire and get cremated on the spot.

So much for police shrinks. Some neuroses were justifiable, particularly in the emergency services. The difficulty, she knew too well, was in controlling them.

Stay calm, you can do this. Back to basics. Work the scene, from the outside in.

Despite the beginnings of fine drizzle, portions of the garden continued to smoulder. Police tape cordoned off most of the Castle Hill road, restricting the number of curious onlookers. Ambulance officers waited, backs to their vehicles. Two other white sedans were parked in the area, along with a fire-truck and investigator's station wagon.

The arrival of a television van at the blue and white tape caught her attention. Damn reporters were like tow-trucks and blowflies. The uglier the carnage, the faster they appeared and multiplied. More used to feeling irritated than vulnerable, she looked around for her new partner while continuing to dictate: 'At eight thirty am, four local constables maintain crime scene. Fire investigators present. Press pack beginning to push their luck.'

'Detective Sergeant Farrer?'

A slim, tall man in a grey suit adjusted his lilac tie. His fair hair was cropped close to his head, without looking too military. 'Oliver Parke,' he said, with an outstretched hand. In the other, he held two takeaway coffee cups in a cardboard tray. 'Hello, and good to meet you.'

Kate had been briefed about her partner the previous week when she was asked to cut short her leave. The unit's long-term issues with chronic understaffing and old-style attitudes had led to the recruitment of new blood, mostly academic types. The last thing she wanted was an inexperienced partner with no common sense and a university degree that had nothing to do with the real world. She had no say in the matter, though, and at that moment just wanted to re-establish a healthy work routine.

She shook the newly-promoted detective constable's hand and noticed the strength of his grip. He was obviously trying to make a good first impression.

'I took the liberty, seeing as though I went right past the coffee house. One's black, the other's white.'

4

Mouth dry, Kate had to admit he had good timing. She accepted the black.

'Thanks, but don't make it a habit.' She resented the buddy-buddy, your turn, my turn, routine. Partners didn't have toilet breaks together, so why should they always drink at the same time?

'How many cases have you worked?' she asked.

'If you mean homicide, two so far. This could be three.' His chest deflated, just perceptibly.

She felt hers do the same.

'How was your break?' His voice was hesitant.

The female detective had no patience for small talk. Banal conversation was something she tried hard to avoid, even more so lately.

'What do you know about the scene so far?' Kate said, unsure whether she saw a smirk flash across her partner's face. He had probably heard stories about her. If they came from the chief inspector, they should have been positive, but anything from the male detectives would be less flattering.

'Fire's just about out. An engineer is checking the place for structural damage. Local boys have sealed off the street, as you can see.'

The neighbours in pyjamas tut-tutted and spoke eagerly to a camera crew leaning into the barrier at the cross-street three houses down. Their witness statements would probably be broadcast before the police had a chance to interview them.

'Make sure we get all that footage,' Kate said, a little too briskly. She needed to be calmer; she was supposed to be in charge and that meant being in control. The only advantage of the media was that they often recorded vital information. 'And we need to check all witnesses. Anyone with amateur videos, digital photos. Make sure you check the mobile phones for images.' The familiar patter was beginning to feel comfortable. 'Any survivors?'

Oliver shook his head. 'Apparently there's one body on a bed. The firemen left it in situ.'

Kate nodded and sipped her coffee. If there'd been any chance of saving a life, the fire crew would have pulled the victim out. That meant the body had to be in pretty bad condition. She used to think that dying in a fire would be one of the worst ways to go, before discovering what it was like to be tortured. The only reassuring thing about a house-fire was that the poisonous gases were more likely to kill than the heat or flames. At least dead bodies couldn't feel pain.

'So we're waiting to get the all-clear from the engineer?'

Oliver nodded. 'He's still assessing whether it's safe for us to go inside.' He cleared his throat before launching in to the facts he had uncovered so far. 'The house is owned by a Doctor Gorman and his wife, from Mosman. It's an investment property but apparently they've never had long-term te-nants. One of the neighbours reckons they planned to knock it down and rebuild. And before you ask, Doctor Gorman's receptionist says that he and his wife are away in Nepal and can't be contacted for a couple of weeks. Seems he does charity work in hospitals there.'

A blue Monaro growled up behind Kate's car. Dr Peter Latham, forensic pathologist, climbed out.

'Welcome back,' he smiled through his salt and pepper beard. 'You've been missed.'

'Thanks,' was all Kate could muster. She respected Peter Latham and did not want to offend him. But if he offered some meaningless platitude about her time away, she might just snap, or worse, burst into tears.

'This is Oliver Parke. He's pretty new to homicide,' she added, hoping to draw the attention away from herself.

'We've already met,' Peter said, removing items from his car boot. He stepped into a white plastic body suit. 'How's the family?'

'Growing by the minute, only four weeks to go.' Oliver beamed.

A forensic services vehicle swung into the remaining space at the crowded end of the street. Crime scene officer John Zimmer peeled himself from the driver's seat and shoved a police baseball cap on his head. 'Looks like the gang's all here.' He became serious as he took in the house. 'Something caused some fast, impressive heat in there.'

Kate assumed he was referring to the fact that big, intense fires always destroyed the most evidence. What the fire did not obliterate, the thousands of litres of water poured on it by the fire crews did. Investigating fires was, in many ways, more art than science.

An hour later, the fire investigator and a younger man who Kate guessed was the engineer appeared from around the side of the house, accompanied by a black labrador.

'You're clear to go in,' the investigator assured the group. 'We're looking at an accelerant spread through the house. Fire boys smelt it when they arrived. And Bella here agrees.' He bent down and patted the dog's shiny black coat. 'Don't know how we managed before the old girl joined us. Have you all met our number one expert witness?'

'How do you swear her in for court?' Oliver smiled.

'Detective, you are in the presence of the first four-legged creature whose evidence is totally acceptable in a courtroom. She's more trusted than any other witness.'

Oliver bent down to give the dog a scratch. Her handler was like a doting parent.

'She's highly trained, and with that sense of smell, she can detect accelerants up to days later, even if surfaces or clothing have been washed. She's what we call a passive identifier. Instead of barking or becoming agitated she just sits when she detects an accelerant. We couldn't budge her once we got to the back door of this place,' he said, looking around.

'So we're looking at arson?' Kate asked. Any suspicion of a deliberate fire meant the body inside would be a homicide case until proven otherwise. Local detectives were off the hook.

'In most cases that's extremely difficult to prove, but this stuff was spread all over the house and finished, or should I say started, in the bedroom,' the investigator said. 'My guess is our guy used petrol.'

'Kate, it's been far too long.' John Zimmer had reappeared. He sidled up to her with his camera hanging around his neck. The CSO fancied himself and assumed every woman shared the same view. Kate felt her skin prickle at his proximity. This was going to be a very long morning, she thought, as he handed her a flashlight.

Returning to work was supposed to be like getting back on a bike, or so everyone had said. By the look of the gutted house, and knowing there was a homicide victim inside, it would be more like getting on two wheels without brakes, gears or handlebars. Kate braced herself for what would come next.

'Let's get this over with,' she managed, and put her half-empty coffee cup on the hood of the car.

Fire crews packed up their hoses and equipment as a small gust of wind spread some ash across the lawn. Kate pulled her suit jacket around herself and protected her eyes with one hand.

The group stopped at the front window. Glass shards lay on the outside, either blown out by the heat of the fire or smashed out by someone in a hurry to escape. Kate bent down looking for traces of blood on the fragments. John Zimmer clicked away, placing small yellow tags on the ground for scale and location in his photos. Kate looked closely at the windowsill. No sign of blood there either.

The CSO photographed that too. 'We sometimes find fingerprints in the window putty,' he said.

For Oliver's benefit, Kate added, 'Anything the fire softens can show up prints.'

The new detective seemed to be paying attention – in fact a little too closely. She felt his breath on her neck and told him not to crowd her. Like a scolded schoolboy, he blushed and apologised. Zimmer seemed to find something about that amusing.

Working the house from outside in, they followed the CSO down the driveway and around to the back door. Peter Latham trailed behind.

'There's no sign of a break-in so far. This was closed and unlocked,' the fire investigator announced before opening the white wooden door. 'Stay,' he instructed Bella, and she obeyed.

'He could at least have left the door open,' Kate muttered.

'Is that because soot would have got onto the outside surface if it had been open during the fire, highlighting any fingerprints?' Oliver enquired.

John Zimmer turned and grinned. 'There's that, but if our guy poured a trail of petrol, he would have been surrounded by a cloud of vapour. When he lit the match . . .' He made his large hands into a ball then opened them quickly. 'Kaboomza! He'd be easier to find, flash-burns and all. It's the most common mistake arsonists make.'

'He poured petrol over the threshold, shut the door, then lit it under the door.' Oliver seemed impressed by the planning. 'So he knows something about fires.'

'Exactly,' the CSO said. 'Which means?'

'He's probably done it before.' Oliver nodded and took notes in a small pad pulled from inside his suit jacket.

Kate ignored the obvious deduction, preferring to concentrate on what she saw, smelt and heard. The stench of death was always stale and heavy, but burnt flesh had a distinct, noxious odour, like nothing she could describe. Bile rose in her throat and she gagged, quickly coughing to keep face, hoping no one noticed.

Stepping across the threshold into the hallway, she saw that the burnt wooden floorboards had two distinct markings – dark and lighter wood. The darker shade was in an almost straight line, in the centre of the hallway, the discolouration strongly suggesting where the accelerant had been poured. They followed it into the kitchen, relatively unscathed apart from paint hanging in tabloid-sized sheets from the blackened ceiling. The soot began at hip-height on the walls of the hallway and around the room, and continued across the open kitchen door, as if someone had drawn a line on the walls with a marker and coloured everything above that line black.

Kate rubbed the linoleum floor near the skirting board with the sole of her shoe and revealed a red and white checked pattern. Soot, not burnt lino, covered most of the floor – again, a sign that the arsonist had travelled in a line with the accelerant.

On the table a plastic tablecloth had shrivelled into a ball, but the table legs were remarkably untouched. Heat, flames and gas must have stayed in the upper section of the room, she thought, given the state of the floor.

Near the open door, Zimmer snapped more pictures, then moved to an overnight bag sitting on the soiled kitchen floor. He recorded it from various angles then bent down and with gloved hands removed something protruding from a side-pocket. It looked like a credit card.

'Name here says Audrey Lambert.' He checked the other side-pockets. 'No driver's licence, key-cards or even receipts. And no cash.'

'Which means no photo ID,' Kate observed. 'If someone broke in, robbed her and took money and everything else, you'd think they would take the credit card as well.'

'Unless,' Zimmer said, 'she's been robbed before and keeps one card separate for emergencies. That's what I did after my wallet disappeared last year.'

'Don't mean to rush you, but I've got court in just over an hour,' Peter Latham said from the back of the group. 'Which way now?'

The group moved along the accelerant trail to the end bedroom. Kate checked her mobile phone to buy a moment and steel herself. She took a couple of deep breaths and entered.

In the middle of the bed was a blackened adult-sized figure lying on its back with arms and legs bent towards the ceiling. The face was bloated and the lips were swollen. The tongue protruded in an almost defiant gesture.

Oliver excused himself and left the room.

Zimmer took photos and Peter Latham studied the remains.

'The hair is dark,' he said, pressing on the pillow. 'There's a clump at the back, untouched by the heat. We can get samples from here.' With plastic tweezers, he extracted some hairs and placed them in an evidence bag opened by Zimmer. He then leant sideways, allowing the CSO in for close-up photographs. They had obviously worked a lot of cases together, which helped speed up the laborious process.

The pathologist plucked tiny pieces of clothing from the creases at the deceased's bent elbows and bagged them too. At least they might be able to identify the colour and type of clothing he or she was wearing.

Kate had seen all she needed for the moment and retreated to the kitchen. The post-mortem, which she would be present for, would be tomorrow or the next day.

Relieved to be out of the bedroom, it occurred to Kate that the firefighters had been careful not to soak the house. At previous fire scenes she had worked, they had blasted their way through the blaze at high pressure, kind of like the way most men solved problems – the bigger the equipment, the greater the force, the quicker the solution. On this occasion, they appeared to have taken a more strategic approach and used smaller hoses with a wide-angle spray that delivered spurts of mist. It was enough to take the heat out of the fire with minimal water damage, and it made a homicide investigation that little bit easier.

Putting on the fresh pair of latex gloves she kept in her jacket pocket, Kate bent down and unzipped the overnight bag. It contained nappies, wipes, baby bottles with patterns partly scratched off, formula and two squeaky toys. Unscrewing the lid of one of the bottles, she gently sniffed. As far as she could tell, it was either unused or had been well cleaned. Replacing the lid, she returned it to the bag and got up to check out the rest of the house.

With a pocket flashlight, she navigated through fallen beams and debris, staying as close as possible to the middle of the hallway to avoid getting soot on her clothes. She checked inside two more bedrooms, both with double beds, the next room with what had to have been a circular bed. There were no other human remains. There was also nothing in the bedrooms that resembled a cot or bassinette; just a pile of melted DVDs and videos in a burnt-out cabinet against one of the walls.

She opened a door and found herself in the garage. Fluid had been poured on the cement floor but igniting it hadn't done much damage. The sparse contents included relatively undamaged rakes, a hoe and lawn mower. Against a wall sat the scorched remains of a large, top-opening freezer, the sort used by people who buy food in bulk. Crime scene had already cordoned off the area with police tape.

Back at the main bedroom, she addressed the group. 'We could have a problem. The bag Audrey Lambert kept her purse in wasn't an ordinary overnight bag. It was a nappy bag, full of baby stuff.'

'Shit,' the fire investigator said, almost under his breath. 'I'll go check the outside bins.'

'I'll take the cupboards,' Zimmer said, matter of fact.

'I'm thinking the victim is a woman, but I won't be able to tell for sure until we're back at the morgue and can examine the pelvic remains.' Peter sighed. 'At least we can use the good bit of hair for DNA sampling, and hopefully we'll get some dental records.'

Kate felt her temples throb and her breathing quicken. There was no easing back into work. In less than an hour they had a body, possibly female, with a credit card but no other identification. The only other evidence so far was a nappy bag. If the unrecognisable body was that of a mother, then where the hell was her baby?

Sl.. ... ...
... ...
... ...
... ...
... ...
... ...
... ...
... ...

2

Outside the house, Kate found Oliver squatting by the back fence, his face pale.

'I remember the first time I saw a burns victim,' she said, scraping the bottoms of her shoes on the grass. 'Teenager had a fight with his girlfriend. After a few drinks, he took off in his father's car.'

The male detective stared at the ground.

'Only trouble was, he misjudged a bend and hit a tree. The car went up in flames.'

Oliver turned his head towards his partner.

'I was on general duties when they took him in to casualty. I still remember the shock of seeing burnt flesh and the disgusting smell. You never get used to it.' She removed the latex gloves and shoved her hands into her trouser pockets. 'Look, some things just get to you – I mean, to everyone.'

Peter Latham came out the back door, doctors' bag in hand. 'The body is pretty fragile. It has to be moved carefully or we'll have bits falling off and getting lost. Must run. See you both at the PM?'

Kate gestured with her hand. They would be there. Moments later, the sound of his V8 engine broke the tension.

'We've got to ID the body and find out whether or not there is a missing baby.'

'What baby?' He stood, smoothing the creases in his suit pants.

'The bag in the kitchen had nappies and bottles in it. What do you think we should do first?'

'Canvass the neighbours. See if they know who was here, whether they saw or heard anything . . .'

'Well, what are you waiting for?'

Oliver nodded and seemed almost enthusiastic about the grunt work ahead. Maybe he disliked the gory side of the job, or was still too sensitive. That would have to change if he was going to last in homicide.

In contrast, Kate disliked the monotony of soliciting information by doorknocking. Busybodies outnumbered reliable witnesses and asked more questions than they answered, eager for any gossip they could extract. She followed the side path towards the road and watched the black labrador wandering slowly amongst the gathered crowd. She could imagine the dog making a monkey out of a defence lawyer on cross-examination. The idea made her smirk. She was beginning to think that coming back to work had been the right thing to do after all.

Bella weaved her way around the pairs of legs but this time failed to stop and sit. She remained on passive alert, sniffing for the arsonist who may have stayed to watch the aftermath of his handiwork. If she detected accelerants on any of the bystanders she would simply and silently sit. After a few minutes, she returned to the fire investigator by the station wagon.

'Nothing so far in the crowd,' he said to Kate, and handed Bella a biscuit. 'Sorry we couldn't give you a slam dunk.'

Kate had a feeling that nothing about this case would be easy.

In the foyer of police headquarters, Oliver pressed the button at the lifts.

'See you up there,' Kate said and headed for the stairwell door.

'But that's more than three floors,' Oliver mumbled.

Six flights of stairs later, at the entrance to the crime lab, the male detective puffed, hands on his belt.

'That was . . . refreshing.'

Kate gave him a sly look but concentrated on her breathing. She did not want to let on how much her leg muscles burnt, and even less that she wasn't ready to go into a confined space like a lift.

John Zimmer greeted them inside, dressed in fresh blue crime-scene overalls. 'Hope you know something about babies,' he smiled.

Kate felt her heart sink. It was one of the topics she knew least about.

'What do you need to know?' Oliver offered.

'We need to get some kind of idea how old this kid is, or was.'

Oliver glanced at the paraphernalia Zimmer had laid out on the bench. Two white cloth nappies, two empty bottles, a bright yellow bib and a sachet of formula.

'Any disposables?'

Zimmer reached his gloved hand into the overnight bag and extracted two nappies, holding them as though they had already been used.

'Well, one's meant for a newborn, probably in the first eight weeks or so, depending on the child's size.'

Zimmer shot Kate a glance and raised his eyebrows. 'And the other?'

Oliver laid out the second one. 'Next size up. I think these go up to about six months.'

'So we still don't know how old this baby is.'

'It's possible the newborn one was left over. It's been unfolded, so maybe the mother tried it on and realised it was too small. In the packaging they come in, they are always squashed flat. Or, the bigger one could have been a sample.'

'Aren't you either for cloth or against it?' Zimmer leant against the benchtop and gestured at the cloth nappies. 'My sister carried on about having to choose cloth for the sake of the environment when she was pregnant. I had no idea babies caused that many carbon emissions.'

'Cloths are one size fits all, so they won't help us work out the baby's age. They can also be used for wiping up regurgitated milk and vomit.'

Zimmer looked repulsed. The man thought nothing of wading through rivers with decomposed bodies, or extracting maggots from a deceased's nose, but the idea of baby vomit made him sick. It was something he and Kate had in common.

'If you look carefully, there's an old milk stain in the corner of that one. The baby might be a refluxer. Some types of formula are thickened, to try and prevent it all coming back up.' Oliver looked inside the bag and in the side-pockets. 'No pins or nappy clasps. The mother used disposables, at least while they were out. And no clothes either, worse luck. That would have given us size and probably gender.'

'Don't the bibs mean the child is eating?' Zimmer asked, confirming that he knew even less about kids than Kate.

'It's a lot easier to pull off a bib than change a baby's clothes. If it throws up or regurgitates milk, bibs are an essential.'

Kate slumped against the bench. 'Great. We don't know if the child is missing, alive or dead, or how old it is.'

'Not necessarily,' Oliver said as he grabbed a pair of gloves from a dispenser on the nearest wall. 'Can I look at the teats on the bottles?'

Zimmer reluctantly handed them over. 'They were both empty.'

Kate watched her partner study the tip of the teat, with no idea what he was looking for.

'The size of the hole in the teat varies depending on the age of the child. A pinprick size is for newborns, whereas older babies can handle a faster flow, so you find teats that are punctured with an "X" shape. There aren't any teeth marks on either of these, and the openings are tiny. My guess is, these are for a pretty small baby, one who hasn't developed teeth yet.'

Kate hated to reveal her ignorance but asked the question anyway. 'How old are they when they start getting teeth?'

Zimmer raised both hands, surrendering to the new detective.

'It varies, but usually around four to six months. Is there anything else in the bag, like a tiny comb, or hair gel?'

Zimmer shook his head.

'That's a shame. If the mum did its hair, there might have been hairs left behind. At least we'd know the colour, whether it's straight or curly.'

Kate had to concede that her partner was a logical thinker. She was beginning to respect him. In a few minutes, he had provided information that would have taken her hours of research to discover, not to mention embarrassment at having to ask experts such basic questions.

Outside the lab, Oliver went to press the lift button, and hesitated.

'Stairs, it is.'

Inside the stairwell, their footsteps echoed. 'How do you know so much about kids' stuff? Didn't you say your partner was expecting?'

'Haven't you heard?'

Kate paused and turned around. 'I suppose you only hear things if you're listening.'

'Or if people choose to tell you.' Oliver came down to Kate's level. 'My first day here, someone called me the drover's dog.'

Kate was familiar with the expression, which referred to the working dog – all prick and ribs. In their brief few hours working together, Oliver had not struck her as someone who slept around. Then again, she never was a good judge of male character.

'That's your business,' she said, and continued down the stairs. 'I just have to work with you.'

'It's because we have four kids already. This will be our fifth. And before you pass judgement, they are all to the same woman, my wife. It may be old-fashioned but I have a large family and every child is wanted. No mistakes, no accidents. They were all planned.'

Kate stopped. Four children. No wonder he knew so much. Then again, most fathers were clueless when it came to what was involved in looking after kids. Oliver was already very different from her previous partners. She was almost beginning to like him.

'All right, now that's sorted, let's find out who Audrey Lambert is.'

Oliver's mobile rang. During a one-sided conversation in which he agreed to what the caller was saying, he propped his notebook against the stairwell wall and scribbled something before hanging up.

'Audrey Lambert has a passport. Her appearance is described as five foot four tall, with medium-length brown hair, medium build. Fits with the burnt body. I have the parents' address.'

'We'd better go find some dental records and confirm the ID.'

'Before we do that,' Oliver closed his notebook, 'I need to know. What happened to the teenager in the car who hit the tree?'

Kate sighed. She was sorry to have brought it up now.

'He never had a chance. Burns were too extensive. They pulled the plug on the life-support once the family had had a chance to say their goodbyes.' She continued briskly down the stairs. 'Which is more than the Lamberts will ever get.'

3

In the leafy suburb, birds sat on telephone wires despite the ample foliage. Parked in the driveway of the cream brick home was a hatchback. From the sloping chocolate roof of the house, solar panels reflected the midday sun. The owners were obviously conscious of the environment, and for some reason that made Kate feel even worse. A box hedge had been damaged, sections looking burnt. She glanced around the street. No one else had damage to the front of their property.

This was the worst part of the job, she thought as she pressed the doorbell. The people inside might be about to have their lives shattered. She had double-checked the address and Oliver opened the letterbox, confirming they were in the right place. An energy bill had been addressed to Mrs T Lambert.

Oliver stood behind Kate, deferring to his superior officer. If Kate had had any choice, she would have done the same thing.

Before she had a chance to knock, the white door swung open. A middle-aged woman with neat brown hair wiped her hands on her apron.

'Can I help you?'

Chicken was roasting, with loads of rosemary and garlic, judging by the aroma. The place could not have been more homely. The detectives introduced themselves and Kate asked if they could come inside.

When they stopped in the lounge room Mrs Lambert looked nervous. 'I bet this is about those boys down the road.'

'I'm afraid that's not what we've come about. It's about Audrey.'

The woman turned an ashen colour and sat on the edge of her sofa. 'No, I don't want to hear this. I want you to go. Now.'

Oliver stepped forward. 'We need to speak with you, Mrs Lambert. Is your husband here?'

The woman pointed to the back of the house. 'In the garden, weeding.'

Without another word, Oliver walked towards the back of the house. He returned with a small, hunched man who immediately went to his wife's side.

'What's this about?' he demanded.

'We need to ask you, when was the last time you saw Audrey?'

Mrs Lambert ran her hands down her apron. 'Why do you want to know? Tom? Why are they here?'

'I'm afraid you're upsetting my wife. Can we talk outside?'

'We apologise for the interruption, but we are investigating a – an accident.' Kate stumbled for the right words. 'There's no easy way to tell you this, but there's been an accident and we need to know if Audrey was involved.'

'Is this some kind of joke?' The man stood, clenching his fists by his sides.

Oliver appeared as stunned as Kate felt. This was not the reaction they had expected. She tried again.

'We are detectives investigating a fire. Believe me, we wouldn't bother you unless it was important.'

Mrs Lambert buried her face in her apron while her husband spoke.

'Haven't we been through enough? Did those idiots down the road send you here to torment us? They set fire to our hedge and you harass us.'

Oliver showed his badge and stepped closer. 'I think we need to take a minute to calm down. Please, sit down, Mr Lambert.' Oliver knelt on one knee by the wife's side. 'We weren't sent by anyone. This is our job. That's all we're doing.'

'There was a fire this morning at a place not all that far from here, and a young woman died,' Kate explained.

'Oh God, no.' Mrs Lambert's bottom lip trembled.

'I don't understand, we just spoke to Audrey early yesterday morning.' The man collapsed onto the three-seater sofa.

Kate hesitated, then sat next to him. 'I know this is a terrible shock, but we need to ask you a few questions. Do you know the name of your daughter's dentist?'

'She's been seeing someone in Knightsbridge, I think. Charges a fortune.'

Kate had heard of it. 'That's in Castle Hill, isn't it?'

'All I know is that it's in the posh part of London. One of her colleagues referred her.'

Oliver shot Kate a glance. 'When was she there – in England?' he asked.

'She was at her flat when she called us, about to go to work.'

'Hang on,' Kate interrupted. None of this felt right. 'Are you saying she was in London just yesterday?'

'That's where she's been living for three years. When our son died in the accident, she needed some time away. Her last visit home was about six weeks ago.'

The man's expression was impassive when he spoke, almost as though his face could no longer show emotion. Now their behaviour made sense. They had been visited by the police once before, with the news of their son's death. Tears welled in Kate's eyes as she felt this couple's pain. Years ago, she had lived through the same thing.

Turning away, she noticed framed photos on the mantelpiece and in a cabinet beside the television: a young man in leathers posing against a motorbike. She felt her blood chill at the sight of the motorbike. The image was so similar to Billy, her first boyfriend, who had died in a smash years before. She struggled to push Billy from her mind and studied a posed portrait of the four family members, the standard kind done at any shopping centre.

She faced the Lamberts again, surprised to find that she was only just holding back her own tears. She used to have no trouble controlling her emotions. 'I think there's been some kind of mistake. We found Audrey's credit card in a house that burnt down, here in Sydney. Does she by any chance have a baby?'

The mother lifted her face. 'A baby? She only just broke up with her boyfriend.'

'Don't you think we would know if we were grandparents? This is absurd. Is our Audrey safe or not?' Mr Lambert wiped away a tear with the back of his hand.

Oliver patted the woman's hand. 'Can you call her, now?'

'Her number's over in the teledex. She might still be asleep but we can try.' Mr Lambert shuffled to the phone and slowly dialled. His hands trembled as he held the handset.

'She works long hours,' Mrs Lambert explained, 'in a big department store.'

Kate's heart-rate picked up as she hoped, for this couple's sake, that their daughter was alive.

Then Tom Lambert's face broke into a smile. 'Hello, Audrey? It's Dad.' His voice became louder, as if the distance between them warranted it. 'No, we're fine. Love, your mother wanted to hear your voice, that's all. Oh, and someone found one of your credit cards.'

There was a pause before he spoke again. 'No, it's turned up, but I still have to notify the bank . . . Do you have any idea where or when you lost it? Not to worry, we'll sort it out from this end.'

With that, Mrs Lambert stood, took the receiver and sobbed into it.

'Audrey didn't even know she'd lost it. She's always losing things, like her keys, sunglasses. Knowing her, she would have paid for something then left it in the shop.' The man sounded as if he were describing a positive character trait.

'We are so sorry to have caused you unnecessary distress,' Kate said to Mr Lambert.

'No, I'm sorry,' he said, looking down. 'There's some other family about to go through a living hell. Believe me, we know what that's like.'

Kate's hand unconsciously touched her back pocket, where she kept her wallet, and the ragged photo of Billy.

Two and a half days after the fire, Kate Farrer led the way into the autopsy room. Oliver Parke followed, less than enthusiastically. They were depending on Peter Latham to give them clues as to the identity of their victim.

Neighbours had not recalled anyone in particular coming or going, and they needed some direction before tackling the piles of missing persons' reports. Calls to every midwife, hospital and baby clinic failed to result in anything useful. Without a positive ID, the next step would be to check Medicare records looking for babies born in the last six months, and then locate every one of the mothers. Either way, they had an enormous amount of information to sift through.

A technician in blue scrubs and white gumboots hosed down a steel bed to their right. At the other end of the room, Dr Peter Latham sat at a bench making notes. The charred body lay on a steel bed behind him, still in the bent position in which they had found her. The stench overpowered the air-conditioned space – not that the pathologist or technician appeared to notice.

Kate readied herself for an unpleasant couple of hours, though she would never show her distaste at what she was about to see.

'Glad you're here,' Peter Latham said, hunting around on the desk for something. 'Sorry about the delay. We've only just cleared the backlog from the latest round of gang shootings.'

Kate silently tapped her head, and Peter Latham located his glasses where he had last left them. Pulling them down over his eyes, his cheeks flushed. 'Before we start . . .' He offered the pair a bottle of eucalyptus oil. Oliver declined.

'Your choice.' Kate dabbed some onto her finger then rubbed it under her nostrils.

'I heard from Anya this morning in New York. Sounds like she's shaking up their Special Victims Unit and working on some fascinating cases.'

Kate smiled, comfortable discussing this one topic with the pathologist. 'She always makes a big impression.'

Peter had mentored fellow pathologist and forensic physician Anya Crichton, who was also Kate Farrer's closest and – realistically – only true friend. During the detective's time away, Anya had accepted a six-week stint in New York. Kate had to admit that the sooner the pair could share a meal and an ethical argument, the more settled she would feel. Emails and letters were short, and Kate not being a phone person meant that recent contact between the two of them had been minimal.

Peter pulled a white plastic apron over his scrubs.

'The smell,' Oliver ventured. 'Why is it . . .'

'So vile? Like nothing else you've ever experienced?' Peter tied the apron at his back and pulled on gloves. 'That's an excellent question. Normally, we're used to the odours released by cooked *portions* of animals. Each component has its own unique smell. For example, burning muscles smell a bit like beef on a barbecue, whereas the aroma of burning body fat is similar to burnt pork. A big difference is that we're used to cooking meat with most of the blood drained in the slaughter process.'

The technician, dressed in a lead apron, wheeled in a machine and lined it up with the head of the body.

'We'll need whole body X-rays on this one. We're looking for any projectiles that entered the body before or after the fire.'

'Like a bullet, for example?' Oliver offered.

'Or metal fragments if an explosion occurred.' Peter motioned for the three of them to step into the corridor for a minute, saving them exposure to the radiation. 'In a fire, you're smelling the full body and that includes blood, which is rich in iron. That's why you get a metallic sort of odour mixed in. On the other hand, burning skin is a bit like charcoal, and hair has an almost sulphurous smell about it, which is what I find particularly unpleasant. It lingers for days, if I remember our university pranks correctly. It's less common, but if the fire penetrates the internal organs, then you get something a bit like burnt liver. Not many people cook that anymore.'

Kate tried not to listen. The smell was one thing, but analysis of the constituents and comparisons to cooked food might just have been worse, particularly for a meat-eater like her. The next hamburger she had would become a salad roll if he kept talking much longer.

'Now that makes sense.' Oliver nudged her once Peter returned inside. 'Can I ask for that oil this time?' She showed him where the bottle was kept and collected gloves from the dispenser on the wall.

'There are some things I want to show you,' Peter began.

They surrounded the rigid, disfigured form. In better light, Kate thought the body seemed more damaged but, ironically, the sterile environment made it easier for her to remain detached.

'She has the typical posture of someone burnt in a fire. You can see why it's described as pugilistic, or the boxer's position.'

Kate thought it looked more like someone sitting up and begging. Either way, it was a totally undignified way to die. For a moment, she wondered how the relatives would deal with identifying, then burying, their loved one. Would the smell still be present in a coffin? How would the funeral director get her into one in the first place? She shuddered at the thought of putting the remains into a wooden casket and incinerating it again. Taking a breath, she tried to stop her mind racing around unnecessary distractions.

The pathologist pointed to the upper limbs. 'The arms are bent at the elbow joint, and the legs are bent at both the hip and knee joints. As you can see, the hands are clenched into fists.'

Oliver fiddled with his tie. 'Is that because the fire and heat cause the muscles to shrivel as the water inside them evaporates?'

'That's exactly why,' Peter answered, sounding pleased that someone understood. 'The specific posturing occurs because of the strength of the muscles that cause the arms and legs to flex, or bend. They're stronger than the opposing muscles. Biceps are stronger than triceps, as you can see.'

He collected a scalpel from a silver tray next to the table and Kate stepped back.

The first incision was through the chest in a Y-shape. She tried to focus on the blackened countenance and protruding tongue, which today gave the face a pained expression. The features looked more like a caricature than a person. She wondered about the last thing this woman had seen and whether this expression was one of true agony.

As a child she had been afraid of fire, but had later revelled in evenings spent around a campfire. Her father had always said fire should be treated like a weapon – with respect and appreciation of its power. It was still difficult to believe how something that aided survival and provided so much comfort and warmth in the cold could cause such devastation to life. Even harder to accept was how someone could deliberately cause that kind of devastation. Pyromania was a whacko psychopathology she would never understand.

'The good news is that this young woman wasn't killed by the fire.'

Peter clipped through the chest bones and removed the breastplate, exposing the chest cavity and internal organs.

'Sorry,' Oliver interrupted. 'How is that good news? She's still dead.'

Peter smiled. 'We have a pragmatist in our midst. I think we'll get on very well. The level of carboxyhaemoglobin, or carbon monoxide, bound to the red blood cells was less than two per cent. That suggests this woman had died before the fire started.'

Kate tapped her right foot, slightly agitated. Arson was definitely one of the most frustrating crimes and almost impossible to get a conviction on. 'So what was the cause of death?'

Peter moved around to the head of the distorted figure. 'This is where it gets interesting.' He moved some of the hair and instructed each detective to feel part of the scalp.

Kate put her gloved hand beneath his and felt a craggy indentation. Oliver put down his notebook and did the same, keeping as much distance between him and the head as he could manage.

'That's a depressed fracture,' Peter informed them. 'You can feel where the skin is split and the bone was pushed inwards, so we need to see what's underneath.'

He moved to the top of the bed and pulled out the stryker saw to cut through the skull. The whining noise prevented conversation, which did not resume until he had peeled the scalp forward over the victim's face. Kate moved to the other side of the room and looked away during the process, which was one of the most grotesque things she had ever witnessed. The sound of the saw still rang in her ears.

Removing the top section of the skull exposed the remains of the cooked brain. A long section of brown hair, like a foot-long rat's tail, was still attached to the back of the scalp, without the singed appearance of the rest of the hair. Oliver looked away and cleared his throat while Kate stepped forward. The brain looked to her like one very large blood clot.

The technician silently wheeled over a stool and Peter sat to study the mess. 'Heat can cause bony fractures along with sub and extradural haematomas. How long did you calculate the fire burnt?'

Oliver pulled the notebook from his pocket and flicked through it. 'Between the neighbours first hearing a noise and the bulk of the flames being extinguished, ten minutes tops. A separate flare-up occurred but at the other end of the house, away from the bedroom where we found the body.'

'Timing is very important. Haematomas,' Peter said, pointing to the area of blood on the brain, 'occur within that period whereas skull bone requires at least twenty minutes of intense heat before it fractures.'

'What exactly are we looking at?' Kate asked, keen to get to the precise cause of death.

'The skull was fractured and there's been bleeding on the brain directly beneath, as you can see. The scalp was split in one section, which might have been due to heat exposure, but if the fire burnt for less than twenty minutes, the fracture had to be caused by something else.'

'Like a head injury,' Kate deduced.

'Exactly. The split in the scalp is most likely the result of blunt force trauma, and the severity of subdural bleeding was enough to be fatal. It makes sense if the body wasn't in the fire for that long.'

Someone had murdered the victim, and attempted to destroy the evidence by setting the place on fire.

'Any identifying features you can help us out with?' Kate needed to know who the victim was before they had any chance of catching her killer.

Peter frowned. 'Nothing as helpful as tattoos or joint replacements, I'm afraid. Growth plates have fused so she's beyond adolescence. And in terms of teeth, they are in excellent condition. No cavities or fillings. She hasn't got any wisdom teeth yet. I'd put her age at late teens to early twenties. Measuring the length of the bones, she's about a hundred and sixty centimetres and had brown hair.'

Oliver, who had hurriedly removed and binned his gloves, scribbled notes as though he would be examined at the end of it.

'So in terms of time of death?' he asked, still writing.

'That's a more nebulous question. The internal organs are in remarkable condition considering the external state. Incidentally, John Zimmer was here earlier and tried to lift some fingerprints, but I'm not sure how successful he was. The skin is pretty badly damaged.'

Fingerprints would only be helpful if the victim had hers on file, anyway. Kate could not get the image of the nappy bag out of her mind. 'Is there any way you can tell if she had a baby?'

Peter rubbed his hands together, as if about to announce a major advance. 'Let's find out.'

Again, Kate stayed back, hoping to avoid all the visual aspects of the procedure. Peter opened the abdominal cavity and pulled out large sections of bowel before reaching down into the lower section and pulling out an organ not much bigger than a fist.

'This is quite remarkable, given the exposure to the fire. The organs, including the uterus here, are intact, which is not what you would expect to see.'

Oliver glanced up. 'What were you expecting?'

'Organs contain water and are prone to dehydrate and shrivel in fires, down to what we call "puppet organs". Most of these appear normal size.'

After running his fingers over the surface of the uterus, Peter placed it in a steel bowl that the technician held and then transferred onto a set of scales. The weight was recorded on a whiteboard mounted on the wall.

Peter Latham moved over to the bowl with a scalpel and sliced the organ open.

'No fibroids, no obvious abnormality, but it is a little larger than I'd expect to see in someone this age. I'll have to check the histology but you may just be right about this woman being a mother. The womb expands dramatically before birth, for obvious reasons, then takes around six weeks to involute, or go back to normal. It's entirely possible that she gave birth, but it has to have been within the last six weeks. I can't help you out with whether or not the baby ever took a breath.'

The nappy bag now made sense. The child had to have been born alive. The milk stains on the cloth nappy confirmed it.

Kate swallowed hard. They were no longer just looking at a homicide. They were on the hunt for a missing newborn who was probably in the hands of the murderer.

4

When Kate arrived at the homicide office the following morning, her partner's desk was already strewn with notes and papers. A clear-desk policy each evening meant Oliver must have been there for a while, but he was nowhere in sight. For a moment, she felt nervous about greeting the other detectives.

Liz Gould stood at the printer, more curvy in shape than before. She had been on maternity leave and returned during Kate's absence. The detective had worked right up until she had gone into labour, keen to finish off her caseload. Unfortunately, her waters had broken in the middle of a house search and was caught on a video recording of the scene.

Kate watched Liz walking towards her. Even with the extra kilograms, the thirty-something's face looked thin and her skin was mottled with acne.

'Welcome back,' Liz said warmly. 'I was sorry to hear what happened, but it's great to have you back.'

'How did you go?'

'We had a boy, Max. He's gorgeous, but being a twenty-four hour milking cow isn't my idea of a good deal.' She pointed to her cumbersome breasts and readjusted a bra-strap beneath her collar. 'To be honest, the hardest part is losing control. I can't organise when to eat or sleep and these hormones have a life of their own. If it wasn't for work, I'd have gone totally insane by now.'

Kate wasn't sure how to respond. Although she had suffered sleep deprivation during her kidnapping, their experiences couldn't have been more different. Kate didn't envy Liz at all right now. Managing her life was challenging enough without a child to look after.

'Better get back to it.'

The new mother returned to the printer, readjusting the other bra-strap on the way.

Sitting quietly at his desk was Detective Sergeant Laurie Sheehan. He had no desire or chance of further promotion – middle-aged and bordering on obese, he had refused to sit further exams or apply for other jobs. Homicide was where he had always wanted to be, and he was good at his job and obsessed with documenting everything 'by the book'. Laurie was also unusual in that he was a consummate gentleman. He was old school – or at least seemed to have gone to a different school from his peers. As a species, the older detectives were deemed dinosaurs and were rapidly being made extinct. Laurie Sheehan was more of an inoffensive herbivore than certain others in the office. He noticed Kate, stood and pretended to doff a hat in respect.

'How's the house?' she asked over ringing phones.

'Kitchen a chef would die for,' he grinned.

One of the few things Kate knew about Laurie was that he loved to spend his days off working on renovations to his house. He never seemed to run out of projects.

Kate glanced at some of the missing persons files open on Oliver's desk.

'Good morning,' he announced as he came up behind her.

His enthusiasm had to be because he was still new, she thought.

'What have you got so far?'

'Not a lot. I've narrowed it down to a hundred and fifty women who might fit our criteria for age, height, weight and hair colour. Not one of the missing persons cases I've gone over was pregnant or had a baby when she disappeared. Any number still could have gotten pregnant after going missing.'

Kate hung her grey jacket over the back of her swivel chair and rolled up the sleeves of her white shirt. 'What about those who could have gained or lost weight since they disappeared? Cut or grown their hair, changed the colour.'

She combed the back of her hair with her fingers, a habit she had developed since having it cut short, as if pulling on it made it feel longer. After escaping her kidnapper, she had been determined to change her appearance, anything to separate herself from the victim she had been. That meant a physical overhaul: more gruelling physical training, more weights and endurance running, and a new hairstyle.

Gone was her dark bob, replaced with a more modern, fresh look, or so the hairdresser justified with a cut, copper colour and a bill for two hundred dollars. Her first thought when she saw it was that Billy would have hated it. Over a decade since his accident, and she still considered what his opinions would have been.

Oliver sank in his chair. 'Did you know there are over thirty thousand people reported missing every year, and half of those are kids younger than eighteen?'

'I had heard that,' she said curtly, unlocking her drawer and removing a wad of papers.

'Sorry.' Oliver stumbled. 'I wasn't suggesting—'

'Being reported missing doesn't mean there's been a crime.'

'But don't you think what it does to the family is criminal?'

Kate turned to him. 'I don't know what your background is, but it doesn't take long in this job to know that disappearing is the best thing for some people. A lot of the women on your list probably had to get out for their own safety, or had mental illnesses and weren't receiving treatment. Nothing's ever what it seems. There are always three sides to every story: his, hers and the truth. We're supposed to find out the truth, usually after being fed all the lies.'

Two other detectives arrived and greeted the pair. Bert Fiskars had been in the force since he left school. From his point of view, police culture was changing too fast and for the worse.

'Early start, Drover.'

Kate cringed at the insulting nickname. 'Grow up,' she said under her breath but loud enough for Oliver to hear.

'Ah, Detective Farrer, glad to see you back,' Adam Rench chimed.

He and Bert made a good pair, each threatened by younger, better educated and more intelligent officers working their way up the ranks.

'Love what you've done with your hair,' Fiskars declared. 'It's so . . . feminine.'

Absolute jerks.

Rench, the elder of the two, sported what looked like a new suit and a trendy light blue shirt with white collar and cuffs. He thought the open-necked shirt and gold chain made him look younger. But no matter how hard he tried, his face still resembled the evil Chancellor in *Star Wars*. Today's effort only made him look sleazier than usual, Kate thought. No wonder his three wives – all richer and smarter than him – had left and his kids had opted to live with their mothers.

'Nice outfit,' Kate replied. 'Did a pimp die and leave it to you?'

Fiskars laughed, and received a silencing stare from Rench for his trouble.

'Oh, I forget you've never been part of our *social* club,' Rench goaded. 'As it turns out, last month we had our annual weekend at the races. My lucky two hundred bucks just couldn't lose. Farrer,' he tapped the side of his sizable head, 'it's all about smart investments and marrying wisely. A cop's wage won't keep you in retirement.'

Rench had a knack for being painful, and judging by the shape of his cranium, it began the moment he entered the world. Gloating about money and investments was just another weapon in his arsenal, one that Kate was sick of hearing.

'Pity you didn't invest enough time in your marriages, or you could have saved yourself a fortune in spousal support,' Kate sniped. 'The way I figure it, with my humble salary and lack of investments, I'm still better off than you.'

Oliver looked up from his list, interested in the banter.

Too slow to think up a comeback, Rench slunk off, his sycophant in tow.

'No one told me about a social club,' Oliver said quietly.

'They'd love to welcome you into their fold, if you don't mind being called Drover and treated like dog-shit.'

'How many times did you say Rench has been married?' he asked. 'I mean, once is more than enough for me.'

'Not sure. At least three, I think. You'd reckon women who have money would have more bloody sense.'

Oliver returned to his paperwork. Kate felt irritable; the day was going to be busy enough without the Evil One and his apprentice, as she had dubbed them, taking up their valuable time.

The chief inspector had phoned her early that morning for a favour. He wanted Kate and Oliver to personally handle a sensitive case. In police-speak, that meant some wealthy or powerful figure had a 'little problem' that they didn't want the media to find out about. The errant daughter of a friend of the inspector's had run away again but this time had failed to make contact. It should have been shunted to the missing persons unit, except for some 'sensitive' issue the inspector alluded to but failed to elaborate on.

Kate's immediate priority, however, was to find the murder victim's missing baby.

'Have you got the statements for the credit card we found?' she asked Oliver.

'Went over them this morning. Audrey Lambert really had no idea she had lost it. When she's away she uses a UK credit card to save paying conversion fees. She pays it off in advance, so doesn't really check the bills. My guess is that when she accidentally left it somewhere on her last trip home, our victim found it.'

Phones started ringing as the office filled up with staff.

'What was bought on the card?'

'Small amounts, so as not to arouse suspicion, I assume. Thirty dollars' worth of groceries, each at different major supermarkets miles apart in Castle Hill and Macquarie. Twenty dollars' worth of petrol, last one two weeks ago.'

Kate leaned back, hands clasped behind her head. 'Doesn't sound like a card-stealing syndicate. There are no extravagances, just basics on that list. My guess is, our victim ran out of money, or financial support, and was desperate. She could have lifted the card, or found it somewhere, as you say.'

That did not help their case. Kate knew that no one at a supermarket would remember a mother and baby buying a small amount of groceries. The number of shoppers each day meant the assistants didn't even make eye contact most of the time, despite robotically uttering 'Have a nice day'.

'Video surveillance footage from the shops is bound to be wiped by now unless they caught a shoplifter the same day and kept the footage for court.'

Oliver looked thoughtful. 'It's a long shot, but what about another aspect of shopping centres – some have mothers' groups.'

Kate's mobile phone rang. 'Go on, keep talking,' she said and checked the caller ID. 'Shit. Hang on a sec.'

Oliver tapped his pencil on the desk as Kate took the call.

'Yes, sir,' she said finally. 'We're leaving right now.' She hung up and grabbed her coat. 'We've got a "little problem" job I haven't told you about yet. I'll explain on the way.'

Oliver dutifully followed her down the stairs to the basement and climbed into the unmarked white Commodore. Kate drove, screeching out of the car park. She only spoke once they were in traffic. 'The mothers' group thing?'

'The centres are huge with lots of public transport access. What if she had no support and hated being home all day with just her and the baby? The shops are a way to get out of the house. If she drives, parking is free, and for the cost of a coffee she can sit for a few hours, watch, talk to other mothers, and not feel so alone. I know plenty of wives who do that when they have kids.'

Kate realised how little she knew about motherhood, despite being godmother to Ben, Anya's four-year-old. When anyone started talking or whinging about parenthood, she automatically switched off, especially when the parent described every tedious detail of the 'wonder' child's development. It always amazed her that so few people understood: parenting was *not* an enthralling spectator sport. So far, she was grateful that her new partner had refrained from babbling away about his brood. She hoped it stayed that way.

She pulled up at an amber light and removed a road map from the glove-box and dropped it on her passenger's lap. 'We need Irwin Street, Kenthurst. What do you think we should do about the baby?'

Oliver fumbled to find the street name and compose his thoughts. 'Go via the bridge, then take the M2. A public appeal, maybe?'

Once over the bridge, she manoeuvred the car across three lanes. 'What if the father killed the mother and took the baby? He's not going to come forward if there's been some kind of custody dispute.'

Oliver went quiet, and Kate tried to think of the best way to approach it. On the freeway, she put her foot down and set the cruise control. They could check the number of children born in the city in the last six weeks, then try to narrow it down to mothers fitting the victim's physical description.

She exited the motorway left to turn right on to Pennant Hills Road and smirked when her partner's right foot shot forward, as though he was applying the brakes from the passenger side. At the intersection, they waited.

'I don't think it was a custody fight,' Oliver said, 'because if it was, wouldn't the father have taken the nappy bag? Unless . . .' he hesitated.

'Unless what?' Kate said, accelerating faster than necessary when the lights changed.

'What if it was just a spare? Remember it didn't have clothes or anything else in it? There wasn't a wallet or purse either.'

'In other words, the baby might never have been at the house at all. She could have gone there to meet the killer, alone. We know she wasn't living there because there weren't any clothes or basic toiletries in the house.'

Kate knew that publicity about the 'mystery mother murder' was probably the fastest way to find out who the victim was, but it was risky. They would get thousands of false leads, and would be tied up for weeks going through them all.

Oliver directed her down a few more major roads, then what turned into a semi-rural drive. Kenthurst seemed to have more trees than houses – or manors, more accurately. Eventually they arrived at number 36, which had the name 'Jerilderie' on the letterbox. Unable to see the house from the road, Kate followed the tree-lined drive and parked in front of an ornate Spanish-style home. A red Lamborghini was parked outside a quadruple garage.

Oliver whistled. 'Not bad.'

'Don't get settled. This shouldn't take long. We're interviewing the parents of a runaway as a favour to the commissioner.'

What Kate didn't understand was why *she* had been chosen, and after only one day back on duty. She knew the sorts of people who could pull favours from the top brass and, judging by the house and property, these people were extremely wealthy. There had to be something to the teenager's story that the family wanted kept quiet.

5

Kate rang the intercom and noticed a camera in the apex of the arched brickwork framing the entrance. After they'd introduced themselves, the front door buzzed and Kate gently pushed it open. Inside the foyer, a curved staircase showcased a six-foot-tall chandelier suspended from the ceiling. It would need a specialised ladder just to change one of the hundreds of bulbs. Marble floors diverged into three large rooms. An attractive woman in her mid-forties appeared from the room to the left, clutching a lace hankie.

'Thank you so much for coming,' she said, shaking hands with the detectives. 'We appreciate how busy you must be.' She gestured towards a small cabinet near the door. I hope you don't mind taking off your shoes.'

'Pardon?' Kate felt as though they should have come by the servants' entrance. Oliver looked surprised.

'The white carpets are impossible to keep clean.'

Kate rubbed the toes of her ankle boots on the backs of her trousers, suddenly conscious of how unpolished they were. She unzipped them and moved to place them next to a small cabinet but the owner slipped beside her and opened up the door. Two shelves inside held shoes. Kate placed hers at the front, feeling odd about the ritual. Her home was the complete opposite to this. Filled with clutter and all the paraphernalia of life which, in her view, made it exactly that – a home.

Oliver was slower removing his shiny leather lace-ups and Kate noticed the heel was worn through on one of his socks.

They were shown into a formal lounge room where white leather sofas and a white marble fireplace complemented the pristine carpet. Kate wondered whether it was new, or just cleaned constantly.

'Why didn't you tell me they were here?' A striking figure in a navy suit strode into the room and extended his hand to the visitors. On his feet were socks and grey slippers. It seemed only Mrs Penfold had the privilege of wearing shoes in the house, although judging by their appearance, her patent-leather courts had never been worn outside.

'Robert Penfold. I see you've met Janine. Can we get you anything?'

'No thanks,' Kate said, not wanting to waste any more time. 'I gather your daughter is missing.'

'Stepdaughter, actually,' Mr Penfold said, ushering them all to sit. Kate glanced at his wife, who seemed to approve of the gesture. 'Both the girls are Janine's from a former marriage but I have always treated them as my own.'

A grand piano took a prominent position near a bay window. The piano was covered with a lace cloth and silver photo frames. Mrs Penfold chose one and handed it to Kate. In it were two young women who couldn't have looked less similar.

'The one on the left is Lesley. She's twenty-one and has been studying in New York for the last year. Candice is two years younger.'

Kate studied the faces of the girls, who were sitting next to each other. Lesley smiled through perfect teeth and shiny platinum blonde hair, a younger version of her mother. Candice stared at the camera with a sullen expression, her mousy hair pulled back into a ponytail, fringe hiding her eyes.

'Candy is the shy one and isn't what you could call a high achiever,' Mrs Penfold added. 'She has never had many friends. She wanted to work in child-care, or did until about a year ago.'

Oliver crossed his ankles, presumably to hide his worn sock while the attention was on him. 'Did something happen?'

'She disappeared overnight and refused to tell us where she had been.' Robert Penfold stared at the carpet. 'There had been some words . . .'

'I had a fight with Candy. It was over a crush she had on a man we don't approve of.' Janine squeezed her husband's hand. 'He's the reason we're concerned now.'

Candice Penfold wasn't the first girl to run off with a boyfriend her mother didn't like, Kate thought. She began to jiggle her right foot. This could be investigated by the missing persons unit. There was no reason to involve homicide at this stage. Kate's time would be better spent finding out the identity of the burnt corpse. If the woman had been killed at another location, the baby might have been abandoned, or worse. At a few weeks of age, the child would need constant warmth, food and stimulation. Kate's foot jiggled faster.

Oliver seemed calm and interested. 'What bothers you about this man?'

Kate tried to check her watch without being obvious. A few minutes would turn into an hour if her partner decided to show too much empathy and asked open-ended questions that gave the parents room to waffle. She could not get the murdered mother or the baby out of her mind.

Robert Penfold walked to a bureau drawer and pulled out a pile of letters bound by a rubber band. ' *These* bother us.' He reached across and handed them to Kate, who removed the elastic then flicked through the letters. They were all written to Lesley and signed with love and kisses. The things that struck her were the immaturity of the handwriting and childishness of the number of kisses.

'His name is Mark Dobbie,' the father continued. 'For a short time he was a water polo coach at the girls' school and had a brief relationship with our elder daughter. He denied it began while Lesley was still at school, but he pursued her for months before they started seeing each other publicly. Just before Candy stayed out all night, the first time, we said we'd take out a restraining order if he ever came near the family, and Candy became distraught. I think she had an adolescent crush on him.'

'You see . . .' Mrs Penfold sniffled and dabbed her nose with her handkerchief. 'He wouldn't leave Lesley alone, even after she broke it off. He said they were soul mates and were meant to be together. That's why she went away to study, to get away from him.' Her eyes welled with tears. 'We think he may have been using Candy to get to Lesley, trying to talk her into coming home from New York.'

'So she could have run off with him then?' Being immature and love-struck was not a crime. So far the Penfolds hadn't given her anything to suggest Mark Dobbie was a stalker or had crossed the legal line. An intimate relationship between an ex-student and coach might be inappropriate, but it didn't constitute rape of a minor if Lesley was over sixteen at the time. Kate needed to hurry this up.

'When did you last see Candice?'

'It was twelve days ago, on her nineteenth birthday,' Robert Penfold said, his voice wavering for the first time. 'We had dinner here. After she spent that night God knows where and wouldn't talk about it, she became pretty antisocial and lost touch with the few friends she had. She just wanted to stay home where she felt most comfortable. We understood her, I guess, better than anyone.'

Janine Penfold shot her husband an angry look and clicked two of her manicured fingernails together. 'I believe she has been depressed, but Robert disagrees. He thought it was just a phase, until she went missing.'

'We've always been close,' the girl's stepfather interrupted.

Kate wondered why he sounded defensive.

'Candy enjoys the same sorts of things as me. Her learning disabilities meant nothing when we watched sport together or went sailing. She's wonderful company but not very worldly at times.'

'A real Daddy's girl,' his wife added. 'We're worried because she hasn't touched her bank account or used the credit card we gave her. She doesn't answer her phone either.'

If she was living with this Mark Dobbie character, he could be supporting her, Kate knew. That did not mean she had met with foul play.

Oliver sat forward. 'Is this the most recent photo you have?'

'No,' Janine Penfold answered, extracting a photo from an art book on the coffee table. 'This was taken the night of her birthday dinner.'

Kate found it difficult to believe that she was looking at the same girl as the one in the photo with her sister. In the recent shot Candice seemed twenty to thirty kilograms heavier. 'She looks so different in this one,' Kate managed.

'Yes, you could say she's had food issues at

times,' Mrs Penfold said, a note of disapproval in her voice.

'There are no issues,' Robert interjected. 'The child's got a hearty appetite. She looks better with some meat on her bones, not like the anorexic teenagers you see everywhere.'

Oliver stood at the same time as his partner, seeming to sense the tension in the room.

'May we borrow this?'

'Of course. And here is her latest bank statement, which confirms what we've said about the account being untouched.' Mr Penfold shook the detectives' hands. 'Please, bring my little girl home.'

His mouth looked grim. Kate knew what losing a person close to you meant, and how difficult it was to cope with.

Janine Penfold led them back to the cabinet where they had left their shoes. She twisted a handkerchief in her fingers.

'Candy changed after the first time she disappeared overnight. She began to eat, out of boredom, loneliness, frustration with us, who knows? Some children get tattoos, use drugs and run wild. She didn't do any of that. Candy's way of rebelling was through food.'

As she zipped up her boots, Kate felt sympathy for the couple but wondered how much of this was a family problem. It could not be easy living with a fastidious mother who saw her daughter's weight as a problem, and a stepfather who openly praised her curves. Either way, the girl's photo suggested she was more than just shapely. And behind the immaculate surface of this family, there was likely to be some serious dysfunction.

Kate was about to say goodbye when Oliver spoke: 'Mrs Penfold, your garden is incredible. Would you mind showing us around?'

Kate clenched her hands tightly. What the hell was he doing? They had done all they came to do, and all they could for the moment. She had the letters and bank statement. They would run a check on Mark Dobbie back at homicide and decide how to proceed from there. But before she could stop her partner, he was escorting Mrs Penfold out the door.

Oliver chatted away about types of trees, bushes and flowering plants, and the importance of native vegetation. Janine Penfold had a fixed, polite smile on her face. Kate suspected she wasn't the gardener of the family. The sooner they left, the less chance they had of offending or upsetting the Penfolds. The chief inspector had requested a visit, not an interrogation. Parke was an unknown quantity and she could not control what he might say. Mrs Penfold was already looking drained.

Before Kate could signal to him, Oliver moved close to Mrs Penfold and leant down to her eye level. Kate could just make out what he said: 'I know how hard this is for you, but we need to know. What exactly makes you so concerned that Mark Dobbie has hurt Candy?'

'He's an evil man, a real manipulator who preys on young girls. He made it clear he wants Lesley back but she told him the only reason she would come home was if someone in the family was seriously ill, or for a funeral.'

6

Oliver wound up the passenger-side window and shivered. 'Is the heater working in this thing?'

'It's on,' Kate said curtly, as her partner noticed her open window. No matter how cold the weather, she could not bring herself to completely close herself in. She needed the fresh air.

Oliver took a sip from his personal travel mug.

Kate screwed up her nose. 'What's that smell?'

'A carrot and watermelon smoothie. Great way to start the day.'

When she thought about it, Oliver seemed preternaturally chirpy in the morning. For a man with four kids and a pregnant wife, he looked clean, ironed and lacked the requisite black bags under his eyes. Kate wondered how he had escaped the house without one of his children wiping dirty hands on his suit, or jumping all over him and creasing his shirt.

Running late this morning, Kate silently thanked all those clothes designers who had discovered iron-free, pre-wrinkled fabrics, and hoped they never went out of fashion. With a dry-cleaner for her suits, she hadn't used an iron in months.

Just pull things out of the washing machine, twist them in a ball and leave them out to dry. Today's white shirt was only unravelled minutes before she left for work. Time efficiency at its peak, she thought.

Oliver removed the contents of a brown paper bag sitting on his lap. He munched on one of two salad sandwiches cut into halves.

'Where do you get the time to be so organised?' she asked.

'My wife, actually,' he answered with a full mouth.

Kate deliberately exited the corner faster than she should have. The remains of Oliver's meal slid around his lap. He caught the paper bag just before it hit the middle console.

'Do you get some sort of vicarious thrill out of being childish?' he admonished.

Kate smiled and revved the engine. His reflexes were fast and maybe that's how his clothes stayed so clean.

Oliver clutched what was left of his sandwich. 'If you wanted some, you only had to ask.'

Kate slowed to a stop at a pedestrian crossing. A group of disabled children were being escorted across the road by two carers. 'Any mayonnaise on it?'

'Home-made.' He handed her a half.

After her breakfast of a takeaway egg and bacon roll, which was still repeating on her, this tasted moreish. The mayonnaise made it.

'I don't have a wife, so Mr No-Name Brand makes most of my sauces.' She licked her fingers to collect every drop of the creamy dressing. It reminded her that she would have to do something about her fridge sooner rather than later. The only things left in it were a rotting banana, some expired yoghurt and a bottle of tomato sauce.

'Do you realise how many artificial additives are in that stuff? It's full of thickeners, vegetable gum. The list is endless.'

Kate waited until the last carer had left the crossing before accelerating. All she needed was a health food freak earbashing her all day. And with traffic grinding to a standstill thanks to roadworks ahead, the day was about to get longer.

Oliver continued to speak. 'My wife makes me something every morning. And before you think I force her do it, she says she enjoys it.'

With four kids and another on the way, Kate doubted that any woman would be happy creating extra work for herself. More likely, Oliver's wife would swap places with him in a snap.

'Did you see the papers?' She reached into the back while keeping her eyes on the brakelights in front of them, and handed him a copy of the tabloid *Daily Mail*. The headline they had run with was 'Young Mother Burnt in Horror Blaze'. If that didn't grab attention and heartstrings, nothing would.

Oliver scanned the article. 'Your quotes don't say anything about cause of death or murder. Just concern about where the baby is.'

'There's a reason for that.' She tapped the horn to alert the car in front that the lights had turned green. 'Murders are mostly committed by someone close to the victim. If the killer knows her, he might not come forward if I called it murder. The way that reads, it's not obvious how she died. If he set the fire to destroy evidence and he thinks it worked, he may be cocky enough now to make contact.'

'That's clever.' Oliver finished off his sandwich. 'But if someone killed *for* the baby, we would have needed to appeal to a wider demographic, to see if someone has just turned up with a child somewhere.'

'You'd be surprised how little attention most people pay to others, and how many keep to themselves. A wife disappears and the husband tells friends she left him and most people don't think twice.'

More than once Kate had been hindered by the time lag between people going missing and someone reporting the disappearance. The first twenty-four hours following a murder were the most critical and had already passed, which was why they needed to identify their mystery woman as quickly as possible. With each day, they were less likely to get a result.

Oliver finished his smoothie. 'Maybe someone will complain if they have a problem like the sound of a crying child waking them. Mind you, it's sometimes hard to pick ages in the first few weeks.

A small baby could easily be mistaken for a new-born who has just come home from hospital.'

'Let's hope someone out there is more observant than the average punter,' Kate said. Someone had to know the dead woman. Later today she would chase up the DNA database and see if they got lucky with that.

A few minutes later they entered the fire investigators' office. John Zimmer was helping himself from a plate of muffins.

'You should try the chocolate chip,' he enthused through full cheeks.

Kate glanced over to see only savoury muffins left. Typical, she thought. Crime scene beat homicide to the good stuff every time.

'Thanks for coming, detectives. I'm Inspector William Maloney. We met at the fire. Can I get you anything before we start?'

'No thanks.' Kate followed him into a meeting room and wedged the door into a fully open position. She swung her jacket over a chair and sat. Oliver chose a seat at the round table directly opposite her. Zimmer grabbed a china mug from a cupboard and made himself a cup of tea.

Inspector Maloney was an experienced arson investigator. Independent of the police, members of his unit were used to working with insurance companies and were invaluable in cases of fire involving homicide. Maloney had a reputation for being like an auditor when it came to details. He had begun as a fireman and worked his way up.

Age and years of more sedentary work did not disguise the man's massive frame. He would have been formidable at his physical peak, Kate thought.

From the way John Zimmer seemed to know his way around the office, it was clear the fire investigation unit had liaised with crime scene more frequently than she had realised. With better-informed criminals, the result of shorter prison sentences and tricks gleaned from crime shows, an increasing number attempted to destroy evidence of their handiwork with fire.

Maloney sat toying with a laptop while the others waited. 'Anyone know how to work these things? It's just flashing at me,' he appealed, and Oliver went to his aid. After a quick check of the laptop, the junior detective plugged it into a power point.

'Battery's low, that's all.' Oliver switched off the light and returned to his seat.

Maloney apologised. Technology was obviously advancing faster than he could keep pace with, but no one minded. He began his presentation.

Slides of the outside of the house appeared first. 'We'll go over the scene from the outside in.'

Kate watched the images projected onto the wall. The ferocity of the fire seemed more evident now than when she was at the site. Without the distraction of smoke, sirens and camera crews, the scene was more chilling. She could not help but wonder what the dead woman's last thoughts were, or whether she had seen her killer.

'There was no sign of breaking or entering. No glass inside. The windows have blown out from the intense heat, shattering onto the ground. It doesn't appear that anyone smashed one to escape.'

Zimmer nodded. 'No blood or fingerprints found on the sills, glass or putty.'

The next few photos focused on the back door. 'As we all saw, the outside of the door was not burnt and was soot-free, which means it was closed during the fire.'

They viewed sections of the floorboards in progression. 'We removed samples of the different types of flooring where we believe accelerant was used, and then compared this to samples taken from other areas, where there was less or no fire damage.'

Oliver sat forward in his seat. 'Why don't you simply test any suspect piece of flooring for accelerants?'

'The problem with that is when some materials break down in a fire they release hydrocarbons and can be mistaken for accelerants like methylated spirits, turpentine and lawn mower fuel. It's also why we took samples from various spots on the bed. We need these other pieces as controls, to confirm that a separate accelerant was used.' He shrugged his broad shoulders. 'Arson is more difficult to prove than people think.'

He continued the slide show. 'Now, the trail of the accelerant is closer to the right-hand walls in most cases. If you look carefully, when it crosses rooms, like from the bedroom to the corridor and then into the living area, it curves a little to the left.'

Kate had always been fascinated by evidence and how the smallest things could mean the biggest breaks. In this case the pattern minimised the risk of the arsonist splashing petrol on himself.

'It's not a fixed rule, but my guess is it's unlikely to be a left-handed person,' Maloney said.

The scene progressed to the bedroom. The body of the unknown mother lay in her peculiar position, arms ready to fight. After enduring a head injury, maybe the victim was trying to tell them something about her killer. But what? When Kate was close to being killed, she made sure to leave behind bits of herself – torn fingernails, bits of skin she dug out, anything that could help the police learn of her fate. Maybe this woman did the same. Once the body had been removed, they examined the bed.

'The body was fully clothed, which explains why some of the mattress appears less damaged – the parts she was lying on suffered less direct heat.'

'Which is why her back was not burnt as much as her front.' Oliver seemed to be thinking out loud while he stared at the image on the wall through squinting eyes.

Kate realised they had been staring at the scene for more than an hour now, and needed to stretch.

Zimmer unpeeled himself from his chair and stood up. 'I don't know about everyone else, but I need a coffee.'

Oliver raised both eyebrows at his partner, as if asking permission. She nodded.

'I'll get them.' He stood and flicked the light back on.

Maloney showed Oliver where to find the coffee and John Zimmer followed Kate out the door.

'How's the new partner working out? Looks like you've already got Drover well-trained.'

'That's because he's intelligent,' she retorted. 'Let's just say that he is a pedigree, whereas some-one like you is . . .'

Zimmer grinned. 'A junk yard dog?'

'Ah . . .' Kate forced a smile. She pulled out her mobile and flipped it open. 'Insight as well – admirable.'

As the crime scene officer laughed, she dialled Peter Latham. His secretary said he was unavail-able. There was a mechanical problem in the mortuary he had to sort out but she would defi-nitely pass on the message.

'Oh, wise homicide detective,' Zimmer bowed. 'Any luck with the canvass?' His tone had become serious, which Kate much preferred.

The pair returned to the meeting room, where Oliver had coffees ready. Normally, she didn't like being waited on, but today she would not show it.

They resumed their seats as she began. 'Neigh-bours didn't see or hear anything unusual. No screaming, yelling, no visitors. You'd think they all had blinkers on.'

'Mrs Gorman, the owner's wife, drives a yellow Porsche but none of the residents of Moat Place could remember when they last saw it,' Oliver added. 'One man I spoke to thinks it might have been there a week or two before the fire.'

'Are you sure she's not missing?' Zimmer had a spark in his eye, like a child who was awe-struck by anything to do with a crime.

'Not exactly, the Gormans are still overseas and out of contact.'

Maloney finished off the last of a muffin. 'That would explain why no one has contacted the insurance company yet,' he said.

'What does Mrs Gorman look like?' Zimmer asked.

'Unless the killer somehow took six inches off her height and removed two large breast implants, she doesn't fit the victim's description.'

Everyone stared at Oliver. 'What? I asked a neighbour what she looked like.'

'Don't suppose the petrol was unique in any way?' Kate asked.

Maloney checked his watch. 'What we have is unleaded petrol, nothing unusual, that was poured in a trail which started at the bed and led out towards the back door. The garage was largely untouched. We assume our person then closed the back door and lit the petrol, which caught fire and travelled under the door. My guess is this wasn't his first fire.'

'Or whoever killed her then did some research before coming back,' Kate added.

'All we know is that there is a remote possibility that our arsonist could have burns to his arms, face and hands. That is, if we've overestimated his abilities.'

Kate had already alerted doctors and hospitals in the area to be on the lookout for anyone with burns.

Zimmer coughed, as though wanting attention. 'We went right over the place. There's no sign of a child's body in or under the house. No blood underneath floorboards either, as far as we could tell. And no sign of a murder weapon in the debris.'

Kate knew that made it almost certain the woman had been killed somewhere else. Head injuries were notorious for causing significant blood loss. If the victim had been hit inside the house, she would have bled on the floor. A large volume of blood would have seeped through the wooden boards. Kate also remembered that the body did not smell of petrol. It had been poured on the mattress, but not on the body. She wondered why someone would go to that much trouble to incinerate the woman as quickly as possible, but not pour petrol on her.

'Can you estimate how much petrol we're talking about?' she asked Maloney.

He scratched his bulbous chin. 'About five litres would have done the lot. You would find that kind of quantity in a garage normally, but we couldn't find a tin. And as I said, the garage was pretty much untouched by the fire.'

'How about checking the local petrol stations to see who filled up into a tin?' Oliver asked.

Zimmer frowned. 'Petrol's so common. Often people fill up the tank then the can for the mower. No one ever looks twice at them. Do you know how many people go through a petrol station in an hour, let alone a day? Trying to get the solo attendant to remember any of them is pretty pointless, especially if they paid with cash. That's why arsonists like this are so hard to catch.'

Unless you had a specific time frame, Kate thought. Surveillance tapes at stations caught numberplates. It was a very long shot, but might be worth requesting from the stations in the area of the fire. Images of hire or stolen cars might just give them more than they already had if the fire was premeditated and the killer well prepared.

She felt the buzz of her mobile in her pocket and excused herself from the room.

'Peter Latham here. Can you talk?'

'Have you got good news about an ID?'

'No, dental records will take weeks. But there's more information about the body.'

Kate started to pace. Maybe the woman had left them something after all.

'I checked the histology for our unknown victim. There was notable cell rupture and crystals present in the liver.'

'Peter, can you make this simpler?' she said. Pathologists might have understood the implications, but she had no idea where this was headed.

'Sorry, I'm getting to that. At first I thought it was an error in the slide preparation so I checked

71

the other organs. Each specimen showed the same thing. It was even in the vitreous humour, the fluid behind the eye. It means that the organs reached freezing point at some stage.'

'Before or after they got to you?' she asked. The secretary had mentioned a mechanical problem in the morgue.

'I checked the fridges. We have to record them every shift to prevent any problems. I've been through all the temperatures for the last week, for every one. None of them had any aberrant recordings. I spoke to the others and no one has had organ specimens with cell rupture or crystals.'

Kate felt her pulse quicken. She had a bad feeling about what was coming next.

'It makes sense now,' Peter continued. 'The organs were in such good condition. Normally they shrink in a fire that severe.'

Kate stopped pacing. 'Are you saying the body was frozen?'

'Completely. It must have been totally frozen to have sustained that degree of cellular damage in the organs.'

'So when did she die?'

'We have no way of knowing how long she was frozen for. All we know is that she died from a head injury, not from the fire.'

Kate thought about the baby. Please don't let it have been killed, too. 'What about the uterus? Does freezing affect that?'

Peter sighed. 'No, it just means the body was frozen within weeks of giving birth. It's confirmed by the presence of foetal squames and lanugo in the lungs.'

Kate had no idea what that meant. 'In English?'

'Lanugo is that down-type hair that covers a foetus and squamous cells come from foetal skin. I found them and vernix fat globules in the lungs. They're the hallmarks of what's called an amniotic fluid embolus. It's where a bolus of the fluid in which the baby grows gets into the venous circulation and gets trapped in the lungs. It usually happens during labour. The effects are similar to a blood clot, if you like.'

Kate paused, confused by what she was hearing. 'I'm not clear. Are you saying she died while giving birth?'

'No. An embolus of amniotic fluid can be fatal, but this one wasn't big enough to obstruct blood flow to the heart or cause significant lung damage.'

'Did she know she had this? Would she have had to see a doctor for it?' A medical record might be their only chance of identifying her.

'Possibly not,' Peter explained. 'She may simply have experienced shortness of breath, which she could have put down to being at the end stage of pregnancy. It would have been reabsorbed over time so wouldn't necessarily have caused any long-term problems.'

Kate tugged on the back of her hair. So the unknown woman had a baby then, after surviving a clot during labour, she was murdered and her body frozen for God knows how long before being set on fire. She could barely believe the scenario herself.

'Is there any way of determining how old the baby is now? I mean, meat goes an odd colour in the freezer after a few months. Do humans do the same?' She was grasping for means to narrow the time frame. 'Can't you tell anything more about when the woman died?'

Peter sighed again. 'Unfortunately, it's impossible to tell. I couldn't even begin to guess with any certainty.'

Kate rubbed her eyes and thought of the media articles seeking a motherless baby. The case had just become far more complicated. They still had no idea who the victim was, where she was killed or what damn month it happened. They didn't even know how old the missing child was. Unless they found answers soon, the murderer was likely to get away with it.

7

Back at Goulburn Street police headquarters, Kate and Oliver stood outside Inspector Gareth Russo's office.

'You wanted to see us, sir,' Kate said from the entrance.

'Come in, close the door,' he said without looking up. 'And take a seat.'

'Sir, I'd prefer to stand if you don't mind.' She remained in the doorway, half closing the door for privacy while leaving it open enough for air. Oliver assumed an at-ease stance. Kate wondered if he had some kind of military background. Then again, he was 'nice' enough to have been a boy-scout leader in his youth.

The triathlon-obsessed head of homicide sat with white sleeves perfectly and symmetrically rolled. To describe him as fastidious would have been an understatement.

'There's been a development in the Penfold case.' He looked up over half-moon reading glasses. 'The girl's car has been found, abandoned, with her mobile phone in it.'

Kate closed her eyes. That didn't bode well. No

nineteen-year-old would voluntarily leave behind her means of communication with the world. Teenagers seemed unable to function without texting friends every few minutes. But then, from what her parents had said, Candice may not have had many friends.

'Crime scene is going over the car,' her boss continued.

'Preliminary testing with luminol has found something positive on the driver's and back seats. The car's been cleaned, but they're swabbing to confirm whether it's blood.'

Kate felt her pulse gallop. The chances of finding the Penfold girl alive had just got a lot slimmer.

'Do you have any real leads yet?' Russo asked, putting his glasses into an open case by his paperwork.

Oliver cleared his throat. 'The mother suggested looking into a former boyfriend of the sister who lives overseas. Apparently this guy was obsessed with Lesley and would do anything to get her to come back. She told him that she'd only come home for a funeral or family crisis.'

'I'd say this constitutes a crisis, wouldn't you, Detective?'

Oliver nodded, like a boy in front of the headmaster.

'I'm taking you off the burnt homicide victim.'

Kate held one foot against the door and jammed both hands into her pockets. 'But the woman gave birth. There is a baby we have a duty of care to find.'

'I've got people manning the phones, collecting leads. I'll reassign the case. With the abandoned car, I need you two on the Penfold job. You've met the parents and already have the background info. And they've personally requested you stay on the case.'

Kate felt her anger rise. They had attended the fire scene and canvassed the neighbours, and been through the autopsy. The murder case should have been theirs, with maximum effort put into finding the child.

'You can write up your reports later but give Fiskars and Rench a handover as soon as possible. Where are you with it so far?'

Kate clenched her fists out of sight and tried to sound calm. No doubt Russo would be looking for any signs of stress or inability to cope with the job. The police psychologist would have made sure the chief inspector complied with occupational health and safety criteria.

'There's a complication with the body.' She felt her face colour, but tried to ignore it. 'The pathologist says it's been frozen.'

'What do you mean exactly by "frozen"?' Russo sounded impatient. He must have been under more pressure than usual, presumably with the Penfold case. The media frenzy over the incinerated mother and missing baby would not have helped.

'As in frozen solid. The organs were still intact, which was surprising given the degree of heat the fire generated. Dr Latham said they had formed crystals in their cells, which means that whoever killed her put her in some kind of freezer.'

The veins in Russo's neck began to bulge. 'Killers who do that usually dismember the bodies first, at least so they'll fit.'

'Well,' Kate continued, 'she was completely intact. We've no way of knowing how long she'd been dead, or—'

'So there's no time of death, no ID and no idea how old the child is, or was? If you ever find the killer, you'll never pin him down to a window of opportunity. We'd better pray someone turns up with a tape of the killer caught in the bloody act.'

Kate hoped Russo was finished with them, but their boss sat forward and tapped his index finger on the veneer desk. 'And I suppose you don't know where she was killed, either. The papers are going to crucify us, and the radio shock jocks will be scaring every parent in the state.'

'About the media,' Kate said tentatively, 'have you had much of a response from people claiming to know the victim?'

Russo's face deepened in colour.

Oliver looked like he wanted to melt into the carpet.

'Ancillary staff have been running around like blue-arsed flies chasing all the false leads. People are ringing up about missing neighbours. A woman who allegedly disappeared with her baby was in hospital with her kid. Another helpful citizen claimed the pregnant woman down the street came back with twins, and she must have stolen a baby because she didn't look that big when she was pregnant. So I had some uniforms check out the ultrasound photos – of two waving sets of hands.' One vein in his neck looked like it might burst. 'And did you know this was a terrorist attack? Oh yeah, and a psychic reckons the woman and the kid spontaneously combusted.'

As annoying as crank calls were, Kate thought, at least people had noticed the stories. Amidst the calls might just be the one that would identify the mother and child.

Russo leant back in his chair. 'Forget about the burnt victim for now. Fiskars and Rench have wrapped up two of their cases and can carry the extra load for a few days. You just deal with the Penfold disappearance. It doesn't look good, but there may be a chance she's still alive. You can start by letting the parents know about the car and gauge their reaction. If you think you'll need phone taps approved, let me know.'

'Excuse me, sir. Is there reason to suspect the parents?' Oliver asked.

Kate felt the heat in her face rise again. If there was something relevant to the case, why hadn't she been informed? Her fingers dug into her palms inside her suit pockets. Calming down wasn't as easy as the police therapist kept telling her.

'Remember the first rule of homicide, detectives. Start with those closest to the family and work your way out. Don't always assume the obvious.' He sat back and placed both palms on the desk. 'And, Farrer, try to be diplomatic. I don't want complaints about harassment from the family.' He put his glasses back on and resumed his paperwork.

Kate didn't move. She was not some kind of beginner, she was an experienced investigator, and a bloody good one. Three months off hadn't affected her mind. So why was she being treated like an incompetent fool?

'Farrer, do you have a problem? If you're not up to the task, I can assign you desk duties.'

What the hell was he doing? Did he want her to fail? She wasn't about to give him the satisfaction.

Oliver almost pushed Kate out of the room. She headed straight for the women's toilets. Inside, she paced, counting to ten to control her temper. On the count of nine she gave up and swung her boot into a cubicle door. Pain shot through her foot.

She took the weight off it and tried to decipher what was happening. She had felt paranoid about returning to work and should have been flattered when Russo asked her to help out on the Penfold case. Now she wondered if she were being set up to fail, and whether Russo was somehow involved. Maybe they wanted her to resign because they thought someone like her was a liability. Was she being blamed for her abduction? It made sense if Oliver was the only one willing to partner her. She wasn't popular before, but now she was like damaged goods, and bad luck as well. If she was being lured into a tainted investigation, Oliver and his career would be affected in the process, unless he was part of the plan.

God, she thought. Now she really did sound paranoid.

I choose not to be a victim. I am a survivor.

She took her boot and sock off and the cool floor soothed the pain.

I choose to be a survivor.

She splashed some cold water on her face and wiped it with a paper towel. Her foot was red where she had connected with the door and the top portion was swelling, but she could still bear weight on it. Nothing was broken.

Kate had worked under Russo for a couple of years and, up until today, had nothing but respect for the man. He was friendly without being overly involved or intrusive, and gave his detectives a long rope, but not long enough for them to do damage with. Occasionally known to drink with the boys after work, he had never once made Kate feel intimidated or unaccepted. He'd approved her application to join homicide, ahead of numerous applicants who had already acted in the job. He had also asked her to come back, specifically, to his unit . . . Her conspiracy theory was ridiculous. No one had it in for her. They were all preoccupied with their own jobs.

Back in control of her temper, Kate quietly returned to her desk, trying to hide a grimace when she stepped on her self-inflicted injury. Oliver had an instant coffee waiting for her that had gone tepid. This time she didn't complain about the gesture, but thanked him and drank it.

Oliver wheeled his chair across to her. 'What was that all about? Do you two have some kind of coded language?'

'What's that supposed to mean?'

'I assumed that warning about the family was for my benefit. For some reason he couldn't come out and say what he knew in front of me.'

'It wasn't just you,' Kate said. 'He's withholding something, but expects us to solve the case ASAP.'

'Is that what you thought? I got the impression he was trying to warn us about the family without specifically saying why. My guess is that he found out something illegally, or off the record.'

Oliver sounded like a journalist, but he might just be right. Today's behaviour was definitely bizarre for Russo. He'd mentioned the possibility of phone taps on the family. Perhaps Russo's office was being monitored, and that was his way of letting Kate know. Internal investigations went on, and the Commission Against Corruption was not above bugging colleagues, at any level. Anyone in the department could be the target and might have been for the last few months. With her three-month absence, it was no wonder she was excluded from rumours about surveillance, but it still helped to know if their conversations were being monitored.

'Either way, he wants us to investigate the parents first, so that's what we'll do. Let's break the news to the father.'

'You mean stepfather,' Oliver said, as though it made a significant difference.

'His office is in town, and it saves us a trip out to Kenthurst and back. We can "gauge" him from there.'

Kate paced the white-tiled floor, trying to minimise the pressure on the ball of her foot, while the receptionist phoned Robert Penfold. Oliver stood calmly taking in the view of Darling Harbour through a glass wall. Boats and water taxis carried people across to shops and restaurants from the redeveloped wharf area. A commuter catamaran from Circular Quay headed west towards the Parramatta River, the afternoon sun reflecting off the water.

Up fifty-three floors in the Market Street suites, Kate had no intention of wandering closer to the glass. No window was thick enough to make her feel secure when she was up that high.

'At least they haven't asked us to take our shoes off,' Kate said, trying to lighten the moment.

'If you had one of these, you would never need to go anywhere,' Oliver said, mesmerised by a massive plasma screen showing collages of technological advances.

What was it with men and televisions, Kate wondered. Oliver was more interested in that than the attractive receptionist. So far, he was completely different from all of her previous partners. Each of them would have been dribbling at the sight of the pretty brunette.

Kate continued to pace the office foyer. With its vast space and expensive views, it resembled a media company more than an IT business. Robert Penfold was obviously successful, or at least that was what he wanted people to think. She made a mental note to look into his business dealings, whether he was being audited, or investigated by the Securities and Investment Commission. Did he owe money? Had someone kidnapped his daughter as payback, or was someone trying to extort money from him? Did he have any shady business dealings? Something had aroused Russo's suspicion, but what?

Kate wondered whether the Penfolds were hiding something when they requested homicide investigate their daughter's disappearance. They had to have excellent contacts either in politics, the police force, or both. But some secrets could not be buried by power. Most could, but murder could not. Secrets that big destroyed lives and eventually one of the stakeholders cracked. Kate wondered again whether she and Oliver were being set up to botch the investigation. A traumatised detective and an inexperienced sidekick might just help a murderer get away with it, if that's what the Penfolds wanted. Her temples began to pound.

'You can go in now.'

The receptionist flashed a smile at Oliver, but he barely acknowledged her, despite her long legs and very short skirt. Either he was not normally flirtatious, or he had a lot on his mind as well. For some reason she didn't fully understand, that impressed Kate.

Robert Penfold appeared from a corridor and shook their hands. This time he wore black leather shoes and an open-necked shirt. But instead of looking more relaxed than he had at their first meeting, he seemed nervous and a little unsure of himself.

Inside his office, he stood by the door, waiting to close it, until Kate used her shoe to wedge the doorstop into place.

'Can my assistant get you anything? Tea, coffee, water?'

'No thanks. We need to discuss something with you.' Kate took the lead.

'Have a seat.' He directed them to leather lounges configured in a square around a glass coffee table, not unlike the one in the Penfolds' home. At one end of the penthouse-sized room, a treadmill faced another large plasma screen. There appeared to be a bathroom off a nook behind the desk, and two more doors. One could have been a wardrobe, or even a bedroom. This office was bigger than Kate's place, and perfectly set up for someone who worked long hours – or wanted privacy away from home.

'Do you have any news?' Penfold pressed his hands together. 'My wife is a mess. She needed sedation overnight. Actually, we're all pretty distressed by this and just want Candice home.'

He was stalling, probably not wanting to hear what they had to say, not that Kate could blame him for postponing bad news. If they had found his daughter alive, he would already have heard by phone.

She cleared her throat. 'We've found Candice's car. It was abandoned and her phone was inside it.'

Kate paused and studied his face. His eyes darted between the detectives, as if waiting – pleading – for more.

'Where's Candy? Is she hurt?'

'I'm afraid we don't know any more at the moment.'

There was a knock on the door. The receptionist entered with a tray of glasses and a bottle of water. Without a word, she filled three glasses before leaving.

'Was the car in some kind of accident? Or did it break down?' Penfold sat forward, his face in his hands. 'It was always overheating, or Candy just ran out of petrol. She doesn't appreciate that cars don't fill themselves or that they need to be maintained.' He looked up, his eyes misting over.

Oliver edged forward in his seat.

Penfold could barely control the tremble in his hands. 'You're here because you think something terrible has happened, aren't you?'

'We don't know,' Oliver said. 'It is unusual to leave a phone behind, but it may have dropped out of her bag. She may be intending to come back for it.'

'The phone battery was flat and your daughter may not have needed it anymore, especially if she ran away and isn't ready to make contact.' Kate decided to stick with the concept of Candice having run away rather than disclosing the possibility that her blood had been found in the car. That could wait until formal lab confirmation.

The last thing the family needed was misinformation and added anxiety, particularly when blood wasn't the only thing luminol reacted with: it also picked up numerous other substances, like plant matter, some paints, metals and cleaning products. Given that Mrs Penfold was obsessed with a clean house, there was a chance the luminol results would turn out to be 'false-positives'. Waiting for confirmation was the only sensible option. Or so Kate reassured herself.

Oliver took out his notebook and asked Mr Penfold if he minded being asked some questions. Kate listened as she wandered over to the desk, looking carefully at the number of photos displayed there. Images of Penfold hugging his two girls at various ages filled the frames. Candid portraits of the three laughing, in black and white and colour, adorned the walnut desk. Oddly, there was only one small photo of his wife. In one shot, a small square picture of the kind printed in the seventies, Penfold squatted down with three children, two boys and a girl. The girl didn't resemble Candice or Lesley. Kate felt curiously uncomfortable looking at the photos.

'How would you describe your relationship with Candice and Lesley?' she asked. 'Judging by these snapshots, you three are, or were, very close.'

Robert Penfold joined her at his desk. 'We always have been,' he said, picking up a picture taken when his daughters were aged around eight and ten. 'This one's my favourite,' he said. 'It was taken on holiday in Hawaii. Candy had been through a tough time, not doing well at school, and she had just been diagnosed with a learning disorder. She had trouble losing weight and got teased a lot by the other kids.' He wiped a smudge off the glass. 'This was the first time I saw her really enjoy herself. We all shared a room and had a ball. She was eight and a half when this was taken.'

'Do you think it's possible that she has a boyfriend you don't know about?'

The father's tone turned sombre. 'No way. She was a terrible liar and would get a rash on her neck every time she tried to distort the truth. She told me everything and promised me that she had never been sexually active.'

Oliver flicked Kate a look of surprise. 'I'm close to my daughters,' he began, 'but I hope that they'll confide in their mother about that sort of thing. Having been there herself, I guess she'll be a bit more understanding.'

'Well, Candy and Lesley's mother is a perfectionist, Detective. She expects a lot from her children. Sometimes that's hard on them. I tend to be the fun parent, the one they can relax and make a mess with, wear shoes in the house if they want, the stuff their mother doesn't allow.'

Kate noticed the way he neglected to mention his wife's name, referring to her only in the possessive form. Perhaps the marriage wasn't as united as the couple had made out at their home.

'Don't get me wrong,' Penfold added. 'She is a wonderful mother and would do anything for her family. That's one of the reasons I married her.'

Kate tried to sound casual, but wasn't sure how to pull it off. 'Has your wife ever been jealous of your closeness to the girls?'

Thankfully, he didn't seem to infer anything from the question. 'The girls were close to their mother when they were little, but as they grew, they loved coming into the office, and even going away on business trips with me. Janine preferred to stay at home and she thinks sometimes I spoilt them, Candy more than Lesley.' He put down the picture, eyes welling again. 'I tried to protect them from the world, but I've let them down. First Lesley, with that Dobbie character, and now Candy.' He turned his face away and began to cry. 'I never knew that the children you love could hurt you so much.'

8

Kate and Oliver left Robert Penfold's office in silence. At a nearby café, Kate ordered lasagne and a black coffee, while Oliver succumbed to a bran muffin and soy milk decaffeinated latte. Kate wondered why he didn't just order fibre and brown water if he wanted all the good stuff taken out.

They had long missed the lunchtime rush and managed to secure a corner table with no other customers nearby. You never knew who could be listening, Kate thought, especially if they mentioned Penfold by name.

'Checking his background is our first priority.' She poured two glasses of water from the bottle on the table. 'See if he has a history of paedophilia.'

'Pardon?' Oliver pulled his wooden chair closer. 'Did I miss something in there?'

'You heard him, the way he talked about his "stepdaughters". And all the photos of them hugging. There was only one of his wife, whose name he only mentioned once, by the way.'

Oliver put both elbows on the table and glanced around. 'So that automatically makes him a paedophile? I can't believe you'd jump to that conclusion. Didn't it occur to you that those photos had to be taken by someone, and most likely Mrs Penfold? One parent usually takes on the role and actually misses out on a lot of the fun by filming it.' He looked down and shook his head. 'And how often have you heard me talk about my wife? I see that as a form of courtesy, like not bringing your kids' names into every conversation.'

Kate could barely believe her partner's naivety. Maybe she had completely misjudged him. How could he possibly have thought Penfold's reactions and comments were normal?

'Maybe you just haven't been in the game long enough, but what we saw in there was perverse. How many teenage daughters do you know who spend more time with their father on business trips than their mother? Or who confide in their father about their sex life or lack thereof?'

Oliver took a sip of water and looked directly at her. 'You should listen to yourself. When you were a child, who was the fun parent?'

'This isn't about me,' she snapped. 'My mother died when I was four years old. I only had one parent.'

Oliver let a breath out. 'I'm sorry. I was just trying to make the point that most fathers work, and the mother is left with the responsibility of raising the kids, even if she works full-time as well. That means she becomes the disciplinarian, and is the one who has to be the bad guy most of the time.'

He waited a moment while the waiter delivered the food and coffees. When he was out of earshot, Oliver continued: 'A man like Penfold has to invest a lot of time to make a business that successful. My guess is that he wasn't at home much and so could afford to be the fun, generous, less strict parent. By attempting to compensate for his emotional and physical absence, he ends up spoiling them and puts a wedge between the girls and their mother. It happens even more with divorced fathers.'

Kate had to admit there was some merit in what he said. His habit of making sense was becoming annoying. She had seen children from broken families used as emotional pawns by game-playing parents. But she still felt that Penfold's manner and the way he spoke was different from a normal parent. She took a bite of the lasagne and swallowed it quickly so she could make her next point.

'Even if that is all he did, he certainly screwed things up for his wife by putting a wedge between her and the kids. Mind you, Mrs Penfold gets to decorate the house with her white carpets and live off his money.'

Oliver picked at his muffin with a fork. It looked even less appetising than his imitation coffee. 'Life is never that simple,' he said. 'Parents do what they can for their families. I've seen it from both sides. Being a stay-at-home parent is bloody hard. It's unrelenting, and if your partner is always at work or away, it's a lonely job.'

Kate shovelled another bite of cheesy meat into her mouth. 'Are you saying you were a house-husband?'

'I did it for a while, after we had the twins. My wife – Lucy, if you really want to know – was a litigation lawyer and she was earning more than me. For us it was partly financial, but she didn't think she could be a stay-at-home mum, and didn't want to farm the kids out to daycare.'

With Oliver's wife going to the trouble of making homemade mayonnaise, she had pictured them as a traditional 1950s couple, totally alien to anything she had known in her family or personal relationships. Her cheeks flushed with shame at having made the assumption so readily.

'So that's how you know so much about nappies?'

'You learn fast on that job. Anyway, Lucy hated being back at work. Instead of going for big pay-outs, she spent most of her time negotiating compromises. And she really missed being with the kids. She's a high achiever *and* a fantastic mother.'

It had never occurred to Kate that Oliver's wife was a professional with her own career. She looked down at her plate.

'Even as a dad, I'm very aware of how people perceive me and how I am with the kids. If I take one of the girls out and hold her hand, you'd be amazed how many people in the supermarket give me second looks. You can't even show normal affection to your kids now without someone thinking you're a paedophile, and that harms girls.'

'How? Surely it protects them.' Kate thought of her own father's difficulty showing affection. She learnt to be independent very early, and in some ways was grateful for that.

'Did you know studies show that girls who have a healthy, loving relationship with their father hit puberty at a later age and, as a result, are less likely to be promiscuous or have teenage pregnancies? On the other hand, girls who don't have a good paternal influence go through the physical changes of puberty at an earlier age and are much more at risk of pregnancy in their teens. Father–daughter relationships are obviously complex, but a good one is critical to a teenager's development and future.'

Kate was shocked to think that loving a father could alter physical aspects of growth. The idea of a daughter's hormones being influenced by a father's affection seemed almost obscene.

Oliver slurped the last of his brown water.

'Penfold didn't do or say anything disturbing to me.'

'I still disagree. First thing we do is look into his background. I'm betting there's more than one skeleton hiding in there. And my gut tells me he had something to do with his daughter's disappearance. That loving father routine is anything but normal.'

9

That evening, Kate just made it to her kickboxing class, her sore foot tightly bound with strapping tape, the magic panacea. Strenuous exercise had been a stress reliever over the last few months, but tonight she felt every muscle in her neck and back tighten, despite the workout. It wasn't the run-in with Russo, or being taken off the homicide–arson case. She could not shake the feeling that Robert Penfold might be a paedophile who was masquerading as a loving father. With only reruns on television and nothing at the local cinema apart from a period drama and a science fiction marathon, she decided to make better use of her time and drive back to the city office after the class.

Though it was nine-thirty, the security officer didn't seem surprised to see her, barely looking up as she buzzed in. He knew her by surname, but she couldn't remember his. She had never been good with names and now no one expected her to be. The advantages of being standoffish, she thought. No small talk or having to remember people's birthdays or anniversaries, and no insincere 'hi, how are you, have a nice day' bullshit. Why waste time saying something no one cared about or meant?

The air-conditioner hummed in the empty office, pointlessly pumping carbon dioxide into the atmosphere. The bloody thing ran at about 35 degrees Celsius in winter, and 10 degrees in summer, so being inside was never comfortable. She checked her desk drawers, a habit she developed on her first job. They were still locked. Detectives were some of the biggest thieves out. Any loose change, pens or paper vanished if an officer left their desk unattended for even a minute. She switched on her computer and waited while it booted up. Her swollen foot throbbed faintly.

She thought about Oliver defending Robert Penfold. It was easy to jump to the wrong conclusions about men and children. She thought of the difficult time she had given her own father during adolescence. He would threaten that if she didn't show him more respect, she would end up drug-addicted, pregnant and alcoholic by the time she was fifteen. Out of her high-school class, only four girls escaped that fate, so he did have a point. Not that she conceded that until years later.

Once she had logged on she typed in 'Robert Penfold' for a search of recent news articles. A number of titles described the titan of the local computing industry basking in unparalleled success. She supposed that business journalists had to make boring topics sound fascinating somehow, but the language was ridiculous. There was nothing titanic about Robert Penfold, in her opinion. He had probably been in the right place at the right time, or had great financial backers and advisors. Nothing she could see suggested dodgy dealings or falling share prices, and a check of the annual report showed the company had a good credit rating and its business loans were with reputable local banks. The Penfolds were photographed in the social pages alongside other prominent business people and, in one photo, the deputy commissioner of police, who appeared to be looking down Janine Penfold's exposed cleavage. Perhaps the powerful political connections were with Mrs Penfold rather than her husband.

Her search on Janine Penfold revealed she was a former model, the de rigeur label for anyone married to money. She might have been a shoe or foot model in her day, but why spoil a glamorous description with the truth? Her first husband and the girls' biological father was 'wealthy horseracing identity, Elliott Archer'. His name didn't trigger any alarms for Kate, but there might easily be shady dealings in his past or present. The divorce barely made the newspapers at the time.

Switching to the police database, Kate checked whether Janine Penfold or her former husband had been charged with or convicted of any crimes. There was nothing. Not even an outstanding parking ticket.

Kate heard movement behind her and swung around, expecting to see the cleaner. Instead, she saw Oliver striding into the office dressed in a black AC/DC T-shirt and faded jeans.

'What the hell are you doing here?' For a moment she wondered if he'd followed her. Or had he been here all along?

'I could ask you exactly the same question. My excuse is I couldn't sleep. What you said about Penfold got me thinking. According to my wife, who shall be nameless just for you tonight, women's instincts are supposed to be right about these things.'

Kate smiled. She had wondered if her partner's instincts about Penfold were more in tune with the truth than her own. 'So we both had the same thought. You'll never make the squad's social club if you keep that up.'

He pulled out his chair and sat at his own computer. 'I don't gamble, so it's no great loss.'

'Neither do I. Not even a lottery ticket. Anyway, I'm just checking on the wife, so you might as well start on Penfold,' Kate said.

She didn't feel comfortable being at work with Oliver this late. Surely he would want to be with his family, and there was no authorised overtime for basic computer checks like this. Or maybe, she thought, he was as angry as she was about being kicked off the homicide case and wanted to clear the Penfold disappearance as fast as possible.

The pair sat in silence, apart from the hum of the air-conditioner and the tapping of fingers on keyboards. For the first time in her working life, Kate was actually starting to enjoy being with her partner. They shared the same work ethic and in just a few days he had shown more common sense that all her previous partners put together.

Turning her attention back to the archive of news articles, she found a feature that included a photograph of Lesley and Candice, back when they were cute kids with ponytails, with their stepfather. Robert Penfold had a fuller face and more hair, but he was still unmistakable as the quintessential family man, offering opportunities to the 'mum and dad investors'. It wasn't enough to sell shares in a successful business, Penfold had to sell his wife's children as well. He could have been a politician.

'Kate, you need to see this.' Oliver rubbed his eyes and pushed himself away from his screen. 'You were right all along.'

Kate wheeled over and felt the surge of cold air from the duct above the desk. She zipped up her tracksuit top and squinted at the screen. The fine hairs on her arms stood upright.

Robert Penfold had been charged with sexually assaulting his son and daughter from his first marriage, though no conviction was ever recorded.

10

After a night's sleep, Kate's foot was no longer swollen or sore. Despite the early hour, the fresh breeze made her feel free. As she ran along the vacant footpaths, lights flicked on inside the inner-city terraces, and she picked up the pace. Both legs ached with lactic acid, so with each long stride her elbows pumped down and back, improving strength and blood flow. Every step brought her closer to being in more control of her life. Only two kilometres and she would be home, in time to shower and change for work.

She thought of how little progress she had made on the homicide case and wondered if she had lost her ability to think broadly enough to make a difference. Three months off work had given her so much time to contemplate life. During the time away she had rediscovered some of the joys of isolation. Not confinement, but the freedom to be alone. Other people feared it. But when it was your choice, seclusion was empowering and the ultimate liberation. No one to worry about, no expectations to meet, just you and your dreams.

For a while, she had forgotten how to dream. When you constantly faced the consequences of criminal ambitions – the murder of loved ones for money, revenge, power, control or, worst of all, so no one else could have them – it was easy to become hardened and cynical about your own hopes and aspirations.

Perspiration dripping from her hair and chin, Kate cut through the park and slowed to watch a group of mothers with three-wheeler prams power-walking their offspring. She could never imagine being tied to a child every minute. Perhaps she was too selfish. Billy's death changed everything. People often assumed being single at twenty-nine meant loneliness, but not since Billy had Kate met anyone she wanted to be with – or more importantly, anyone who could put up with her.

Stopping to stretch her hamstrings on a bench, she wondered what might have been different had he lived. They'd had dreams and plans all those years ago, wiped away in a split second by his motorbike accident. He was her first and only love. If they hadn't had a stupid argument about which team would win the football premiership, she would have been on the bike too. Instead of one funeral, the town would have mourned two twenty-year-olds.

The hatred in Billy's parents' eyes when Kate moved forward to place a flower on the casket showed everyone how little they thought of her. If it hadn't been for her, their son might still be alive and they would not let her forget it.

She tried hard to push Billy from her mind, only to be vividly reminded of the photos of the dead Lambert boy and his bike. She thought about how dismissive she had been of the Penfolds. Oliver was right to ask more questions. The former boyfriend did need to be investigated, but the father remained the prime suspect.

Kate changed legs and felt the full stretch of her muscles before heading home, determined to find out why the old sexual abuse charges against Penfold had been dropped. Then she would work out how to deal with Mark Dobbie. From what Janine Penfold had disclosed, there could be a reason to fear him, and Kate could not afford to ignore anyone who might have been involved in Candice's disappearance.

After a steaming hot shower, Kate put on another pre-creased shirt and headed for the office. Again, Oliver's desk was littered with notes, but he was nowhere to be seen. He had obviously come in even earlier, despite the late night spent searching the databases.

On her desk sat a cling-wrapped bagel with a note. Oliver's wife had made extra this morning in case his partner was hungry. Kate sat down, suddenly uncomfortable about being included in his wife's production line of meals. She wondered what Oliver's wife thought of making breakfast for the single woman who spent all day with him.

It was too early to pay a call to the Penfold home, so she tried to locate the arresting officer, despite the alleged offence occurring years earlier. There was no listing for the officer in the current police phonebook, and there were over a hundred people with the same initial and surname in the metropolitan white pages.

Kate pushed the bagel aside and switched on her computer. After logging on to the internet, she googled 'Mark Dobbie' and about fifty hits came up. She clicked on the local sites and located one to do with personal training. A muscle-bound man with folded arms stared out at her from a photograph. Mark Dobbie's website was simple, without fancy graphics. Essentially it was an ad for his business specialising in personal training for women.

She studied the man in the photo. His tan seemed too orange to be natural, the chest hairless enough to have been waxed. The half-smile, small dark eyes and slicked black hair made him a virtual caricature of the many men who frequented gyms to pick up women. Apparently Dobbie was single, passionate about bodies, health and being the best. At what, the website did not say. It briefly alluded to coaching young women's water polo but gave no reason why he had left that 'truly worthwhile task'. The testimonials from satisfied customers sounded suspiciously the same, all citing Dobbie as the inspiration for their makeover.

The site included some before and after photos of clients.

The first was an overweight woman with brown hair who had supposedly transformed into a minuscule blonde bikini-babe. Kate studied the two faces, which did not seem to bear any resemblance to each other. Two more case studies looked equally dubious, and each finished 'product' seemed to have attended the same fake-tanning salon as the trainer.

Notably absent from the site was any information about how much this transformation would cost.

Kate clicked on a link which took her to a page where Dobbie answered simple questions about weight loss and body shape. He even sold his own 'guaranteed' weight-loss powders to personally selected customers. Who knew what criteria he used? She suspected it meant these customers weren't considered to be undercover police. If Dobbie failed to cooperate with any questions Kate had, the fraud and drug squads could always look into the contents of the miracle powder.

Ten minutes later, after a couple of blogs and video postings of his weight-lifting skills on YouTube, Kate had a wealth of information on Dobbie and his character. She ran a check on him through the police database. Bingo! The guy had a charge sheet. Just over a year ago, he was caught for indecent exposure following a drunken incident on an island holiday. Security staff reprimanded him and he agreed not to drink alcohol for the rest of his time at the resort.

Kate googled the name of the island and quickly found a travellers' website listing incidents that tourists claimed had occurred on their holidays. They ranged from sexual assault to disappearances – presumed to be suicides or accidental drownings. She wondered who the target market was, so clicked on some of the site's ads. Partially-clad women cavorted on pristine beaches, and each advertisement closed with a group of giggling women holding cocktails, begging real men to 'come on over'. It was exactly the sort of thing that would attract a man deluded about his looks and sexual prowess. More than that, it would seem like a smorgasbord for sexual predators.

Dobbie had also escaped a conviction for assault two years earlier, when the victim dropped all charges before the matter went to court. The photos showed a man with an almost unrecognisable face, swollen and bruised. The alleged victim recanted his statement and claimed to have acquired his injuries by walking into a wall.

Bullshit, Kate thought. More likely, Dobbie or one of his friends intimidated the witness into changing his story.

Suddenly they had two suspects. Kate's head began to pound.

11

'Wore my best socks today.' Oliver grinned as they waited at the Penfolds' door. Kate pressed the intercom again and stepped back. Eventually, Janine Penfold came to the door, tugging at her washing-up gloves.

'Sorry, is this a bad time?' Kate asked.

'Oh no, it's fine. We have a cleaner, but I like to go over the floors again once she's gone, to make sure.'

Kate thought that was bizarre but tried not to show it.

Janine Penfold peeled off one of the rubber gloves and patted her hair, checking everything was in place. 'Do you have good news? Have you found Candy?'

'No news yet. We're still making enquiries.'

'Whatever that means,' she snapped. 'Our little girl is missing while that thug Dobbie is still out there seducing innocent girls. Have you spoken to him yet?'

Kate knew Janine Penfold was about to get a lot angrier when they raised the real reason for their visit.

'May we come in?' She was already unzipping her ankle boots.

Mrs Penfold fiddled with the gloves. 'Of course. Where are my manners? You'll have to excuse my outburst. This has been such a stressful time – for us all.'

She led them into a kitchen-cum-family area and ushered them onto wicker bar stools facing a raised portion of the granite kitchen bench.

'I just have one more tile, it'll only take a second. Please, make yourselves comfortable.'

She disappeared down the hallway and Kate realised there was no mop, only a bucket and a cloth the woman used to clean by hand. She really was fanatical about cleaning, beyond anything Kate considered normal. Cleaning a floor after a cleaner had just done it suggested a significant obsessive-compulsive disorder.

Kate swivelled round and took in the room with its rustic ten-seater table. The feature wall had a tropical fish-tank mounted within it, and glass doors leading onto the deck revealed a landscaped garden and an abundance of native trees. The place would have cost a fortune, but although the décor was tasteful, the absence of pens, note-pads, newspapers, letters or magazines made it seem like a display home awaiting inspection at any moment.

Mrs Penfold returned a minute later and poured the contents of the bucket into the sink, then washed her hands thoroughly under the tap. A waft of ammonia hit Kate's nostrils and the strength of it took her breath away.

'Coffee?' Unaffected by the smell, their host had already begun pulling demitasse cups from a cupboard. Kate assumed Janine Penfold needed to keep busy to cope with Candice's disappearance.

'That would be nice,' Oliver answered then cleared his throat. 'Mrs Penfold, this is difficult to tell you, but some information has come to light and we'd be negligent not to check it out. Your husband's secretary said he would be here.'

The machine clicked in and began to crunch coffee beans.

'Secretaries don't know everything. He left a while ago. What is it, Detective?'

Kate braced herself for a change in attitude. 'We need to find out why someone filed a complaint about your husband supposedly abusing his children from his first marriage.'

'Is that all?' She waved her hands in the air as if pushing away a cloud. 'That was his vindictive ex-wife, trying to get a bigger settlement.'

'It's still a very serious complaint, Mrs Penfold.' Kate had known women to fabricate assault claims to retain custody, but in other cases, the accusations were justified.

Mrs Penfold activated the machine again. 'Short blacks?'

Kate wondered if the subject had just been closed. The coffee gurgled away then stopped.

Mrs Penfold placed two coasters on the bar followed by two saucers and small cups. Kate thought that the whole point of granite was that it didn't stain or mark.

'I met Robert when the marriage was over, but his wife kept clinging to the hope he'd come back. In the end she said that if he left her, she'd make sure he never saw his children again. There were two boys and a girl just a bit older than mine at the time.' She picked up a cloth and began wiping the bench. 'Of course, he couldn't live with her anymore and moved in with me. That's when she screamed child abuse.'

Oliver sipped his coffee.

'Did your husband fight the claims and contest custody?' Kate asked.

'We talked about it, but at the time his business was taking off and the bad publicity would have ruined him. And for the sake of the children as well, he made the ultimate sacrifice and gave up custody and access. Robert couldn't bear to drag his kids into court and so, true to her word, his wife withdrew the charges.'

'Didn't the police or child protection unit investigate?'

'Of course, but the children had obviously been told what to say by their mother and their stories fell apart under questioning. The police knew as well as I did that nothing improper happened. Robert is an incredible father. That's why our girls took his name.'

Oliver put his cup back on its saucer. 'That must have been horrific, giving up access. The kids would be adults now – so does he see them?'

Janine Penfold placed her cup and saucer in the sink. 'He tried a couple of years ago but they don't want anything to do with him. Their mother poisoned them, playing the deserted victim all those years, and they feel he abandoned them for us. She never remarried and died of alcoholism late last year. The kids don't seem to consider the child support he's paid, or the fact that he paid for their mother's funeral.'

Kate stood and flattened the front of her trousers. The story sounded plausible, but she was surprised that a father would relinquish visiting rights to his own children, yet happily adopt two stepchildren. 'Thanks for your time, you've cleared that up for us.'

Back inside the car, Kate wanted to know what Oliver thought of the explanation.

'It makes sense. Wouldn't be the first time a scorned woman has threatened to cry abuse to secure a better settlement. She knew that was the one thing likely to ruin him, not to mention damage the kids. In some ways, it's the deserted woman's most effective weapon.'

Kate had to agree, but if Robert Penfold had been guilty of abuse, he was smart enough to give in to all of his wife's demands, to make the problem go away. After all, he had a new wife and two stepchildren. And the fact that the children seemed coached didn't exclude abuse. Plenty of social workers and concerned parents emphasised what kids should say when interviewed by police. She would make sure any children of hers were prepared for the brutality of cross-examination if necessary.

Kate put the key in the ignition. 'He's either a loving father, or a sick and twisted abuser.'

'Maybe that's a much finer line than we realised.' Oliver buckled his seatbelt. 'Maybe it is possible to love your children too much.'

12

Leo Penfold looked a lot like a younger version of
his father. Tall and thin, the only heavy thing about
him was his eyelids, which drooped slightly over
large brown eyes. The effect made him appear sad.

'Can I help you?' he asked as they entered the
shop.

Kate had never been inside a scrapbooking shop
and until Janine Penfold told them that's where
they'd find Leo, she had no idea such a thing
existed. As far as she was concerned, scrapbooking
meant sticking newspaper clippings into an oversized book of plain paper. This was a whole new
world. Photos attached to large, patterned papers
embellished with ribbons and writing, were displayed in transparent sleeves pinned to the walls.
Kate had to admit the effect was impressive, and
that a lot of work was involved. A customer with
two baskets already full of items headed down
another aisle.

'We're looking for Leo Penfold,' Oliver said,
showing his badge.

'That's me.' The man behind the counter
rubbed his hands on a dark green apron of the

112

kind hardware shop assistants often wear. 'What can I do for you?'

'I'm Detective Sergeant Kate Farrer and this is Detective Constable Oliver Parke. We'd like to ask you some questions about your father, if you don't mind.' Kate leafed through a book with a wooden cover containing embellished pictures. It seemed a lot of trouble to go to for something no bigger than a notebook.

'They're one of our newest lines and that's all we've got left. The small albums are great presents and stocking fillers.'

That made sense, Kate thought, and closed the tiny scrapbook. 'About your father.'

'I barely know him. Haven't seen him for years,' he said, stacking square sheets of coloured cardboard on the counter.

'Can we ask why?'

'It's no secret. He left us for that rich bitch and her kids. End of story.' He lowered his voice and gestured for the customer who had finished shopping to come to the register. 'Why? Has something happened to him?'

'No, but his stepdaughter Candice is missing.'

'Hardly a surprise, having that witch for a mother,' he said, scanning the customer's purchases. 'That'll be $86.50, thanks.'

From what Kate could tell, for a few coloured textas, sticky tape and pieces of paper, the amount was exorbitant.

Oliver muttered, 'This is a multi-billion dollar

industry in the US alone. Most of the businesses are run by women – housewives and mothers with a passion for scrapbooking. They even have these enormous conventions. Impressive, don't you think?'

Kate stared at her partner, stunned by his admiration for something she would never understand. They waited as the customer signed the sales receipt then disappeared further inside the shop to browse again.

'Not a cheap hobby.' Oliver flipped through a magazine on a stand.

'Scrapbooking's addictive, and all our materials are guaranteed acid and lignin free. They're the best money can buy,' Leo said.

Kate failed to see the significance and raised her eyebrows.

'That means they're archival quality and won't damage the photos or fade.' He rolled his eyes. 'Thankfully, our regulars keep us in business.'

Oliver shifted from foot to foot. He suddenly seemed more uncomfortable than Kate felt. 'Did your father ever treat you inappropriately?' He almost blurted out the words once the customer was well out of earshot.

'You mean like walking out on us? Sure, he paid for things, but he broke Mum's heart.' Leo pointed to a display on the wall that featured a grey-haired woman looking wistfully to the side of the camera. 'That's Mum, not long before she passed on. She wanted us to know how much she loved us. That's how she got involved in scrapbooking, so we decided to honour her memory with this place.'

Oliver lowered his voice. 'Did your father ever physically abuse you?'

The son leant forward. 'I don't know what this has to do with his spoilt brats, but he wouldn't have dirtied his hands by touching us. When he walked out, he didn't ever want to see us again.' He glanced back at the image of his late mother. 'Now tell me that's treating your children appropriately.'

A young woman came out from a back room with a box of papers she deposited on a work table in the middle of the store. She smiled and wiped her hands on a green apron, identical to Leo's. 'Everything okay?'

Kate nodded and said they just needed to ask Leo a couple more questions.

'I'm the co-owner, Madeleine Penfold. Is there a problem?'

'One of the ugly stepsisters is in hiding and these police officers are asking about the sperm donor they call our father.'

Madeleine Penfold's smile faded quickly. 'Leo, could you please grab the other two boxes so we can set up the new display?'

Her brother seemed more than happy to oblige.

'Sorry, Leo's the oldest so he bore the brunt of Mum's bitterness. Some of it rubbed off.'

Kate walked towards the shop entrance, out of Leo's earshot, and Madeleine followed. Oliver studied items hanging from a stand.

'You've never heard your father's version of what happened or why he gave up custody?'

'I assume there are two sides, but out of respect for Mum, we never initiated contact. Our other brother lives up north and, as far as we know, feels the same. Please understand, this is painful for all of us. I'm sorry if one of the girls ran away, but I have nothing more to say about our father. None of us does. He made his choice a long time ago when he left.'

Kate thanked her and opened the door, which jingled and made Oliver look up. Based on one brief meeting with two of Penfold's biological children, they had not done or said anything to suggest they had been abused. It was possible that the mother really had lied about the sexual abuse and Penfold may have spent all his energies on his adopted family to compensate for the loss of his own.

13

'What makes you so sure he'll be home?' Oliver asked as the detectives drove to the outer suburbs address on Dobbie's driver's licence. 'Let's say he is expecting a new female client,' Kate said with a grin.

Oliver had not returned to the office until late morning. He had unofficially been at the shopping centres nearest Moat Place canvassing mothers and children. Without a name, face or age of the baby, questions about the murdered woman and her child had proven futile.

They pulled up in front of a gymnasium situated above a homemakers shopping centre, the kind that had furniture, light fittings, bedding and carpets in the one location. Dobbie lived opposite in 22A, part of a red brick federation-style semidetached house. Outside the adjacent property, an elderly man pruned rose bushes.

'You have a lovely garden.' Oliver stopped and admired grass, cut in half by a tiled pathway that led to a covered verandah. Lining the periphery were rose bushes with leaves that looked a little scorched at the tip.

'Did have, before all these water restrictions,' the man responded, removing a dead bud with a gloved hand. He paused and squinted from beneath a straw hat. 'I'm guessing you're here for next door?'

Kate nodded. 'Do you know the resident well?'

'Does anyone?' The man pushed his hat back onto the crown of his head.

'What do you mean?' she asked, revealing her badge. The man leant forward to take a good look at it.

'We reckon he's one of them drug pimps. You should see the number of cars that park outside my place, day and night. The council won't do nothing about it.'

'That's got to be pretty annoying.' Living in the inner city where car-parking was at a premium, no one would dare complain if someone's car was outside their home. It was expected. Kate sensed this man believed the space outside his home should be free for him or his friends to use.

'Why do you think it might be drugs?'

'I wasn't born yesterday, and I've got the wrinkles to prove it. I know what young people get up to today, with things like marijeewaana.'

Kate didn't dare correct his pronunciation. Nosy neighbours had their advantages at times. The man stepped forward. 'These muscle men go inside and are out in minutes. Except if there's a woman inside, that is. Then they all stay. Wouldn't have happened in my day,' he said.

'Thanks so much for your help, sir.' Kate led the way around to 22A and knocked on the door, sure that the old man would keep watching for as long as he could.

Mark Dobbie greeted her in bare feet and shorts. His smile vanished when she showed her badge and introduced herself: 'Detective Sergeant Farrer, and this is Detective Constable Parke. We'd like to ask you some questions.' She didn't wait for an answer and pushed past him.

'About what? Unless you have some kind of warrant, you can leave.' He leant out the door and scanned the driveway.

'We won't take too much of your time,' Kate said, fully aware that she could take as long as necessary. 'If you want to change, we can wait.' She wandered into the living area and Oliver moved towards the kitchen. It looked like the place had one bedroom and bathroom – four rooms in all. Dobbie seemed to be alone.

'Listen, I'm expecting a new client any minute now.' He folded his arms and flexed both biceps.

Bare-chested was obviously how he intended to greet his new 'client'. Kate shook her head and glanced around the place. Mirrors were visible from almost every angle. And people thought women were vain.

'You must take pretty good care of yourself.' She noticed a set of shiny barbells. 'You work out a lot?'

'I do what I can. The way I see it, the skin is

119

nature's own shrink-wrap, and it shows *everything* that's going on underneath.'

Oliver crossed his eyes, out of Dobbie's line of sight, and continued to scan papers on the kitchen bench.

Kate tried to get him to relax and talk about his favourite topic – himself. She squatted down and touched one of the weights, noticing the acne on his shoulders and back, one of the signs of steroid abuse.

'How much can you lift?'

'Bench press, over eighty kilos. Leg press, one twenty kilos.'

Oliver whistled then commented, 'Impressive.'

Dobbie turned towards the male detective and looked him up and down. 'I could help you get in shape in six weeks. You'd never know yourself.'

Kate suppressed a grin. 'I'd love a set of these, but they're way too expensive. Personal training must pay better than police work.'

'You should try eBay. I never pay full price for anything.'

Kate doubted that Dobbie's place had been furnished through internet auction sites. Even if the plasma screen mounted on the wall was a bargain, the surround sound and installation would have cost a packet. His job must have more perks than he declared on his tax return.

'What's going on? What do you want?' He sounded irritated now.

'We're investigating the disappearance of a young woman, Candice Penfold,' Kate responded, looking hard at his face. Even in the low light, she noticed his pupils contract – a sign of the fight or flight response. He crossed his arms tighter. As her father always said, people were just like animals when cornered.

'Don't look at *me*. If she ran away from those sicko, controlling parents, who could blame her?'

Kate had obviously hit a nerve. 'When was the last time you saw her?'

'Dunno. Maybe a year ago. She was hooked on me but I wasn't interested.'

He broke eye contact. He had to be one of the worst liars Kate had seen.

Oliver stepped forward from behind the bench and whistled through his teeth. 'A young girl throwing herself at you? Must have been tough to resist. No one would blame a man for giving in. Know what I mean?'

'Mate, even you wouldn't go there.' He moved away. 'I make it a rule never to sleep with anything that weighs more than my old greyhound. She was one fat, ugly, dumb bitch. Wouldn't get a root in a brothel full of blind sailors.' He glanced at Kate and winked. 'You're more my type.'

If flesh could crawl, hers would have been inter-state by now. This guy was just stupid enough to get himself in deeper. A year ago, Candice was svelte. If she had not gained weight until the last few months, he had to have seen her recently.

'I hear her sister, Lesley, is more your type.'

'What if she is?' He glanced at himself in the

121

living room mirror before sitting at the round dining table. 'And she'd still be here if her father hadn't bundled her off, to break us up.'

Kate joined him, helping herself to a chair. Oliver stood leaning against the kitchen bench. She noticed a yellow and white photograph envelope on it.

'Why do you think he would do that?' she asked.

Dobbie clasped both hands on the glass table top. 'The Penfolds think they're better than me, that I'm not good enough for their golden girl.' He grinned through whiter than white teeth. 'Well, my rich women clients don't think the same way. I've fucked nearly every one of them.'

Kate assumed she was meant to be either shocked or awestruck. She was neither.

'Did you have a sexual relationship with Lesley?'

He looked at the female detective as if she was simple. 'Daddy's little girl was no virgin. She came on to me with those Bambi eyes and see-through shirts. I thought she was a tease, but she could really put it out, if you know what I mean.'

'Oh, I know *exactly* what you mean,' Oliver echoed.

That took Kate by surprise. Gone was any hint of the meek, mild family man she had met only days before. Either her partner was a misogynist like Dobbie, or a reasonable sort of actor.

Dobbie responded to the bait and kept talking. 'At first it was a bit of fun. We'd go out; she'd give me blowjobs in the car outside her parents' place, almost as if she wanted them to see. She was on fire.

You do know the old man's loaded, don't you? Got lucky with some computer gadget he invented, now he thinks his shit doesn't smell. You know the type.'

Oliver nodded. 'Sure do. They think they can run the world, and make it even tougher for guys like us. Bet that made you pretty angry, particularly if you loved Lesley and she loved you.' He leant back and stretched one hand towards the photo envelope. 'Guess you would do anything to get her back. And if it hurts the old man, it's a bonus. Know what I mean?'

Dobbie's eyes flashed towards the packet on the bench. He stood up. 'Listen, I told you what I know and now I want you to leave. That client will be here any minute.'

Kate asked if she could use the bathroom, and did not wait for permission. She hoped Oliver would keep him distracted for long enough to allow her to have a look around while they were there.

She heard Dobbie raise his voice: 'I can get a lawyer who'll do you for harassment. You can't just stroll in here and take over.'

'You wouldn't want to waste money on lawyers. They cost a fortune. Then we'd have to start asking questions about your income, what you declare to the tax man.'

Kate grinned at Oliver's words as she looked inside the bedroom. A large framed photograph of a nude woman hung above the double bed. Beside the bed was a stack of the latest body-building magazines. They were unlikely to be bargain-priced on eBay. So much for him buying everything cheaply. She heard Oliver continue.

'And then there's that little magic powder in the tin over there. Could have anything in it. Is it approved by the food and drug authorities?'

Her partner had more gumption than she had given him credit for. Inside the bathroom, she closed the door as Dobbie said something about Chinese medicine. A small plastic rubbish bin contained a used syringe. Inside a mirrored, mounted cabinet, she saw a box with vials in it. DHEA, the box read. One vial was labelled HGH. She had the ammunition she needed.

Kate flushed the toilet, turned the taps on full bore and flicked a couple of drops of water onto the mirror before wiping her hands on the towel. If Dobbie ever complained that she had performed an illegal search, at least she could honestly say that she had used the bathroom. As she emerged, she fiddled with the top button on her trousers.

'About time,' Dobbie said and stood with the front door open. 'You can go now.'

Oliver swept the photo envelope off the bench onto the floor.

'God, so sorry about that,' he said. 'Let me get it.'

Dobbie left the door and rushed to the floor, a second too late. Kate had already reached down and opened the envelope. Photos tipped onto the carpet. Dobbie tried to snatch them but again Kate was too fast. In her hand she held photographs of a woman lying on a bed. She was naked and in every shot had both eyes closed.

If Kate did not know better, she would have thought the woman was asleep.

14

With Mark Dobbie safely in an interview room at the station, Kate joined Oliver outside. She did not want to tip Dobbie off about the search warrant she intended to get and execute while he was being questioned.

'Do you want me to apply for the warrant?' Oliver checked his watch.

'We've only got four hours until he has to be charged or released, which means we have to move fast. He seems to relate to the macho act you pulled, so it's best if you stay with him.' Kate stepped towards the wall as two uniformed constables passed. 'Get what you can about the Penfold girls and the family. When he last saw Candice and heard from Lesley. One of the other detectives can sit in. I'll get the warrant. With the neighbour's comment about selling drugs, the needle I saw in the bin at his place and his physical appearance, which suggests steroid abuse, we can get one on suspicion of drug dealing.'

'Aren't the photos more incriminating? Surely we're better off getting evidence to confirm he raped the woman. There's no way she was conscious in those pictures.' He shook his head. 'That has got to be one sick bastard in there. And what about Candice Penfold? He lied through his teeth about not seeing her.'

Kate sighed. Without a complaint from the woman in the pictures, it would be impossible to convince anyone that they had enough evidence to suggest Dobbie was a rapist. And so far they had nothing concrete to tie him with Candice's disappearance.

'I agree, but we can use the illegal steroids as leverage. With a search for more photos, we'd be limited in where we can look. But with a warrant for drugs, we have licence to check out every nook and cranny, the bins, in the damn roof if we need to. Because drugs come in powdered form as well, we can justify searching more places, even under flooring. That means we have a much better chance of finding whatever he's stashed away that could implicate him regarding Candice or other women.'

Oliver smiled. 'And by holding him here while you go through his place, he has no chance of destroying evidence.'

'Right. You get inside and play the moron. I'll get the warrant.'

She climbed the stairs and found Inspector Russo at his desk. Very little happened in the unit without his knowledge, and he always made himself available to staff.

Russo listened with a noncommittal expression as Kate stood in the doorway and explained the urgency of the Dobbie situation.

'Your warrant will be signed,' he said when Kate had finished. 'I have a magistrate on standby with a good record for sentencing drug dealers. You'll have it by the time you get back to Dobbie's house.' Russo stacked some papers into a neat pile and removed his reading glasses.

'And, Kate,' Russo added, 'we're relying on you for this one. Make it your priority.'

Kate wasted no time getting back to Dobbie's house. She hoped there had been some positive leads in the missing baby investigation but didn't stop to ask.

Two uniforms accompanied her and, as Russo promised, the warrant was there, signed, when she reached the front door. This time the neighbour was nowhere to be seen. She wondered how he would appreciate police cars parked outside his property.

With gloves on, logbook ready and a constable video-recording the search, they knocked, waited, then forced open the front door. This time the place assumed an even more grotesque feel. The weights, gym equipment and plethora of mirrors could only be the trappings of a narcissist. Kate headed for the bedroom and the constable with the handicam followed. Recordings were routine to protect the police from accusations of theft or malicious damage, but in this case, a taped record of the costly equipment and furnishings could support the claim that Dobbie's expenses exceeded his income.

'Make sure you get all this,' Kate said, referring to the paraphernalia in the bedroom. Handcuffs, silk ties and a leather mask lay on a shelf near the bed. Under the mattress, she felt for anything out of the ordinary. Inside one of the pillowslips she found $1000 cash. Judging by the obvious hiding place, he'd never been robbed or searched before, she thought, as she bagged and recorded the find in the logbook. Under the other side of the mattress, there were a number of envelopes. Each contained photos of naked women – at least four different women, as far as she could tell. Again, each one had her eyes closed. She showed the cameraman the find and bagged each envelope separately.

Flicking through the magazines beside his bed, a piece of paper with a telephone number on it fell out. Kate wrote it down in her notebook and returned the pile to its place beside the bed. As she stood up, something out of place caught her eye. A cigar box stood up on the shelf, between two sports trophies. She opened the lid and removed a pack of playing cards, condoms and one dangly earring. At the very bottom was a white envelope. Inside were more photos, of yet another naked woman. Kate couldn't make out the face in the first one, but the second showed her head turned to the side, eyes closed. A man was on top of her. All she could see of him was the back of bare shoulders and three small marks on them.

'You bastard,' she whispered, as each picture became more sexually graphic. These ones must have been special to Dobbie, because they were kept separately and most were in close-up. The young woman looked just like Candice Penfold at her slimmest.

15

'You're in deep, deep shit.' Oliver Parke sat with his hands behind his head across the table from the suspect. 'You might as well tell us what you know.'

Mark Dobbie refused to look at the photographs in front of him. 'Never seen them before.' He shifted in his seat. 'Besides, they don't prove anything.'

'True.' Kate leant against the interview room wall, arms folded and ankles crossed. 'But it shows you weren't completely honest with us about Candice Penfold this morning.'

Despite loathing Dobbie and his perverse sexual practices, Kate had no tangible evidence to use for a charge of sexual assault. Not only might the victims refuse to come forward, some might not remember being drugged or photographed. That's why drug-rape cases were so difficult to prove. Even if a victim came forward with drugs still in her system, there was no proof that she didn't take them voluntarily.

'But they sure make you look like a sexual deviant. Any women on a jury would have to see you for exactly what you are,' she said.

'You've got nothing.' Dobbie smiled. His teeth looked even whiter under the fluorescent lights.

Oliver sat forward. 'I agree. Let's just get this sorted out and you can be on your way.' He clicked his pen and opened his notebook. 'Tell us the names of the women in the pictures and we'll check them out. Once they confirm that they all consented to sex and being photo-graphed, we'll know this was just a silly mis-understanding.'

Dobbie's eyes darted between the detectives. 'What about the drug charges?'

'That will depend on how cooperative you are.' Kate pulled up the spare chair next to Oliver and sat down. She looked at the clock on the wall. They still had forty-five minutes left to question him.

'When did you last have sex with Candice Pen-fold?'

'Never. Told you, I don't stoop that low.'

'Well, who is the man in the photo then?'

Dobbie laughed. 'Jesus, you are struggling. You've got nothing. And you'll never be able to prove I did anything to that bitch.'

Oliver flashed Kate a look.

'Then I guess when we find her, we can ask her what happened.' Kate tapped on a manilla folder on the table. Filled with documents that she wanted Dobbie to think were relevant to the investigation, it was a bluff technique she had used successfully before. 'Unless, of course, you know we won't find her alive.' She tapped again. 'Did I tell you we just found her car? There was blood on the seats – cleaned off, but our forensic guys are pretty clever at finding stuff like that, just like on television. A smart guy like you should know that, with your big screen TV and all.'

Dobbie blinked several times in quick succession. He either resented having his intelligence challenged, or she had just hit another nerve by revealing the car had been found.

'We're thinking someone killed her, and you're our primary suspect. You had motive for a couple of reasons. Was she blackmailing you about the photos? Did she threaten to come to us about them and your little drug activities?'

'Or,' Oliver offered, 'did you cook something up that would bring her sister home? Maybe you wanted Candice out of the way for a while, long enough to worry Lesley into coming back and seeing you, but something went wrong. Even the best-intentioned plans can go wrong.'

Oliver was controlled and methodical, Kate realised. He was saving Dobbie's not inconsiderable pride by giving him an opening to confess. 'Best-intentioned'. Hell, Dobbie could admit to what he had done and come out seeming like a good guy, at least to himself.

The clock ticked away. They needed to wrap this up quickly.

'Is there anything you'd like to tell us in relation to the whereabouts of Candice Penfold? If you tell us now, freely, things will go much better for you,' Kate said.

Dobbie picked at a fingernail. His hands shook slightly, despite the façade. He looked up at Oliver and cleared his throat.

A knock on the door interrupted them. Inspector Russo opened the door and asked Kate and Oliver to step outside.

What the hell was he doing? They had Dobbie. He was about to confess.

'Detectives. I need both of you out here, NOW!'

Dobbie exhaled quickly and stared at the closed folder in Kate's hand. She picked it up, slowly stood and walked to the doorway behind Oliver.

Outside, Russo spoke with his head down. Judging by his creased forehead, he was as angry as Kate. 'There's someone you need to speak to. Immediately, before you question Dobbie any further about the Penfold matter.'

He showed them to the interview room down the corridor. Inside sat a blonde woman with petite features, stunning despite puffy eyes. She had clearly been crying.

'Meet Lesley Penfold,' Russo said. 'She's just off the plane but came straight here. She'd like to make a confession.'

Lesley buried her face in a tissue. Her words were only just audible.

'You can't arrest Mark for killing Candy because he didn't do it. We figured that if she disappeared, you'd question Mark about it and scare the hell out of him.' She looked up at them with wet, doe-like eyes. 'I'm sorry . . . we just wanted him to leave us alone.'

16

Kate could not believe what she was hearing. The young women had fabricated Candice's disappearance and had the detectives looking for a nonexistent victim. All the while, a baby was out there somewhere. She paced the small room, clenching and unclenching her fists, trying to calm down. The girl's flood of tears didn't earn her any sympathy. It was too damned late for that.

Oliver stood in silence then leant over the table. 'We should charge you two with creating a public mischief, and make you pay for the cost of this joke of an investigation.' He moved his face close to Lesley's. 'Do you have any idea what you have done?'

His anger stunned Kate, who started to worry he might actually make physical contact with the girl.

He pounded the table with his fist and Lesley flinched.

'Why the hell didn't you tell us this? Or are we part of your little game as well? Is that what you do? Manipulate people, play games with them?'

Lesley Penfold shouted, 'Stop it, you're scaring me! That's what Mark does.' She turned to Kate, pleading, 'I got on the first plane when I heard about Candy's car. She doesn't go anywhere without her mobile.'

Lesley's perfectly made-up face began to resemble a clown's, with vertical mascara lines running down each cheek and red lips puffy with the snuffling and nose-wiping.

Kate decided to play good cop until they had unravelled the story. 'So what exactly was the plan and who came up with it?'

Russo knocked on the door and entered the room. 'The Penfolds are in the waiting room. They want to be allowed in.'

'No chance,' Oliver said. 'This girl is of legal age. We can question her alone, without them, if she refuses legal representation.'

'She asked for them instead,' Russo said. 'I kept them in the waiting room and now they're demanding to be let in.'

Oliver stared at Russo for a brief moment. 'Then aren't they supposed to be present?'

'I'm fully aware of the regulations governing interviews, Detective Parke.' Russo spun on his heel and met the Penfold parents in the hallway, escorting them into the room without another word to Kate and Oliver.

Outside, the pair watched the family reunion through the two-way mirror. Robert Penfold hugged Lesley while Janine rubbed her daughter's back and stroked her shiny blonde hair. Judging by the relaxed body language, Kate suspected that the parents did not know about their daughter's set-up, and they hadn't asked for a lawyer – yet. Neither parent mentioned Candice or where she could be. They were too busy enveloping the prodigal child. What Kate was observing seemed to support the studies that suggested parents treated their good-looking children better than their plainer ones. For a moment, she pitied Candice Penfold, and felt the pang of having lost her own mother so young.

Like any child, Kate had idealised her dead mother, but the only 'memories' she had of her were those constructed from photographs and stories her father told. A family reunion was once her childhood fantasy, but the way the Penfolds were fawning over Lesley, seemingly without concern for Candice, was far from heart-warming.

Kate felt her pulse quicken again at the thought of the days they had wasted on the investigation, time that could have been spent solving a real murder. She would make sure the girls were charged with misdemeanour crimes and their iden-tities made public to maximise their humiliation. Penfold wouldn't be able to keep their names out of the papers this time.

Oliver stood with one hand on the two-way mirror, the other in his back pocket. 'I didn't see this coming at all,' he said quietly. 'How do you want to approach this?'

'Let's leave Dobbie inside his room to sweat for a few more minutes. He may not have killed Candice, but he's hiding something. We have him for the drugs anyway.'

'I could have sworn he was about to confess to hurting Candice. And I'm not sure that what he was going to say was about the photos,' Oliver said. 'This doesn't add up.'

'I agree. Something tells me the plan went awry in more ways than one. How about I start off and you just jump in when you're ready?'

Oliver nodded and went into the adjoining room for two more chairs. When he returned, Kate was leaning over the table towards the young woman.

'Lesley, I understand this is all very distressing, but we need to go over the details about what you and Candice arranged.'

Janine Penfold dabbed her daughter's face after licking her own hankie. Either she couldn't bear to see her daughter look less than perfect, or she was still controlling her grown-up child, or both.

Lesley was more composed now and began to speak more clearly: 'Mark had been writing to me while I was away, and just wouldn't accept that I didn't want to be his girlfriend. He would follow Candy and beg her to get messages to me. She had a crush on him so would have done almost anything for him – even help him win me back. That's why she went to his place. He said he had a present for her, to say thanks.' She dabbed her eyes again. 'Candy loves presents, and believes anything anyone tells her. Anyway, afterwards, she said one of his friends was at his place, drinking, and she thought there might have been drugs there, too. She fell asleep on the floor but woke up and left while they were out of it. There was no present. That's what upset her so much.'

Robert Penfold sat with his arm around his daughter's shoulders. 'Before you think Candy got drunk, Detective, she hates the taste of alcohol and never touches the stuff.'

Kate suspected Dobbie had drugged her with something more powerful. 'Do you know how long ago that was?'

Lesley exhaled through her mouth, her nose still congested from the crying. 'Um, it was after spring break, so it was a month or two after I left. But we didn't think this up until a few months ago.'

Kate opened her folder and handed Lesley the photos of Candice, still inside the plastic sleeve to stop fingerprint contamination. 'These might alarm you,' she warned the parents, 'so you may not want to view them.'

Lesley stared at the image, her hands shaking.

'Do you recognise the woman in the picture?' Kate asked.

'It's . . . Candy.'

'Do you recognise where the picture was taken?'

'God, it looks like Mark's lounge room. I recognise the couch.'

Mrs Penfold leant over and snatched the plastic sleeve, clutching it between her manicured, pink fingernails. 'Candy lied to us and slept with that animal as well?'

Robert Penfold clenched his teeth and stood abruptly, knocking his chair back. 'Where is the bastard? I'll kill him.' Oliver was quick to block the doorway.

'I can understand that you're angry. You have every reason to be, but you have to calm down. Assaulting the prick won't help anyone right now.'

Again, Kate was impressed that Oliver, like a chameleon, could change character in an instant.

'Please sit down, Mr Penfold.' Oliver held up both palms in a calming gesture. 'We all want to know where Candice is. Let's sort that out first.'

Robert Penfold sighed and reluctantly returned to his daughter's side.

'Do you know what really happened that night at Mark's house?' Kate asked.

'I swear,' Lesley said, 'I didn't know she slept with him, or took her clothes off for photos. I just don't believe it.'

Kate suspected that Candy had not known either. If Dobbie had slipped her a date-rape drug, she would have no memory of the event. Without the photos, it was possible that no one would ever have found out. Then again, there was still the remote possibility that Candice had lied to her sister and actually slept with Dobbie voluntarily. No doubt, that's what Dobbie and his lawyer would argue. This far down the track, there would be no trace of drugs in her system, even when they did find her.

Kate checked her watch. They couldn't keep Dobbie in custody for much longer. She would have to get the exact details of Lesley and Candice's plan later. For now, she wanted to know where the missing girl was so she could get back to Dobbie.

'Where is Candy right now? We need to speak to her as well.'

Robert Penfold knelt down and looked steadily at his daughter. 'It's OK, you can tell us. We just want her back safely.'

Lesley began to cry again. 'That's why I came home, when Daddy called me about the car being found. That wasn't part of the plan. She was supposed to just dump the car and go away, like on a holiday, but ring to let me know where she was staying. She'd been saving all her cash so she could have a break from . . .' She glanced at her mother.

'Do you have any idea what you've done?' Mrs Penfold said, still holding the photo.

'None of that matters now. I haven't heard from Candy since she left.' She looked up with those doe-eyes again. 'She was supposed to call and tell me where she was. I'm scared something really has happened to her.'

17

Kate sat on the steps outside police headquarters with her face in her hands. She needed air, even if it was polluted by petrol fumes and smoke from the nicotine junkies. Her first week back had been more gruelling than she had expected, and her body felt as if a flu virus had moved in. Every muscle ached and her neck felt the strain. She had a headache from lack of sleep and clenching her teeth, something she did when she was stressed.

The Penfolds' situation had beggared belief. The girl who tried to protect her sister from Dobbie had been drugged and raped, possibly without ever knowing. Had she realised and gone to the police, there might have been fewer women in the same situation – and the chances of finding the others in the pictures weren't great. She had come back to homicide to investigate murders, not be stuffed around by wealthy debutantes who got caught up with the wrong kind of men to annoy their parents. What had Dobbie said? That Lesley would flaunt their sex acts outside the family home. He might have been exaggerating, but something told her that on that topic, he was telling the truth.

While Dobbie was being booked and fingerprinted before applying for bail on the drug charges, they could forward the photographs to the sexual assault unit. He still had a lot to answer for.

Her mobile rang and she ignored it. Three more rings and voicemail would kick in. This was her breathing space. The smoko you have when you don't smoke. She thought of the unidentified dead mother, burnt to an unrecognisable state. Fiskars and Rench should not have been given the investigation. They were likely to cut corners and that could cost them a result.

'Mind if I join you?'

Kate shielded her eyes from the sun and looked up.

'Sure, boss, it's a free step.'

Russo hitched up his trouser legs and sat with enough space between them to be comfortable but remain private.

'I know these first few days back have been less than ideal. Believe it or not, I'm trying to look after you. You've been through a rough time but we need your skills and can't afford you to give up on the job.'

Kate could barely hide her irritation. 'I don't need shielding or protecting. I was certified fit to work and that's what I'm here for.'

He put his hands up in defence. 'That's not what I meant. The Penfolds have been trouble since they started pulling political strings and, of course, we're expected to dance like performing monkeys.

Forget the genuine cases and pander to them. For God's sake, look at the crime stats and police figures for where they and their mates live.'

Russo was right. On paper the wealthier suburbs needed the most police because of skewed crime figures. The public didn't realise that scratching a car was reported as a crime in those areas, or that a stolen wallet was treated as larceny. Police stations in those areas were overstaffed and the detectives' time was taken up investigating trivial matters that, in other places, would never even be reported. Meanwhile, the disadvantaged suburbs went understaffed, even though they were rife with drug and gang crimes. As long as state and federal leaders lived the high life, nothing was going to change. Russo was clearly frustrated by the system, and Kate wondered if that had prompted the change in his behaviour. Beside her now sat a disillusioned boss who had once energetically revamped homicide and its staff. Maybe Oliver was right. Russo might not have felt able to speak freely inside the confines of his office.

'Is something going on here that I don't know about?'

Russo clasped his hands in front of him. 'Like what?'

'With respect, sir, you're a lot more irritable than I've seen you.'

Russo rubbed his brow. 'Things changed in some ways while you were away. Not because of you, but obviously there was an investigation into

145

procedures to protect officers' safety, which has led to more, shall we say, scrutiny.'

Kate knew that words like 'scrutiny' usually meant an internal investigation by the anti-corruption unit.

'Are you saying the unit and everyone in it is under investigation?'

Russo breathed out. 'I'm not in a position to comment on undertakings by other units.'

Kate could barely believe that police were wasting time investigating them when homicide was so overworked. She clenched her jaw hard and pain shot through her temples. She opened her mouth and the joints clicked. Like any public service, the police was a top-heavy bureaucracy where decision-makers often had no idea about the realities of the jobs of people they criticised.

'You can't get results without manpower. Is this a political stunt to shaft us because of the number of unsolved cases?'

'It's nothing like that, I'm sure. Just be careful who you talk to and what you say. And do your job by the absolute bloody letter of the law, especially with the Penfolds. Nothing else. You never know who's listening.' Russo donned his sunglasses before setting off down the steps and into the street.

Kate felt a mix of anger and relief. Anger at being in a goldfish bowl through no fault of her own, and relief that she wasn't being shafted by her boss. Her instincts told her Russo was a good man but his performance this week had rattled her. At least now she had some understanding of why.

Be careful about the Penfolds? Why the hell should they be tiptoed around just because they had money?

Her mobile rang again, and this time she checked the screen. The number was Oliver's.

'I'll be there in a minute,' she said, standing up and wiping the back of her trousers.

'I thought you'd want to know. Lab just faxed,' Oliver said. 'The substance on Candice's car is definitely blood. We need to get some samples of her DNA for comparison.'

18

Posters from the movie *Pirates of the Caribbean* lined the walls of Candice Penfold's bedroom. Magazine shots of Orlando Bloom were pasted alongside images of waif-like actress Keira Knightley. Ribs and collarbones featured prominently on almost all of the women Candice had chosen to honour on her walls. The exceptions were some before and after ads for diet fads. Other torn-out pages showed photos of Hugh Jackman, Brad Pitt and a tousle-haired Keith Urban.

Fashion magazines were strewn beside and under the queen-sized bed, suggesting that this room was probably off limits to Mrs Penfold. A corkboard displayed a number of childish drawings of horses. A few birthday cards were also pinned to it, including one from someone who described herself as 'Your friend, Polly'. The undated card looked as though it had been penned by a young child. Kate wrote the sender's name down in her notebook.

Candice's wardrobe resembled a shop clothes rack, with items ordered in sizes from eight to sixteen, some with price tags still attached. She had either bought small clothes to give her incentive to lose weight, or just kept them for when she was that size again, as she did with the larger garments. Self-absorption and self-criticism may have been why Candice spent so much time in her room. Then again, it could have been the large-screen TV and DVD player. Her DVD collection included remakes of *Cinderella* and *Beauty and the Beast*, and *Shallow Hal*.

For a room used exclusively by a teenage girl, the ensuite was surprisingly bare, even for a girl with an obsessively clean mother. Apart from a hairbrush and toothbrush, there were few other items. Kate remembered collecting lipsticks and gloss given away with magazines, even though she didn't use them. But in the ensuite there was no make-up, and no hair products of any kind. Unlike most teenage girls, Candice was obviously not obsessed with preening, pruning, dyeing and bleaching parts of her body that nature had already made perfect.

Most striking, the bathroom mirror above the sink was covered in magazine clippings, leaving only a small space for its actual purpose. Kate realised there hadn't been a full-size mirror in the bedroom. It was almost as if Candice deliberately avoided seeing herself. The room had a sad feel to it. She was in no doubt that the young woman had very low self-esteem. To have such an attractive and successful sister, and a former model for a mother, can't have been easy.

Kate thought of Mark Dobbie being so quick and open about condemning any woman larger than a greyhound. Bastards like that had to be punished for what they did. They treated animals better. The photos of Candice having sex made her even more furious now that she could see how innocent the teenager was. But while Dobbie may have been a drug-rapist, it didn't automatically make him a murderer.

Kate picked up the hairbrush and studied it. Some of the long brown hairs clinging to the bristles might still have their roots intact. She bagged the brush and the toothbrush separately for DNA sampling and left the room, gently closing the door behind her.

On the conference room table, Detective Sergeant Hayden Richards examined the photographs of the naked women.

'Your photographer's focused on the pillow, not the face,' he said, squinting at the images. 'Could have been deliberate to make the subjects more difficult to identify.'

He checked the back of each photo through its plastic sheet protector and sighed when he noticed no markings.

'Or,' Oliver suggested, 'the photographer is an idiot.'

The more experienced detective frowned. 'It's not like he was distracted at the time by logical thought. You said they were in an envelope? We could check with the lab that printed them.'

Kate had already considered that. 'The envelope was one available in supermarkets alongside the photo-printer cartridges. These were most likely do-it-yourself jobs.' Besides, photo kiosks and labs were obliged to report any suspicious photographs to police. There was too big a risk taking digital images anywhere for professional printing. Dobbie's house didn't have a printer, but the ones for home use were portable and could have been with his unidentified mate – the one with the three moles on his back, lying on top of Candice.

Kate watched as Hayden Richards continued to study the photographs. The senior detective headed the sexual assault investigation unit and had formerly worked in homicide. The once morbidly overweight man had recently slimmed down to normal weight and even Kate had heard rumours that he was unwell. For the first time she smelt aftershave in his proximity, not the stale odour of tobacco.

Seeing Hayden thinner was a shock initially, but she thought he looked healthy and round-faced, not remotely gaunt or ill. Not that there was any chance the pair would enter into chitchat about health or diets. That's what she respected about the 'moustached ferret', as he was affectionately known in the force. He was completely focused, and his investigative skills when reviewing cases had shamed even the most tenacious officers. Kate still had a lot to learn from him, and Oliver seemed in awe as well.

'Where exactly were these found?'

'On the kitchen bench. We accidentally knocked them onto the floor and some spilled from the packet.' Kate stole a look at Oliver. 'This picture of our missing woman was hidden separately from the others, in his bedroom.'

Hayden sipped from the bottle of water he had brought with him. 'So for some reason Candice Penfold is more special than the rest. Maybe he knew having her photo was risky but couldn't bear to throw it out.'

'Or he was thinking of blackmailing a member of the family with it. Apparently he was pretty desperate to get the sister back from overseas.'

Hayden laid the pictures out neatly. 'Do you know who these other women are?'

Kate sat down on the table and put her feet on the seat of a chair. 'We're hoping you might be able to help with that one. Have you had any intelligence reports? Because we couldn't find any formal statement alleging Mark Dobbie was a rapist.'

'We're working on about seventy-five unsolved rapes in the area, but nothing related to the address you mentioned over the phone. The name Dobbie sounds very familiar, though. Can you wait while I check?' He pulled a mobile phone from his pocket and stepped outside the room. 'Poor signal in here,' he muttered, and walked towards the outside windows in the main office.

Kate and Oliver were grateful to hear anything the detective could tell them and watched him through the glass partition. Within minutes Hayden returned with a grin on his face.

'Mark Dobbie, muscle man and halfwit. I do know him. He was a person of interest on an assault I worked on a couple of years back. It was one of those club holiday island places about two hours off the coast by boat. A seventeen-year-old claimed she woke up naked in a men's room but couldn't identify any of her attackers. Dobbie was on the island with some friends at the time and they were seen by other tourists taking recreational drugs. That same week, a twenty-something woman went missing, presumed drowned, after being seen intoxicated and dancing with one of Dobbie's friends. Her body was never found.'

'Was there any physical evidence on the seventeen-year-old?' Kate asked. Dobbie and his mates could be far more dangerous and perverted than she had realised.

'Problem was, the assault wasn't reported until the girl left the island with her family. She said some men had told her there were whales off the coastline and she could get a great view from their cabana balcony. Mum and Dad trusted she'd be safe on the island so let her roam around and visit the teenagers' club.'

'As most people would,' Oliver said. 'After all, there are uniformed staff who act like friends and who guests would feel safe around. Who wouldn't feel trusting in that environment?'

'I can see what you're saying, but island resorts, like cruises, have a bad name in certain parts of the world. Up until recently there's been a problem with reporting incidents and police getting access before evidence is destroyed. It's not unusual for staff to ignore the claims of a seventeen-year-old girl who couldn't actually remember what happened and wasn't even sure she had been raped. Besides, if she had been drinking, she was underage. It wasn't in the resort's best interests to pursue it.'

Kate was not surprised that Dobbie could have been involved in drug-raping before. A self-contained island was the perfect place for predators like him. Women often travelled in groups, drank to excess and were out for fun. All assumed they were safe to roam around at night. She could see why they might take personal risks they wouldn't consider back at home. Recreational drugs may have been part of their holiday experience, but being raped was not.

'What do you have on Dobbie?' Kate felt even more determined to stop this deviant ruining women's lives.

Hayden sat back, hands clasped behind his head. 'He's slimy. Brags about sleeping around with his clients, who are usually sexually frustrated women whose husbands have moved on to younger versions. I guess it's their way of getting back at the husbands – spending as much of their money as possible before a divorce.'

Oliver paced the room. 'So on top of his other unsavoury pastimes, Dobbie is a prostitute.'

Kate suspected the equipment in his house was too expensive to have been paid for out of his earnings as a personal trainer.

'We couldn't get him for accepting money, if I recall. The women paid in goods – expensive ones.'

'Same difference,' Oliver said.

'Not really,' Kate countered. 'There are plenty of women sleeping their way up the social or money tree, and we can't arrest them for that.'

Oliver rubbed his chin. 'There's something I don't understand, though. Guys like Dobbie are never short of women who voluntarily sleep with them. Why would they go to the trouble of buying expensive drugs and risk getting caught?'

'That's an excellent question, and one which has caused juries to acquit handsome rapists before. But it's a pathological need these men have, and it's about ego. If a girl knocks them back – or, more likely, seems prudish – she becomes a challenge. They don't have to use protection if the woman won't remember whether or not they had sex. That heightens the sexual experience and reduces their chances of being hounded by the woman. There's no emotional attachment or concern about health issues either.'

'You'd think prostitutes would be cheaper than the drugs they're buying and giving away,' Oliver said. 'I just don't get it.'

'That,' Hayden replied, 'is because you're not that kind of man. Remember, these rapists go to

155

extraordinary lengths to make themselves look attractive – the body-building, hairstyles and the way they dress are all designed to attract attention. They have enormous egos, but are incredibly insecure. They don't just want to have sex, they want great sex. And they take the photos to prove they've had it, and to relive the moment, if you get my meaning.'

Kate knew exactly what he meant. And the thought of Dobbie masturbating to the victims' images was as revolting as taking the pictures in the first place.

'We found GHB in his home, along with human growth hormone,' she said, relieved they had got that much on Dobbie given that he had already slipped through Hayden's net.

'Ah, we call it "GBH" because that's what it causes – grievous bodily harm. That and growth hormone often go together. Testosterone is becoming passé because of its negative effects, like acne and shrivelled testicles. It can even cause man-boobs – not the image these Neanderthals want to present.'

Hayden pulled out some pages from the black portfolio he had brought and handed them to the detectives. One sheet contained information on drugs used in sexual assaults. Kate read that Gamma-Hydroxy Butyrate (GHB) occurred naturally in the brain. It was thought to promote the type of sleep during which the body produces more growth hormone, used for muscle development in bodybuilders and movie stars wanting to 'bulk up' for roles.

It usually came as a colourless, odourless liquid but could also be in powder or capsule form. Injecting the drug didn't have any benefit over swallowing the stuff. The reason it was used in sexual assaults was that the drug was rapidly absorbed, with peak blood levels occurring around twenty to forty minutes after being swallowed. The effects lasted from about forty-five minutes to eight hours, depending on the weight and metabolism of the victim and the dose administered. The information sheet went on to explain that the initial effects included euphoria and, some believed, heightened sexual awareness and desire, but there was a very fine balance between a dose that increased sexual pleasure and one that caused extreme sedation, confusion, nausea, vomiting and lack of bodily control. Coma, respiratory suppression, seizures and death were commonly reported.

Kate looked up but Oliver was still reading. Hayden gave them time to absorb the information.

'What some of these guys do,' he began, 'is give the woman a dose and if she doesn't turn into a raving nymphomaniac, they give her another, and another. Any victim who survives does so by sheer bloody luck rather than good judgement on the rapist's part. That's what makes this drug so bloody scary. And when you combine it with alcohol . . .'

'With no taste or smell, no one would know if it had been slipped into a drink or not.' Kate picked up the photo of Candice Penfold. If she was as private and shy as she seemed, she would have been a prized victim for Dobbie and his mates.

'And the worst part,' Hayden added, 'is that because it's used recreationally, the blokes will always claim the women took it voluntarily and turned into sexual animals. When they have photos of the women performing oral sex and other activities which, not coincidentally, are designed for pleasuring the male, juries can look pretty judgementally on the women, in the rare cases when we have enough to go to trial.'

He perused the photos on the table once again.

'Unless any of these women comes forward, there's little you can do to charge Dobbie, or whoever belongs to the back in that shot, with having committed sexual assault. Drug possession is about all you've got.'

Kate knew that as long as Candice Penfold was around, Mark Dobbie was at risk of being caught for premeditated rape. He had a lot to gain by her disappearance.

19

Brett Spender grunted as the carer transferred him to his bed. 'I want the computer,' he barked, irritated that his carer was paid until nine o'clock but cheated him of at least fifteen minutes every Friday night.

'Wouldn't hurt you to use manners.' Rosalie straightened both of his legs and tucked him in like she would a child, top sheet up to armpit level. 'One of those *Scary Movies* is on tonight. You might actually get a laugh out of it and release some endorphins for a change. Could be just what you need.'

He knew what he needed, and it was not staying home by himself in front of a second-rate comedy.

'If you want,' he tried to sound casual, 'you could stay and watch it here. There should be more spritzers in the fridge and a couple of bags of chips in the cupboard.'

She fussed with the sheet some more and pulled it tighter, despite the fact that he couldn't have rolled out of the bed even if he'd wanted to.

'I told my parents I'd stay home with them tonight. They keep complaining I treat the place like a motel since I started working evenings for you. They'll probably make me watch some depressing SBS documentary with them.'

'Bullshit!' Brett hated being patronised and lied to. He felt his blood pressure rise. 'I'm not blind or stupid. I see how you put your make-up on and you drown yourself in that cheap perfume. You smell like toilet spray. It's disgusting.'

He saw the muscles on her face tense, and knew he'd cut her down. The truth was, he didn't want to hurt her. She looked and smelt great. Every time she bent over him he liked to smell the strawberry shampoo in her long, soft hair. The musk perfume she wore on special occasions was subtle, not cheap at all. The only thing wrong was the cherry red lipstick she had trowelled on. When she smiled, it made her teeth look yellow. She must have applied it when she was supposed to be cleaning up after dinner – on his time, not the boyfriend's.

'OK, then, if you really want to know, we're going to dinner in Chinatown then dancing. I'm staying the night with Alfonso.' She licked her lips. 'I'll leave it to your imagination as to what we'll be doing at his place.'

Since she'd started going out with Alfonso, Rosalie had stopped the long discussions they used to have. She was the first girl Brett had ever really got to know and become friends with, rather than just wanting to have sex. Before the accident, he wouldn't have looked twice at his carer, but the chubby woman had grown on him. It was just like they say about fat chicks – she had a good person-ality. Only Brett really meant it with Rosalie. Until Alfonso had changed her – he didn't like what she had become or how vulgar she had started acting.

'I pay your salary, remember, so you can afford to go clubbing, drinking and whatever.' He couldn't bring himself to say what he resented most. He flicked his head to move the fringe from his eyes by using his neck muscles – the only ones left in his body that still worked. Paying for a haircut was no longer a priority for him, especially since being on his back so much meant he had rubbed a bald spot on the back of his head. 'I don't care what you do. I'm thirsty.'

Rosalie straightened and took the plastic cup from the bedside trolley, holding it to Brett's mouth and placing the straw between his lips.

'How many nurses have you worn out over the last few months? Three, or was it four?' She waited for him to finish sipping. 'Look, nobody wished this on you. It was an accident, but you're still young and at least you're in your own place, not withering away in some urine-soaked nursing home.'

Just rotting in here, he thought, totally dependent on cows like you. He jerked his head to dislodge the straw and knocked it out of the cup, his anger welling.

'Suits you, being able to come and go and piss off early whenever you want. I'll be docking your pay for this.'

She leant over, giving him a view of her ample cleavage. 'This whole self-pity routine is wearing pretty bloody thin.' She spoke softly, as though someone else might be eavesdropping. 'If you were civil I might stay and watch a movie with you one night. Just don't expect me to stay and listen to your "woe is me" crap. If you feel better slagging me, go ahead, but what goes around comes around.'

He blew the air out of his mouth in a hiss. His neck arteries began to throb as his anger rose. No one spoke to him like that.

Ignoring him, Rosalie placed the computer mouthpiece to his left, within easy reach when he turned his head. The screen was attached to a metal arm on the side of the bed. Since Brett was incapable of rolling over, there was no chance of him bumping it in the night.

She stood back and sighed. 'Why do we go through this before every weekend? Listen, if you want someone to live in – company – you can always hire a full-time nurse.'

He did not respond.

She left the room for the ensuite and returned with a cup of fresh water. In silence, she moved the bedside trolley close enough for him to turn his head and reach the straw in the night. She took a cigarette from his packet and lit it with his lighter. He stared at the ceiling as she held it near his mouth.

'The local church offered to send visitors for

company, remember? If you want, I can organise it.'

He inhaled as much smoke as he could but with his respiratory muscles so weak, the effect was minimal. Another of life's simple pleasures that would never be the same.

'I'll be stuffed if happy clappers patronise this cripple.'

'Have it your own way.' She checked the catheter bag and turned on the TV suspended from the ceiling to maximise his view, then stood staring at a singing banana in a car ad.

'At least the Christians are doing something for other people. I don't see your old friends going out of their way to come and visit.' Her jeans rubbed together at the inner thighs as she lumbered towards the bedroom door.

'I'll see you Monday.' She paused to flick off the light, the part-smoked cigarette still in her possession. 'Try to have a good one.'

Brett turned his eyes. He didn't need pity. Not from anyone. 'Don't bother coming back, you fat, ugly bitch,' he called out. 'You're fired. Fuck off. Leave the key on the kitchen bench and get the fuck out.'

He heard her stomping around the kitchen, throwing pans in the sink, and then the front door slammed shut. A few seconds later, the boyfriend's car screeched off down the road.

Brett was alone. Like he was for most of every day. If it wasn't for the mouth-operated computer and phone, the outside world might not have existed. He breathed out and in to inhale any residual smoke. Instead, he got the remnants of her perfume. The agency would send someone on Monday to get him out of bed. He'd tell the weekend woman to arrange it. Even better, he could email the agency tonight.

It had been ten months since the diving accident that had shattered his world. When the compensation settlement cleared, his mates were happy to come around and drink more than their share of the profits. Now they all had excuses. Truth was, they were too busy working and having fun to visit anymore. His mother – a real piece of work – had an official stance for her absenteeism. It broke her heart to see her youngest son like that. In other words, even she had better things to do than nursemaid a grown child and wipe his dirty backside.

On the TV, a repeat of *My Name is Earl* had begun. Brett used his chin to hit the volume on the remote. Earl always went on about karma. How doing bad things made bad things happen to you. Brett thought about a *Dr Phil* episode about creating your own destiny. Oprah and Dr Phil had both made a fortune telling other people how to do it. Maybe that was what good karma meant. You boss people around and make a financial killing.

Brett wondered what he had done to deserve his fate. Six of them dived into the water that day, but only he had ended up in a wheelchair. He thought about his friends and the fun they'd had on holidays, especially that last one. Girls would line up to get laid by them, more often than not. Half the time, they didn't even tell you their names. That's what holidays were for. Good mates, lots of alcohol, drugs and great sex.

Brett closed his eyes and wondered if that was the bad karma bit. Activating the computer to his left with the mouth-rod, he sent messages to everyone on his address list – dozens of them – explaining that maybe Earl had a point. Bad karma had to be changed. Otherwise, life wasn't worth living. A few minutes later the rod hit the send button. Then he emailed the agency.

Brett woke to the aroma of hot chips, his all-time favourite. The food you could have anywhere. At the pub, the football, or after a big night out. So long as you worked it off later at the gym. Saliva trickled from his mouth onto the pillow.

A black and white movie was on TV but the room remained dark. Rosalie must have come back to smooth things over with a late-night snack. Maybe she and her boyfriend had busted up. Truth was, he wanted her back, fat arse and all. It wasn't the first time they had argued and she showed up hours later as though nothing had been said. That's one of the reasons he liked her. She was never too proud to come back. He knew she needed the work so he would accept the apology this time, and give her a warning about rudeness. The first bit of good karma.

When she didn't appear in the room, he called out to her, 'Apology accepted.'

No answer. He turned down the sound on the TV with his chin and listened. Nothing. The cow hadn't come back at all. Ungrateful bitch. He wondered if she was the one bringing bad karma. He closed his eyes. His imagination had to be playing tricks. He drifted into that weird place where the past and what could have been merge, still salivating at the thought of food. He remembered when every muscle worked and things were the way they should have been. He had been fit, easy on the eye, and always had at least one girlfriend. And the sex was unreal. A bit of Viagra and he could come as often as he liked.

Women wanted him and he knew how to make the most of it. A couple of drinks and they couldn't wait to get their knickers off. Sometimes it took a little more to get them in the sack, but it was always a cheap root. Why would you pay a prostitute when almost every woman you met gave it away for virtually nothing? Hell, sometimes they even paid for the drinks. His face relaxed into a smile. The memories were almost as good as being there. Except that now his body felt nothing.

Somewhere there had to have been bad karma. One dive off that jetty and his life was over. He wished he'd died in the accident, not been saved from drowning only to slowly wither away. Muscles were no good to him now. Atrophy, flab and fat were all that remained.

What good was sex if you couldn't feel anything? And who'd want to have sex with him now? The only women who came near him were absolute dogs. But he really did like Rosalie.

If he was honest, he wouldn't have looked twice at himself either. He thought about the times he'd made fun of the cripples at the local special school. The spastics and the brain damaged, wheeled along each day. The sight of them made him sick as a kid. Truth was, he was probably a little scared of them, the way they couldn't control their heads or the way their hands curled freakishly near their shoulders. He could not understand how a parent could love them. His mother explained: 'No one else will take them or wants them.' Karma, he thought, grimacing. How did he get to be such a dickhead? Then again, everyone at school was like him – at least all his mates. Or were they?

His head jerked forward with the crashing sound. The TV flickered before he was left in complete blackness. Then he smelt the smoke. He forced out a cough and tried to rub his face against the pillowslip.

'Who's there?' he shouted, then struggled to catch his breath.

Another crash and this time blistering heat hit the side of his face closest to the door. Within seconds, orange and black engulfed the corridor outside his room. He realised what was happening.

'Help me!' The air was thick and claustrophobic and muffled his voice. 'Anybody!'

He willed his legs to move but they ignored his desperate pleas. Nothing from his arms, either. Fucking nothing.

'*Help!*' his voice slurred.

Sweat poured from his face and the flames disappeared behind a sheet of blackness. He tried to reach his computer but his chin could not find it. Each breath became more laboured.

For the first time, he was grateful that his body was completely numb.

Karma.

20

Kate sat on her lounge-room floor scraping the last of the butter chicken from the takeaway container. She cleaned up the extra sauce with pappadams saved over from the night before.

Going for a run had failed to relieve her frustration that the sexual assault unit would not intervene and help out with the Dobbie case. Not that she could blame them. They were in a bind. Without Candice Penfold to file a complaint, they had no right to investigate and their resources were stretched as it was. What Hayden Richards had given her was a better insight into Dobbie's character, if she could call it that. It was more like he had an absence of character if he could plan to drug and rape women, carry it out and then take trophy photographs for entertaining himself afterwards.

Oliver had contacted Candice's few friends, mostly former school colleagues, to ask when she had last been seen, in what state of mind, and whether she had let anyone know where she planned to go. So far he hadn't discovered anything they didn't already know.

Kate decided to spend the evening sifting through the box of documents that had arrived on her desk from Hayden Richards' unit. It contained photocopies of scores of documents from the investigation into the island resort. She looked at a newspaper clipping about the woman presumed drowned. A photograph showed a young woman with a wide smile posing for the camera, glass of wine in hand. The press could have used any photo of the woman – one from school, or with a boyfriend – but they chose one that made her look like a party girl. Public sympathy would have plummeted after the photo was released, which meant that interest in the case was likely to wane faster than if the community was angry about the death of a young woman with an unblemished past who should have had her life ahead of her.

Kate read the article, which mentioned that Lilly Stavos had been known to take ecstasy and smoke dope. In other words, if she drowned, it was likely due to a cocktail of drugs. More articles read along similar lines, until an exposé of crime at self-contained holiday destinations led to a coroner's enquiry and a reopening of the case six months later. That's when Hayden Richards had begun his part of the investigation.

Kate flicked through the large pile of papers and interviews with staff and guests. Lilly Stavos was reported missing at 9 am one morning by her girlfriends, when she failed to return to her cabana.

The two friends denied she had been suicidal and described her as being in good spirits, having consumed a few cocktails in one of the bars. A note pinned to the statements said that the bar staff were given alcohol quotas to sell each shift, and were encouraged to serve alcohol to people irrespective of whether they were inebriated. Kate wondered how their public liability had coped with such an admission. It probably hadn't.

One of the waitresses remembered seeing Lilly leave the pirate-themed disco with two men, identified as Aaron – or Elvis, as he liked to be known – Brown, and a young plumber, Brett Spender.

Kate saw Mark Dobbie's name circled on the hotel guest list and flicked through the papers to see why he had been a person of interest. He had booked the trip with the other two and was given an adjacent cabana. So both of the men believed to have been the last to see Lilly Stavos alive were Dobbie's mates.

None of the other holidaymakers had seen what happened. An elderly guest claimed he had heard that Lilly was a spy and planned her disappearance in a submarine, information he was keen to pass on to police. A note about the witness described him as confused and disorientated, and his wife confirmed the man suffered from early dementia.

The following morning, Lilly's sequinned handbag was found near a wooden walkway bridge, along with fibres from the tasselled dress she was last seen wearing. Tassel threads had adhered to part of the railing, suggesting she had brushed hard against it. Or been dragged across it, Kate thought.

She was beginning to get the impression that Lilly could have been given a fatal dose of drugs and then her body dumped in the ocean during the night. Hayden Richards, it seemed, had developed the same theory. If that were true, Mark Dobbie's mates were as callous and calculating as he was. The night Lilly disappeared, Dobbie was seen roaming naked outside his room. He was apparently knocking on cabana doors trying to find his room because he had misplaced his key.

Kate studied the security report on the search the following morning. Neither Dobbie nor his friends' rooms were searched. All rooms were doorknocked by staff, and announcements made over the PA system, but no one was formally questioned apart from Lilly's friends. The investigation was a total cock-up, she thought, with no forensic evidence collected apart from the dress fibres and handbag. There was no fingerprinting of the rails near where Lilly's belongings were found, and no search for blood.

A cleaner later reported being called to Spender's and Brown's cabana at around 6 am to clean up vomit. It was impossible to say whose vomit it was. The case was a disaster from the start, but then resort security weren't trained in forensics and the mainland police were hours away. With young people pursuing sexual encounters and drinking

172

excessively, even victims would have trouble being taken seriously. The island really was a sexual predator's paradise.

Kate double-checked Brett Spender's address. He lived in a suburb thirty minutes away. She took a final swig from a can of ginger beer. She never bothered with a glass; it saved on washing up. As she gathered up the papers and placed them back into their cardboard box, she knew it was plausible that the young woman had gone for a late-night swim and drowned. But with Dobbie's history of drugging women, Kate felt sure he and his friends were involved. She wondered if one of them had three moles on his back, like the man in the photo of Candice Penfold.

She got to her feet and headed for the kitchen. She threw her fork in the sink and grabbed a glass of water. The oven clock read eleven fifteen.

As soon as she lay down, fatigue enveloped her muscles and feet . . . But the peaceful place she had drifted into was suddenly shattered by the shriek of her alarm. She groped for it and groaned. Four forty-five was her normal time for a run, but this morning she decided to give it a miss. Once awake, though, she was incapable of getting back to sleep so she had a long shower and decided to pay Brett Spender a call.

She wanted to get any information she could on Mark Dobbie and what happened on that island holiday. Though it was still early, catching witnesses, or 'persons of interest', at odd hours often rattled them enough for them to admit to things they might otherwise hold back.

Kate left a message on Oliver's phone telling him where to meet her, grabbed her keys and headed for Brett Spender's place.

21

Kate pulled up outside the weatherboard house, the street still in darkness apart from the pool of light cast by a lone street lamp. The overgrown yard suggested Spender didn't exert any energy in the garden. She checked the file. He was a plumber, but there was no truck in the drive.

She had smelt the smoke as soon as she entered the street, but couldn't see where it was coming from. As she approached Spender's house the outside sensor light flicked on, then off, before she reached the porch. As her knuckles rapped on the front door, she felt searing heat behind it. Something was wrong. The smell of burning oil took her breath away for a moment and stung her eyes. She pounded on the door.

With no answer, she stepped around the front of the house and past the lounge-room windows. As she ran towards the back corner of the house, the force of a blast knocked her onto the grass, her hands instinctively covering her head. Grey and orange flames licked the outside of the house, the window blown out.

She rolled and checked herself for injury. She

had no cuts or grazes but she must have fallen awkwardly because a sharp pain radiated from her ankle. A neighbour from across the street ran towards her and Kate yelled for him to call the fire brigade and an ambulance. Not knowing if anyone was inside, she hobbled around to the back of the house, hoping to find a way in. One of the windows, she saw immediately, was missing its pane of glass. Feeling carefully for any shards, she hoisted herself through the window frame and onto the floor. She yelled out for anyone who could hear. No one answered.

Peeling off her jacket, she wrapped it around her hand and crawled along the floor. The black smoke obliterated visibility and when she lifted her hand to feel for doorknobs, the intense heat was intolerable. Standing, she immediately realised, would be fatal. Almost deafened by the noise inside and prevented from going further by the blistering inferno, she felt for a wall to get her bearings.

Shit! Which way had she come? She felt light-headed and sick to the stomach. She crawled backwards, trying to retrace her path to the window she had come through. Coughing and blinded by the smoke, each small movement she made became a battle against exhaustion. The next thing she felt were large hands grabbing her from behind and dragging her along the ground. The hands pushed her through the window into the arms of the largest fireman she had ever seen. She could have sworn she heard Oliver's voice in the commotion.

Within seconds she was on an ambulance trolley, coughing and wheezing into an oxygen mask. She grappled with the mask, uncomfortable with anything that covered her face.

Someone washed her eyes out with sterile water and the stinging slowly subsided. She closed her eyes and rested.

'What the hell were you thinking?' a voice said.

She blinked and gradually focused on Oliver. The first thing she noticed was how immaculately dressed he was so early in the morning.

'I got here just as it started. Is anyone inside?' he asked.

Her mind raced. How did he arrive so quickly? 'Were you following me?'

Oliver said something about her being confused and that she needed to get to hospital.

Kate shook her head and coughed up some dark phlegm.

'No hospital.' The ambulance officer offered her nasal prongs for oxygen, which she accepted. Within minutes, her breathing rate had slowed and the coughing abated.

'You can't have been inside long,' Oliver said. 'From what the firey said, it's gone up incredibly fast.'

'Oil. I smelt burning oil when I got here. Then there was an explosion.'

A few minutes later, John Zimmer arrived wearing his blue overalls and black toecapped boots. 'Gang's all here, I see. At least some of us aren't lounging around trying to suck up eternal youth gas.'

'Shut up, you shit-stirrer. Kate's been through enough without you adding to her trauma.'

Zimmer grinned. 'What can I say? Some women find my sense of humour endearing.'

'Not this one,' Kate mumbled, her mouth parched from breathing through the nasal prongs, and no doubt from the surge of adrenalin she experienced in the fire. Every muscle in her body felt fatigued – not the usual tiredness, but worse than she felt after running the half-marathon. She smiled to herself.

'What's amusing?' Oliver asked.

'I went over on my ankle before. Now I can't feel it at all. It's probably cured.'

'Or you've burnt through the skin and nerve-endings. Bit of a drastic way to treat a minor condition, I'd say,' Zimmer chirped. 'Remind me not to ask your advice on how to treat a stomach-ache.'

Uncharacteristically, Kate appreciated the attempt at humour. To be honest, she wouldn't have minded what they talked about. She just did not want to be alone right now. Being part of the team made her feel better and the pair's presence was surprisingly calming. She had to admit to wanting them both to stay.

Flames plumed from the side of the house as firefighters hosed it from inside and out. Zimmer stood watching, hands on his hips and legs wide apart. 'That's one hell of a blaze. If there's anyone left inside, they won't have survived.'

A firefighter approached, still wearing his breathing apparatus and fireproof suit. He took off his helmet and revealed sweat-soaked hair. His face bore a silhouette of the breathing apparatus, with soot blackening the uncovered areas.

'You the detectives in charge?'

Oliver and Kate both said yes.

'We have one deceased, in the master bedroom. Large build, bigger than most women, so it's probably a male. And there's what remains of a wheelchair by the bed.'

Wheelchair? Nothing in the police statements mentioned Brett Spender being disabled or incapacitated. He had danced at the disco with Lilly Stavos. Maybe it wasn't Spender's address anymore, or perhaps he lived with a disabled parent.

'And don't think there's anything you could have done to save him.' The man spoke directly to Kate. 'Even with our equipment, we didn't have a chance.' He held up his yellow helmet, which had partially melted.

'The heat was intense enough to do this, so you did bloody well just getting in and out alive, especially in synthetic clothes.'

Kate felt a tightness in her chest. Someone had been inside when she arrived, and could still have been alive now. She wished she could have reached the bedroom, but the heat and smoke had been too much to fight against. She realised her jacket had been little protection and, in any case, she had dropped it somewhere inside. All she had on was a light shirt and trousers. If only she had kept a woollen blanket in her car.

'Maloney's here. We might get some answers.' Zimmer moved towards him and had a quiet discussion before bringing him over to Kate. By now, a neighbour had kindly provided a tray of glasses and bottles of water. She took a sip and removed the oxygen prongs to speak with the chief fire investigator.

'Sorry to hear what happened,' Maloney said. 'But I need to know everything about when you arrived. What you saw, smelt, touched, heard and felt from the moment you got here.'

'It was a horrible smell, like burning oil, coming from inside.'

Kate explained about the heat on the front door and the shattering of the side window.

'Could there have been an explosive in there,' Oliver asked, 'to have that much force?'

'That is possible, but it may be that you arrived just before the flashover occurred. The fire could have started in the kitchen, with cooking oil, by the sounds of it. We'll know when we get inside.'

Kate thought of the body in the bed, next to a wheelchair.

'If the owner of the chair was unable to walk, who would have been cooking in the kitchen? If the deceased had started to cook before going to bed, why did the fire start so close to daylight?'

'Unless he got up to cook breakfast, felt unwell and got himself back to bed,' Oliver suggested.

Kate thought of the window with the missing pane of glass. She had no doubt. This was arson. Somebody broke in and set fire to the place. Someone who wanted to make sure the occupant didn't come out alive.

22

Inside the car, Kate quickly removed her shirt and trousers and pulled on yoga pants and a T-shirt she kept in her gym bag in the boot. One fire unit had left and the other was tidying up. Uniformed police kept voyeurs and TV crews across and down the street.

Oliver had begun interviewing neighbours and witnesses, and the ambulance crew had finally let her off the gurney. She had hobbled with what felt like jelly legs, over to her car.

The change of clothes helped her cope with the next step; they had to go back inside the house with the fire investigators and walk the scene. The sun now shone on the front of the house, showing how much damage had been done by the smoke and flames. Light glistened on the shattered shards of glass on the front lawn. Looking at the size of some of them, Kate was even more grateful to have avoided being cut to pieces as the window blew out.

Oliver tapped on the bonnet and Kate joined him on the footpath.

'This is Evelyn Masters, a nurse who cared for Brett Spender on weekends.'

Damn it. Spender was the one in the wheelchair. Kate knew she had just lost a link to Dobbie, and a possible link to Candice Penfold.

'The other police wouldn't tell me what happened. Is Brett in the ambulance or has he gone to hospital?' The middle-aged woman spoke with a slight English accent, and appeared distressed, fiddling with one of the buttons on her white polo top.

Kate and Oliver exchanged sympathetic looks. Each knew the woman needed to be told. 'Do you have the names or numbers of any of Brett's family?' Oliver asked gently.

'Oh, Lord no.' She covered her mouth and looked at the remains of the house.

'Was Brett disabled?' Kate asked.

'He broke his neck in an accident. It left him a C3 quadriplegic.'

'What does that mean exactly, to a layperson?' Kate rolled up the sleeves of her oversized T-shirt.

'Sorry, I'm not thinking clearly. The fracture was at the level of the third cervical vertebra.' She pointed to the top of her neck at the back. 'It meant he couldn't move his arms, or really feel anything below his neck.'

Kate shuddered at how helpless Spender would have been in a fire. He may have even been aware of it before he died. Even so, she needed to ascertain whether he might have been cooking that morning. 'Was he was completely dependent on you for *everything*?'

'He had some neck movement but no use of his arms or legs. He was totally reliant on help with his ADLs.'

'AD whats?' Oliver asked.

The carer plucked at another button. 'Activities of daily living, we call them. Bathing, eating, cooking, toileting, the things you normally do for yourself in the course of a day, things we all take for granted. I only work weekends. Carers come, to sponge-bathe him, get him out of bed, prepare meals and feed him, change the sheets, that sort of thing. And I suppose we provide a little company.'

The woman stared at the house, seeming to have difficulty comprehending what had taken place. 'You wouldn't wish that kind of death on your worst enemy, not even Brett.'

Kate was taken aback by the comment. Most people were afraid to speak ill of the dead. 'I'm sorry, are you saying that Brett Spender was difficult to work for?'

She tugged on the top button again. 'He could be a real bugger and would give you lip, he would. Never so much as a thank you or kind word.' She continued to stare at the house. 'I can't believe he's gone.'

Oliver escorted the woman to a uniformed officer who would take her details and any information about Spender's family contacts. Now, he and Kate were needed inside the house. Inspector Maloney waved them over, holding up five fingers.

They had five minutes before they went inside. As they slowly walked towards the blackened house, Kate took in Oliver's immaculate appearance, eager for a minor distraction from the job ahead.

'How did you get here so fast after I called? When I left the message, I thought you were still asleep.'

'I'm organised in the mornings.'

'Don't tell me you sleep in a suit?'

Oliver forced a smile. He was probably feeling reticent about going inside the house as well. 'No, but it's laid out on a chair by the bed, just in case.'

The image of him carefully laying out clothes each night was too much. Then again, he hadn't said that *he* was the one who prepared for the next day. Kate rolled her eyes.

'Hey, it's not like I ask my wife to do the ironing. She says she enjoys it. At least I hang the jacket up in the car, to stop it creasing.'

Kate couldn't imagine anyone wanting to iron, not even if they were being paid for it. 'You might do her a favour and cover up with overalls. The place will be filthy inside.'

Zimmer had already anticipated their need and pulled out two pairs of disposable plastic overalls, complete with shoe covers. 'Don't want dopey detectives trashing and contaminating our scene,' he said, handing them over with his usual cheeky grin.

This morning, Kate could forgive him almost anything. As they stepped into the white overalls, she wanted to know more about what had occurred outside the house. 'Did you take note of the people who watched the fire?'

'It's a quiet street, people seem to keep to themselves,' Oliver replied. 'Not many thrill-seekers. There was a male, average build, in a dark T-shirt and jeans who appeared briefly across the road. Couldn't make out his face beneath a dark baseball cap and no one got his details. I took a photo with my camera, but it's too dark to make out a face. None of the neighbours seemed to remember seeing him.'

'Didn't you go after him?'

Oliver stood, hands on hips. 'I was a little more concerned with bringing you out alive.' He collected a clipboard from a pile of crime scene equipment and studied his notes, putting some space between them.

Kate wasn't sure what to say in response, so she took a few deep breaths. The fear she had felt inside the burning house still lingered. She tried to push it aside and prepared herself to go back in.

Inspector Maloney informed the team that Dr Peter Latham was on his way to certify and assess the body. He had set up lights attached to an outside generator to augment the natural light inside the house. The group walked single file and carefully stepped around debris. They stopped at the kitchen.

Their attention was immediately drawn to a pot on the stove along the wall near the window and sink. The black cauldron-style pot had melted and buckled to the level of the fat it contained. Kate remembered the intense heat she had experienced. Now she saw the physical effects of it.

'The first team through eliminated electrical faults, so it looks as though the pot of oil was the flashpoint, where the fire started. Just like around fifty per cent of all house-fires, which are caused by cooking left unattended.'

'Except that Spender was in no position to cook for himself,' Kate pointed out.

Maloney nodded. 'That's why we're here. The flashpoint explains the burning oil you smelt when you arrived, and the black smoke when the window shattered.'

Oliver stepped closer to the stove. 'What sort of temperature does it take to melt metal like that?'

'A typical fire reaches about 1100 degrees Fahrenheit. That's 593 degrees Celsius. Aluminium melts at 660 degrees, and brass at 940 degrees Celsius. Judging by that melted pot, this fire got to a temperature somewhere around that, I'd say.' Maloney spoke with no emotion in his voice.

Zimmer looked up from snapping photographs. 'When you think that a chicken cooks at only 180 degrees Celsius and you wouldn't think of sticking your hand into your oven, you can begin to imagine the heat generated in this place.'

That explained the phenomenal heat Kate had felt when she tried to raise her hand. She immediately thought of the fireman's melted helmet and had more respect than ever for fireys. They withstood these conditions every time they were needed. She was surprised that more didn't lose their lives in the line of duty.

Kate had never before understood how people could jump out of burning buildings when they were multiple storeys up. She had wondered why they would opt for certain death when they still had a chance of being rescued. Maloney's description of the furnace-level heat and her experience of the horror removed any lingering doubt about why they would jump. Given no other option, she would do the same.

As she looked around the kitchen, Kate saw that everything above about two feet from the floor had been destroyed.

A plastic rubbish bin had melted down. John Zimmer photographed it. Maloney instructed a technician to collect the contents, which were preserved inside. 'We need an indication of the way this guy lived. Had he already eaten? Were there food scraps inside the bin, like potato peelings from someone preparing chips? Had he been drinking? We'll also go through the contents of the fridge.'

From the way he spoke, he might have been training the technician. He continued: 'When oil boils, it releases vapours which rise, emitting a distinctive, acrid smell that makes your eyes water. The smoke turns black and very sooty, which our reliable eyewitness here so aptly described. You can actually feel the heaviness of the oil in the air.

You can still smell it, too.' He paused for them to inhale before pointing to the ceiling. 'See the V-shaped pattern made by the smoke? That's further evidence to support the fire starting in here. There's nothing in the rest of the house to suggest multiple points of origin, although we will be taking samples from the flooring, carpet and cupboards to be sure.'

'What about the window that blew out? Wouldn't an explosion have caused that?' Oliver remained near the stove, hands behind his back.

'You usually find a circular pattern with explosions. What Detective Farrer described was a classic flashover. The oil causes tremendous heat, and the gas rises and heats the walls and cupboards as it rolls along the ceiling to the other side of the room. Items like the cupboards start to give off white, wispy smoke and vapours, which ignite almost simultaneously when they reach auto-ignition temperature. We're talking about intense heat now, which causes thermal expansion of the frames around the windows. The frames crack and the pressure inside the room is so high that it blows the windows out. Smashing glass is often the first indication the neighbours have of a fire.'

'What about the smoke detectors?' Kate asked. 'I didn't hear them go off.'

'You would have if they'd had batteries in them,' Zimmer said, moving on to the next room.

A technician bagged the melted plastic smoke

detector in an airtight container. 'We may be able to lift a fingerprint if someone tampered with it.'

Kate watched the technician change into a fresh pair of rubber gloves each time he collected new evidence. The used gloves were discarded along with a seemingly endless supply of plastic tweezers and trowels. The patience required to do the task properly was more than she could have managed.

'Someone would have had to be pretty determined to burn down the entire house if they broke in, went to the trouble of removing batteries and boiled some oil,' she said, examining the marks on the ceiling. It seemed a lot of trouble to go to, but why? The arsonist had probably thought an oil fire in the kitchen would look like an accident, but they clearly had no idea how fast that kind of fire burns. Or how quickly fire crews would arrive. That could mean the arsonist was inexperienced or stupid, or both. With luck, traces of him or herself would be left behind.

'Detective, you said the lights flicked on and off when you arrived?'

'The sensor light at the front of the house.'

Maloney pointed to the remains of a toaster plugged into the wall. 'The insulation in the cord would have been burnt and this would probably have short-circuited the electricity. My guess is that you arrived within minutes of the fire starting. That's all the time it would have taken to flashover in here.'

'So Kate just missed the arsonist, or he was still inside when she got here,' Oliver said.

Kate struggled to think back. She hadn't seen a car outside or in the street, or any movement in the dark, though she must have been close to catching the culprit.

They continued through the house.

'You can see here,' Maloney gestured towards the corridor wall, 'where the gaseous heat layer finished.'

It was the level to which Kate had been able to raise her hand before burning it. Seeing it in daylight was less threatening, but in some ways more disturbing. She realised how close she had come to dying.

'All up, how long did the fire burn?' She needed to know every detail.

Maloney squinted as if calculating in his mind. 'It was exactly eight minutes between receiving the emergency call and the first unit arriving. In the first three minutes they checked the house for survivors, pulled you out and discovered the remains, and it took a total of six minutes to put out the fire. Mopping up and putting out embers in the ceiling took another hour. The open dining room off the kitchen helped the heat and smoke to spread out.'

Oliver shook his head. 'Most of this damage was done in eight minutes. That's incredibly fast.'

'When you look at how much combustible material is in the house, it's pretty standard. Fire needs oxygen, heat and fuel. It had all three in here. The gas just travels through the house raising the temperature of flammable items to ignition point. By the time the victim smelt the smoke, he was pretty much done for, especially if he couldn't get out through his bedroom window. Modern houses are full of flammable materials like nylon, rayon, foam, laminex. In the old days, wooden furniture didn't ignite the same way.'

'This feels like déjà vu.' Oliver moved next to his partner. 'The fire pattern is like Moat Place.'

'Except that here we have burning oil instead of petrol poured through the place,' Kate added.

Peter Latham arrived and forged his way to the front of the group. 'Here we go again,' he said as he brushed past Kate and Oliver. 'Most people die in their beds, but it's supposed to be by natural causes.' Instead of his usually relaxed manner, he appeared tense and frowning.

Kate steeled herself, once again, to see the remains of another victim. The intensity of the burnt-flesh smell was not as bad as she expected. The bedroom door had been open, judging by the amount of soot covering the inside of it.

Maloney moved it slightly, revealing a thin strip of undamaged carpet. 'This can be our control sample of carpet,' he informed the technician. 'You can get it after Dr Latham has finished in here.'

The group silently, almost reverently, entered the room. Peter spoke into his hand-held recorder, noting the position of the body and gross pathological findings. Brett Spender lay there flat, not in the boxer-type position Kate had expected. His face was blackened, as were both arms, which lay on top of the sheet pulled up to his chest.

Zimmer moved forward to take photos as directed by Peter. He moved the sheet a little, exposing relatively clean skin. 'There's a high concentration of soot around the nostrils and mouth.'

Kate closed her eyes and tried to remove the image of a helpless man gasping his last breaths while she was being rescued just metres away.

23

After dropping home for a shower and change of clothes, Kate and Oliver met back at the morgue. Outside the double plastic doors leading into the PM room, Oliver pulled eucalyptus ointment from his pocket and smudged some outside both nostrils.

Peter Latham was sitting at a bench studying a file when they entered. On a steel slab lay the corpse of Brett Spender. Kate hoped that Peter could confirm the ID with either dental records or DNA. On the wall light-box, X-rays of wide open teeth almost glowed. In the background, a radio played an ad for the latest in teeth whitening techniques.

'Hello again.' Peter looked up at them over his glasses. He appeared tired and lacked his usual enthusiasm.

'First thing, it's definitely young Mr Spender. Lucky for us, teeth don't lie, and fires don't damage them. Next thing is the cause of death, which is pretty straightforward in this instance.'

Peter offered the detectives plastic aprons and latex gloves. After putting them on, they stepped closer to the remains. The Y-shaped incision in the chest had been sewn up, and the scalp had already been peeled back then replaced. Kate was relieved that she had taken the time to shower. It meant they had missed the most gruesome part of the autopsy. A summary was going to have to suffice.

Peter Latham grabbed a probe and pointed it towards Spender's mouth. 'The tongue is swollen from dehydration in the fire. This body has been affected like the unidentified woman we saw recently, who still hasn't been claimed, by the way. We're running out of fridge space,' he said, as though they were in a position to fix it.

Kate felt flooded with guilt that they still didn't know the woman's name, let alone where her child was, and whether he or she was still alive. The body would remain refrigerated at the morgue until someone claimed it. The last unknown homeless person had stayed there for two years. Kate was determined not to let that happen to the young mother's body.

Peter continued to probe Spender's mouth. 'The lips are also swollen, as is the pharynx and back of the throat. I've taken some samples and was just about to fix the slides and examine them when you arrived.'

'If he died of smoke inhalation, how long after the fire started would it have happened?'

'He was alive long enough to inhale a substantial amount of the smoke. See the dark soot around his nostrils and mouth? That's when he was struggling for air. There's evidence of smoke inhalation in both lungs, so he was still breathing.'

Kate looked up at the surgical light above the table. He could still have been breathing when she arrived at the house and tried to get into his bedroom. If she hadn't failed, he might be alive now. When she called out to him, he might even have heard her but been unable to answer.

'I tried to get to him, but the smoke was too thick and the fire too hot,' Kate offered, as if apologising.

'I don't believe you could have saved this man,' Peter said in a sympathetic tone. 'The swelling and congestion to his airways is substantial, not to mention the effects from the heat.'

Oliver cleared his throat. 'So without a doubt, whoever started the fire intended to kill him and destroy any evidence. Who would want to kill an invalid that way?'

'Motive is up to you,' Peter said. 'But he might not even have been aware of what was happening to him. The carbon monoxide levels in his blood were around eighty per cent. When they get to twenty to thirty per cent people feel unwell, then they get confused at levels up to about forty per cent. At fifty per cent they start to slur their speech, experience significant weakness, and possibly even vomiting. Unconsciousness happens at about sixty per cent. So by the time the heat from the fire hit, he wouldn't have known anything. And that doesn't take into consideration the damage done to him by cyanide gas from the lounge and mattress materials.'

Kate remembered becoming disorientated and confused about where she had entered the house and how to find her way out again. She hadn't realised she was that close to unconsciousness from the toxic gases.

Peter moved over to a set of scales on which the brain rested. The whiteboard attached to the wall listed the weight of every body organ recorded so far. He lifted the brain and placed it at the head-end of the metal table. Again, he used the probe to point to a large, reddish-looking bruise on the brain's surface.

'Heat can cause epidural haematomas due to a shift in fluid when the skull comes into direct contact with flames, which in this case happened when the headboard and pillow caught fire. This is deep brown and has a jelly-like texture. We normally see that in heat haematomas, caused most likely by the blood boiling, if you like.'

'So there was no head injury at all.' Oliver leaned closer to look.

'There doesn't appear to have been, although I can confirm it by testing the carbon monoxide level in the coagulated blood.'

Kate shook her head. 'And what exactly will that show?'

'If the haematoma occurred before the death and the fire, the blood collection should have lower levels of the inhaled carbon monoxide than in the bloodstream, because that portion of blood was already out of circulation. If it has the same amount as we found in the bloodstream, then it is definitely an artefact caused by the fire.'

As usual, Peter Latham made a lot of sense out of confusing facts. The pair thanked him and returned to the car.

Kate unlocked the doors. 'We know Spender knew Mark Dobbie.'

'Why is it that everywhere we turn this week that guy's name keeps popping up?'

'Because there must be a shit-load of people with incriminating stuff on him. That bastard was about to admit something in the interview room, I'm sure of it. We need to find out exactly what he wanted to confess.'

24

Rosalie Saxton answered the door with uncombed hair and the stale breath that comes from too much alcohol and not enough water the night before. Although it was two o'clock in the afternoon, she still looked hungover.

'If you want a donation, I don't have any money. And if you're peddling religion, you can nick off.' She went to close the door, but Oliver already had his foot inside. He held up his badge and introduced Kate first, then himself.

'We need to talk to you about your movements last night,' Oliver said, moving inside.

Rosalie had no alternative but to let them in. 'What's this about?' She buttoned the top of her grandpa shirt to hide the singlet underneath. The creased pyjama pants suggested the detectives had woken her up.

'Where were you between 8 pm last night and 6 am this morning?'

She rubbed her eyes and clasped the side of her head. 'I was at work until . . . I don't know, nine o'clock, then my boyfriend and I went to dinner and met up with some friends at a club in town.

After that it gets a bit hazy because we started with cocktails and finished with vodka shots. Do you mind if I get a coffee and some aspirin? I've got a shocker of a headache.'

They followed her into the kitchen, which contrasted starkly with her unkempt condition. Two breakfast bowls were placed together in the draining tray, along with two bread and butter plates and two knives and spoons.

She filled a plastic kettle, switched it on and downed two aspirins with water sucked from the tap over the sink. When the kettle boiled, she put four heaped teaspoons of instant coffee into a mug and another three of sugar. After the addition of some water and a token stir, she was ready to talk again. Kate wondered if there was enough water to actually dissolve the contents of the mug.

Rosalie shuffled into the lounge room, where again everything was neatly in its place. When she sat on the twin-seater, Kate chose the other sofa. That left Oliver the rocking chair.

'I slept at my boyfriend's place and came back here at about eleven. Mum and Dad went to the markets, so I crashed in my room.' She tentatively sipped the coffee, clutching it as she would a precious object. 'What is this about? Did I forget to pay a speeding fine?'

'You can relax, it's nothing like that. How was work last night?' Kate asked.

'You know, another day, another dollar.' She smiled to herself.

'Did something amusing happen last night?'

'God, no. Brett, this quad I work for, isn't exactly Charlie Chuckles. He was his usual smartarse self. I fed him, put him to bed, got him a cigarette—'

'What did you do with it after he smoked it?' Kate wanted to know if the carer had had the opportunity to set up the fire and, if so, why she hadn't just set fire to the bed with the smoking butt, then set up the oil in the kitchen as a ruse.

Rosalie sipped some more coffee. 'What are you, the smoking police? I put it out and flushed it down the loo. Don't tell me that tight arse has made another complaint against some poor soul?'

'What did you cook for Brett Spender last night?'

'Oh jeez, is he saying I tried to poison him? Don't tell me he got an upset stomach and he's blaming me? He thinks the bloody world is out to get him.'

'Maybe someone was,' Kate said, watching for some sort of reaction.

She seemed to think for a moment. 'Let's see, Fridays are usually spaghetti night, but he wanted pizza. I heated up one of the frozen low-fat ones.'

'Did you fry anything to go with that?'

She looked across at Oliver as if he was simple. 'Now that would have been pretty stupid, giving him a calorie controlled meal with fried food, for heaven's sake. The dietician orders his meals and I just heat them up, like I'm told. The few times I've bothered to cook for the ungrateful bastard, he's accused me of trying to finish him off.'

Kate and Oliver stared at her, giving her the opportunity to expound on what she had just said, and possibly incriminate herself. Instead, she said nothing.

At that point, the front door opened and an elderly couple came in carrying fresh flowers and groceries in a recycled cloth bag.

'Rosie,' the woman said. 'You should have told us you were entertaining. I could have made muffins this morning.'

'Well, aren't you going to introduce us?' The man walked with a limp but stuck out his hand to greet Oliver, who had stood when his wife entered the room first.

'Dad, Mum, don't get excited, these are the police.'

The woman frowned. 'Is everything all right? You didn't bump into anything with your car again, did you?'

Rosalie seemed embarrassed. 'No, the car's fine. I'll explain later.' She turned to the detectives. 'I'm just staying here while I get enough money together to move out.' When her parents excused themselves to put the groceries away, she spoke in a lowered tone: 'There's no rush to go. I don't have to pay board, I get all my meals cooked, my washing and ironing done and get treated like the prodigal daughter every time I walk in the door. Why would I move out in a hurry?'

Rosalie slurped more coffee and curled her legs up on the lounge.

Kate studied the young woman. She was typical of generation Y, the selfish 'me' generation, as the books and talkback radio described it. So far, Rosalie hadn't even bothered to ask if Brett Spender was all right. Perhaps she already knew he was dead. She was not flustered, or showing any signs of guilt or fear in their presence.

Mrs Saxton returned to the room wringing both hands. 'Please excuse my curiosity, but my husband and I would like to know why you're here. Rosalie is a good girl – though not so good when it comes to reverse parking.' She smiled anxiously at her child.

'Your daughter is helping us with some enquiries regarding her employer, Brett Spender,' Kate explained, then decided to change tack. 'How did you come to work for Mr Spender?'

The mother answered for her daughter. 'Rosalie's been working for that agency for a couple of years now, caring for old people and the disabled. It's wonderful work but doesn't pay well, so we help out where we can.'

'Mum, they don't want to know any of that. They're talking to me.' She raised both eyebrows as if expecting her mother to disappear. 'Maybe the police would like a drink.'

Mrs Saxton apologised for her rudeness and offered tea, coffee or a soft drink.

Kate felt as if she was an adolescent again, over at a friend's house, being waited on by the mother. She held up her hand. 'We're fine, thanks.'

Mrs Saxton retreated. 'Just call if you need anything.'

'What is Spender like to work for?' Kate baited the girl, hoping she would talk about her employer in the past tense, suggesting she already knew he was dead.

'How about a pig, woman-hater and egotistical jerk? That guy could use a reality check. He could have been some great stud once, but no one wants to know him now. He boasts he wouldn't go out with anything that weighed more than most thirteen-year-olds. He treats me like a slave and keeps calling me fat and ugly, but it doesn't stop him staring at my tits every chance he gets.'

'That must be incredibly upsetting for you,' Kate said, trying to sound sympathetic. 'Doesn't that really tick you off? Don't you want to let him know you're better than that?'

'The guy is an arsehole. What's the point, when he has no insight? If he doesn't know by now that he's an idiot, me telling him isn't going to make any difference.'

'So why do you still work for him?' Oliver asked. 'Couldn't you sue him for sexual harassment?'

'Yeah, fat girl sues quadriplegic for harassment. How's that going to go? The guy can't even lift his little finger for a grope. Besides, sometimes he does show that he's trying hard not to be a total dick-head. He asked me to stay and watch a movie last night, but I already had plans with my boyfriend.'

Oliver rocked forward and stopped. 'Was he disappointed?'

She paused for a moment. 'I actually think so. But then he turned back into a pig and yelled at me to get out, that I was fired again. The usual Friday night routine.'

'What did you do next?'

'What do you reckon? I left.'

Kate sat forward. 'Is that the last time you saw him?'

Rosalie unfolded her legs from beneath her. 'You make it sound like the guy threw himself off a cliff after I left. What did he do? Did he send some scary emails, or make threats? I never take him that seriously when he rants and raves.'

'Brett Spender died early this morning,' Kate said, matter of fact.

The empty cup slipped onto Rosalie's lap. 'But he was fine when I left. He wanted to use the computer. I moved it so he could, and I put the telly on.'

'He died from smoke inhalation,' Oliver explained.

The young woman's pleading eyes darted between the detectives' faces. 'But I took his cigarette. He didn't even smoke much.'

'There was a house-fire that started with boiling oil on the stove. Brett didn't stand a chance.'

'Oh my God. I don't believe it,' she said, putting her face in her hands. 'What am I going to do for a job now?'

25

Before going over Spender's medical file that evening, Kate had a soak in the bath. Epsom salts in the warm water eased her muscles. She closed her eyes and let the water wash over her, gently sweeping it around with her hands.

Her mind replayed the events surrounding the fire. Over the last few months she had been obsessive about avoiding situations in which she felt vulnerable. But as soon as she had felt the heat through the door of Spender's house, she hadn't thought twice. All she cared about was saving the life of anyone inside.

The past twenty-four hours had proven to her that she could still do her job. During the fire she had come close to blacking out after inhaling carbon monoxide and who knows how many other poisonous gases. She had probably breathed in cyanide gas as well, but not enough to cause damage. Thank God she hadn't needed to be hospitalised. As small as her home was, it was where she wanted to be. Alone.

Even though she had come close to being killed, Kate knew that she would climb through that window again, without a second thought. That was the real reason she became a police officer; to protect people, especially those who were too helpless to look after themselves. As a child she had detested seeing anyone bullied and always intervened, despite it getting her into more scraps than she could remember. She was just like her father, always defending the underdog. The memories made her smile, especially the times she had come home covered in dirt, bruised from fighting some bully-boy. Her dad would frown and reprimand her but she knew that he was proud of the stand she had taken.

Kate savoured the sensation of the water on her skin, how soothing and reassuring it felt. Where she had grown up, hot water was a luxury, and a hot bath was something had only by people who visited fancy hotels. Slowly lowering herself to water level, she felt the warmth envelop the back of her head, making her feel instantly drowsy.

She thought of Brett Spender, who'd been unable to bathe himself or enjoy such simple pleasures as heat or cold on his skin. She wondered how many people would attend his funeral. If he'd been as unpleasant as Rosalie Saxton had made out, chances were there wouldn't be many mourners. But in death, appearances were important. People he hadn't seen or had contact with in years might crawl from their comfort zones to express the sadness they'd assume was expected. Brett's drama could become theirs, if only for a few hours.

Kate and Oliver would attend the funeral, and ensure everyone there was photographed and identified. There was a chance that Spender's killer would go to the service. For her own and Oliver's sakes, she hoped Spender was deeply unpopular. It would make their work a lot easier, limiting the number of potential suspects.

She wondered who would turn up at her own funeral. That you had to be dead to have one was annoying. There should be pre-death wakes, so people could celebrate their life with others of their choosing. No hangers-on, no one turning up for the sake of appearances. No unwanted colleagues expressing insincere sympathy; just people who really cared.

Kate sat up and turned on the hot tap, reviving the tepid water. Her mind was drifting so she tried to focus on the case.

So far, the first two people they had interviewed had disliked Brett Spender. Each of his paid carers had had the opportunity and motive to hurt him, if he'd treated them as badly as they claimed. Rosalie Saxton certainly showed no compassion, and was the last known person to see him alive. She could have returned to Spender's home and staged the fire after her date. The neighbours didn't hear anything until the explosion. No one heard him calling for help.

Conveniently, Rosalie Saxton's employer was not around to dispute or deny her allegations of harassment. Although she did make a valid point in that there would probably have been little support or sympathy if she sued him or lodged a formal complaint. She needed the job, and no jury would convict a quadriplegic without the use of his hands, arms or body of harassing or intimidating someone who was employed to bathe and toilet him.

Kate hadn't anticipated Rosalie's reaction to the news of Spender's death. No surprise, shock or even hint of sadness. Just concern about herself and her job prospects. But selfishness wasn't a crime, and it didn't mean she bore enough malice towards her boss to commit murder. Besides, if jobs in the industry were that difficult to come by, killing her meal-ticket wouldn't have been too smart.

The weekend carer seemed to have been genuinely shocked by the fire. Although, she too could have come early, set the fire, then returned later in the morning as if everything was normal. Then again, Oliver had spoken to the agency. The woman had been on their books for over ten years and was a model employee. She had not known Spender before accepting the weekend job, and there was nothing in her past to suggest she was violent.

With wrinkled fingertips, Kate climbed out of the bath and released the plug. She quickly covered herself in a towelling gown and towel-dried her hair. Despite feeling physically exhausted, her mind remained active. She made a cup of green tea and sat on a cushion at the coffee table in her lounge room. Opening the case file, she began reading.

She started with the PM report that outlined Brett Spender's past medical history. Born in Brisbane, he was twenty-two years old, previously in good health. As a child he had suffered anaphylaxis due to ingestion of peanuts. She shook her head. Typical doctor. What sort of word was anaphylaxis? Why couldn't doctors just use normal words like 'allergy', words with fewer syllables and a meaning that everyone understood?

She read on. While on holiday ten months earlier, he had dived off a jetty, sustained a neck injury and was airlifted to hospital. The injury involved a fracture of the third vertebra in his neck and severed the spinal cord between the third and fourth vertebrae. Doctors said he was lucky to survive. Then again, she thought, luck was relative. Spender spent three months in rehabilitation, with little improvement. The resort company settled out of court for a confidential amount. All the medical notes said was that the company had covered medical expenses and Brett Spender would be able to live independently for the rest of his life. That is, as far as he could while being completely dependent on others for his basic needs.

In today's world, private care was expensive. Kate tried to calculate how much money would be needed for a house, renovations to accommodate a wheelchair, and private carers. The settlement had to be significantly more than a couple of million dollars. If the money was supposed to keep him for the rest of his expected life, there should be a lot left over. So who stood to benefit financially from his death?

Listed as next of kin was his mother, Nancy Spender. The house had been paid for, so Kate wanted to check whether it was insured for full replacement, and whether Spender had any life insurance from before the accident. If he did, the payout could be even more substantial. Not a bad return for some boiling oil.

Kate waded through various medical consults, for everything from constipation to mouth ulcers. She didn't want to know what a treatment called manual disimpaction meant. It sounded disgusting enough. Being a doctor had to be worse than police work. She suddenly felt better about sitting on the floor late at night, working.

Stretching her legs, she decided to finish up and get some sleep. They could interview Spender's mother in the morning. As she turned one last page, a photo caught her attention. It had been taken during a dermatology consult suggested while Spender was in rehab.

Kate stared at the photo. Spender had three moles on his back, at the level of his right shoulder blade.

26

Nancy Spender was packing her suitcase when Oliver and Kate arrived at her home. The two-bedroom flat had a 'for lease' sign in the window.

The detectives introduced themselves and Oliver took the lead: 'We are very sorry for your loss, Mrs Spender. This must be a difficult time, but we need to ask you some questions.'

'I don't have much time, I've got a lot to organise.'

She led them into what real estate agents would describe as a 'cosy' living area, which led into a galley kitchen. The place smelt like a mix of cigarette smoke and bourbon. Judging by her dark eyebrows and the white-blondeness of her hair, she'd recently had her colour done. Clothes lay strewn across a double-seater bamboo lounge, most items with price tags still on. It appeared that the grieving mother had recently been on a spending spree.

'We understand completely,' Oliver said, hands clasped in front of him like a priest. 'When is the funeral service?'

'I don't know, Monday or Tuesday. Brett suffered a lot. Now he can rest in peace.' Nancy

Spender sniffed. 'You're a man, which one do you prefer?'

She picked up a gaudy pink floral bikini and held it up to her rake-thin body. Then she held up a black one-piece with a cut-out across the stomach. For the first time, Oliver seemed dumbstruck.

'We can see you're very busy. Are you moving house as well?'

She frowned. 'We all grieve in our own way. I've decided to go on holiday for a while, to get away from it all. There's not much left for me here now and too many memories. I sail on Wednesday on the *QE2*. It's very posh so I want to wear the right sort of things. Brett loved the water and beaches, you know. I'm taking his ashes to release into the Pacific.'

Kate studied the woman's weathered face and tobacco-stained fingers. This was a chain-smoking woman not prepared to admit her age.

'When did you last see Brett?' Kate asked.

'Oh, just the other week. He was doing fine and didn't want his mother around all the time.'

'According to his carers,' Oliver challenged, 'you hadn't seen him for over six weeks, and then you argued. What was the argument about?'

She waved the hand holding the bikini. 'A couple of weeks, six weeks, what's the difference? When was the last time either of you saw your mother?'

Kate cut in: 'The argument?'

Nancy smiled and picked up two new items to

compare. 'We always fought. It was how we got on.'

'We were told that you argued about money after Brett's payout. That you felt you deserved your share.'

'It's hardly a surprise, me having struggled to bring him up by myself, that I would expect he should help me out in my twilight years. I gave up everything for him. Boyfriends, a career, the lot.'

The woman felt her child owed her. So she was planning on vamping around in revealing swim-suits bought with his money. If she was travelling alone, the wealthy men on the cruise were probably her targets. Having already spent some of the inheritance, she could easily be on the prowl for another man to support her.

Oliver seemed impatient. 'Where were you on Friday night and Saturday morning, Mrs Spender?'

'With a friend, if you must know.' She sidled up to him. 'Older women have needs, too.' Then she cackled with a hoarse laugh that turned into a productive cough.

'We'll need the name of that friend.' Oliver flicked open his notebook and clicked his pen. 'Are you sure he can substantiate that?'

'I don't like your attitude, Detective whatever-your-name-is. If you plan on keeping that up, you might as well leave right now.'

'Fine.' Oliver retreated towards the door, which was only a few feet away. 'We can do this down at the station if you're not prepared to cooperate. We would have thought you'd want to help, given that your son was murdered yesterday.'

'Get out,' she snapped. 'You have no right to judge me.'

As they left the unit, Kate turned. 'One more thing, Mrs Spender. Are you the beneficiary of Brett's will and any insurance he had?'

The door slammed behind her and almost rocked on its hinges.

Monday morning arrived too soon, after a weekend of sleeping and watching sport on TV. Feeling relaxed and refreshed, Kate watched Oliver study the photo of Candice Penfold and the man with three moles. He used a magnifier of the kind employed by jewellers and photographers. The crime labs had them, but she had never before seen a detective use one. Oliver leaned closer to the photo and squinted. He had seemed tense all morning and had barely spoken a word. She thought she had him figured out, but right now she had no idea what was going through his mind.

Then again, Kate decided, it was possible that he had started out wanting to prove himself and had become swamped and overwhelmed by the job. It wouldn't have been the first time a detective started out cocky then found himself out of his depth.

The job was never finished, and at times it felt like they were drowning in it, with no way to the surface. At best, they were barely treading water. And some tired sooner than others.

'The moles look very similar to the ones the dermatologist photographed on Spender's back. It can't be a coincidence.'

'That's what I thought.' Kate swivelled back to her desk. 'So we think Spender raped Candice Penfold that night?'

'Or was one of the rapists,' Oliver qualified. 'We don't know that others weren't there taking advantage of her as well. Maybe Spender was the only one caught on film.'

'True. So Candice disappears then Brett Spender is murdered. That's no coincidence either. What if she staged her disappearance so she could murder Spender, assuming she found out it was him in the picture?'

Oliver frowned. 'But how do we explain the blood in the car? It's plausible that whoever else was there that night killed her and Spender. Maybe one of them was going to go to the police.'

Kate's phone rang and she answered. 'Send him up.'

A moment later, one of the computer technicians arrived in the office. Don Platt didn't look like the average computer analyst. He was suntanned and had a trim physique – he had once been a champion ballroom dancer, before the sport had become popular. For all the flak he got from the other males on the force, he got as many advances from females. Platt had a reputation for being a ladies' man that Kate suspected was well and truly earned.

He shook Oliver's hand, then hers, which he held for a moment too long. She let go and wiped her palm on her trousers.

'What have you got?'

'Brett Spender's computer. The fire destroyed it, but I've gone through his server and pulled up his emails from the last six weeks. The final one was a group mailout and it's a doozy.'

He inserted a disk into the laptop he had brought with him. Kate and Oliver looked over his shoulders as he pulled up the file.

'It seems this man had a change of heart and wanted to clear his conscience about something before he died.' Kate began to read the email out loud.

Dear so-called friends. I type this with a sore mouth, which at least means I can feel something. It is Friday night, late, and I am alone. Fridays and weekends are all the same to me now. I am alone and there seems little bloody point.

'Come on,' Oliver interrupted. 'Don't tell me he committed suicide, or paid someone to kill him?'

'Wait a minute,' Kate said. 'It goes on.'

Friendships are fickle bloody things. You think you have lifelong mates, joined by some sort of superglue, and then one thing changes. What happens to the friendships? What fucking friendships? I might as well have died in that bloody accident, for all my friends care. Where are you? Have you changed your lives, do you come to visit? The answer is of course not.

You can't catch what I've got and I'm not a fucking freak. I am the same bloke you laughed, drank and had fun with. The best offer I've had is from some old church crone who feels sorry for the cripple. The only other is from some sick bastard on the internet.

I've had enough. Earl is right. It's all about karma. And some of us created some serious bad karma shit in our pasts. If you don't change, something like this could happen to you.

'Earl, who's he?' Kate asked.

Platt answered as if it was obvious: 'It's a TV show where a guy was a crook and he goes back to everyone he hurt or robbed to make amends and create good karma.'

She read on.

From now on, I'm taking Earl's advice and will try to do good stuff, to make things right. This email is my first try. The only way to get any part of my body to work, or get a life back, is to do right and good things. If you're smart, you'll do the same thing. Think about it.

Brett

The technician flicked through some other messages while Oliver spoke.

'It sounds like he's converted to some kind of cult or religion and is spreading the word to the only people he has quick access to.'

'But if you read it in context with what we know about him most likely raping Candice and who knows how many other women with his friends, he could have made them think he was going to the police,' Kate said. 'Look at the timing. He sent it out late in the evening, and he was killed a few hours after. Long enough for the recipient to receive it and react.'

Oliver asked to re-read it. 'It could be seen as threatening. Things like, "you could end up like me". Maybe he did intend to go to the police.'

'Who got the email?' Kate bent forward again to check the screen.

'In total,' Platt stated, 'thirty-two people. Everyone on his mailing list, except the nursing agency. He emailed them separately after sending this message. You'll notice a lot of the addresses in this group email are workplaces, mostly hotels and resorts. The recipients are probably concierges, barmen and other workers. Either Brett Spender was a great guy who everyone loved, or he didn't realise staff get paid to be nice.'

Oliver straightened. 'Nancy Spender isn't on the list, but our good friend Mr Dobbie is.'

That did not surprise Kate, given the pair had been on holidays together, but they would need to interview Dobbie again to find out whether he had an alibi for Friday night.

She also wanted to know why Spender had bothered emailing the agency late at night. 'Can I see the other one he sent?'

'Sure. It's not exactly subtle. He says he never wants that bitch of a carer, Rosalie Saxton, to set foot in his house again. She's fired. Then he demands someone else comes on Monday.'

Oliver scratched his chin. 'It doesn't sound as though he was planning on dying that night, if he's demanding a different carer.'

Kate agreed. 'And Rosalie said he sacked her every week.'

'It shows you what an idiot this guy was,' Platt commented. 'He decided to create good karma and starts by crapping on his nurse. I'm thinking he missed Earl's point.'

'Or maybe,' Oliver added, 'someone missed Spender's point. Karma is supposed to be the doctrine of inevitable consequence. Maybe his life of drugs and rape just caught up with him.'

'That's supposed to be our job and the courts'. Some of us call it justice. Only Spender didn't get justice. Forget your karma and fancy philosophies.' Kate tugged on the back of her hair. 'Whoever killed him needs to be caught and put away for life. *That's* what inevitable consequence is supposed to mean.'

27

'What the fuck do you want?' Mark Dobbie half opened the door, revealing a bare chest. 'Do I have to phone my lawyer?'

'Whoever it is,' a raspy female voice called from inside, 'get rid of them and come back here.'

'No one. I'll be right back.'

'Is this a bad time?' Kate raised both eyebrows. 'Because we're not leaving.'

'I was lucky to make bail because of you bastards, coming in here and screwing with my stuff. The place was a fucking mess when I got back.' He opened the door further and, despite being totally naked, stepped closer to Kate. With a semi-closed mouth, he leered. 'If this,' he grabbed his penis, 'doesn't do it for you, maybe you liked looking at those photos and came back for more.'

Kate didn't flinch despite being repulsed by his stale body odour.

Dobbie didn't back away. 'Are naked chicks your thing? We could arrange a sitting if you want 'cause I could do with some new pics.'

'You could do with some breath-freshener.' Kate looked beyond him into the flat. 'If your friend inside there hasn't said anything, it's probably because she's lost her sense of smell. My guess is, she has absolutely no taste. Did you tell her that you drug girls and rape them?'

Dobbie's eyes flashed angrily. Oliver moved swiftly to put himself between his partner and the man.

'Put some clothes on,' Oliver said, and pushed through the door. 'We're staying.'

Inside, a pair of red high-heeled shoes lay on their side, one on the lounge, the other on the floor beneath the table. A set of keys and a sequinned bag were on the bench. Kate picked up the bag and extracted a driver's licence. Date of birth read 1956.

A still-naked Dobbie stood defiantly, before grabbing his mobile phone and speed-dialling a number, no doubt his lawyer's. Obviously, someone said they would take a message because he demanded they come immediately. 'The police are harassing me! Tell him to get over here now!'

Dobbie hung up and faced the detectives. 'Your arses are fried. You're gonna be on *A Current Affair* tonight, and man are your bosses going to be pissed with you.'

'You mean we might be on the telly?' Kate pretended to be excited at the notion of being on a tabloid program known for targeting scammers, corrupt police and men who refused to pay child support. Then she pulled a piece of paper from her jacket. 'We have a warrant. The team will be here any minute. Hey, maybe you can bring your mother along – the one in the bedroom.'

'Mark, what's taking so long?'

A middle-aged woman appeared in the hallway, naked apart from a gaudy diamond necklace. 'Oh God,' she said, attempting to cover her breasts with one hand and her pubic hair with the other. 'Did my husband send you?'

'No, madam,' Kate said. 'We're the police. From homicide.' She peeled off her jacket and covered the woman's back on the way to Dobbie's bedroom. 'You might want to get dressed before the search team arrives.' She added from the corridor, 'And just in case reporters find their way here.'

In record time the woman was dressed in a black sequinned cocktail number and had located her shoes. Kate handed her the licence, bag and keys, which she snatched before rushing past Dobbie, not even bothering to say goodbye on her way out.

'Let me guess, one of your clients?' Oliver offered, and threw a towel from the home-gym equipment to Dobbie. 'Put this on, you're embarrassing yourself.'

Another rap on the door heralded the arrival of Maloney and Bella, his accelerant-detecting dog.

'What's this?' Dobbie wrapped the towel around his waist and laughed nervously. 'Rin Tin Tin or Lassie? There aren't any drugs here so you're wasting your time.'

'We're not looking for drugs. She'll just go

through the house quietly,' Maloney said. 'We can start outside with the rubbish bins.'

Oliver put on latex gloves and located Dobbie's laptop computer inside a black padded bag on the floor. 'We'll be taking this with us,' he said. 'You'll get a receipt and it will be logged in our book. Now, since we have a few minutes, where were you on Friday night and Saturday morning before sun-up?'

'What the fuck are you trying to pin on me now?' Dobbie sat at the dining table and dialled the lawyer again, this time less cocky in his manner. 'They've got another warrant. I need someone here now.'

Oliver leant over the table. 'Friday night. Where were you?'

'God, I don't know, out with friends, probably. How am I supposed to remember?'

'Try harder. Can anyone verify where exactly you were that night?'

Dobbie rubbed his hands over the stubble on his face. 'Friday night. Wait a minute, I ordered some laksa and was supposed to have a friend over but she couldn't make it. I stayed home and watched a DVD.'

'That wouldn't have taken all night. What else did you do?'

'Had a couple of drinks and went to bed.'

'What time would that have been?'

Kate pulled on gloves and led the way into the kitchen. A uniformed constable accompanied them with a digital video camera recording the search. Maloney opened the cupboards under the sink and Bella sniffed away. There was very little inside them – no cooking oil containers, just a canister of powdered ammonia, a bag of sponges and washing up detergent.

'Probably about midnight,' Dobbie volunteered, craning to see what the detectives were up to.

It struck Kate as odd that there were no dirty plates or even glasses in the kitchen or lounge room. Dobbie obviously hadn't bothered to give his visitor a drink. Judging by how lucid she appeared, he hadn't drugged her either. This woman had come to the place willingly for sex with Dobbie. There was just no accounting for some women's taste, she thought. Even so, she doubted loverboy would be seeing her again in a hurry.

Maloney removed the lid of the plastic rubbish bin and Bella seemed unimpressed by the contents, which comprised energy bar wrappers and left-overs in takeaway containers that looked days old.

They toured the lounge room, again without any response from Bella. Inside Dobbie's bedroom, Maloney started with the laundry basket, although more clothes were on the floor than inside it, including a pair of women's control-support underpants, the kind Kate referred to as 'rawhide undies'. They pushed parts of a woman's body in, shoved other bits out and rounded everything up. The dog obligingly sniffed and passed all the items.

Kate opened the sliding door on the wardrobe and separated some of the clothes with gloved hands. At one end a shirt and a pair of trousers dangled from the same hanger. Bella nuzzled them then sat.

'Good girl.' Maloney patted the black labrador's head. 'Great girl.' He handed her a biscuit from his pocket.

'We've got what we wanted,' Maloney said. 'I'll bag these separately in airtight containers. They may have been washed but they've definitely got accelerant on them.'

Kate returned to the lounge room where Oliver was asking Dobbie whether he knew Brett Spender.

'That poor bastard, yeah, I know him, or used to before his accident.' Dobbie looked up at Kate. 'Am I allowed to get a drink?'

'Help yourself,' she said, and nodded at Oliver, to let him know the search had been successful.

Dobbie made himself a coffee. He checked the fridge for milk, opened the carton then pulled a face before tipping the contents down the sink. He opted for black with two sugars.

'When did you last see or hear from Brett?' Oliver was still playing the nice guy.

'Not for months. I went round to his place a couple of times but he didn't want to talk, just sat there like a vegetable. It was pretty gross. He kinda blamed us for his accident.'

'What happened?' Kate leant against the bench.

Dobbie, looking defeated, moved to the table and sat in a chair, legs extended under the table.

'We were mucking around after a big night, diving off a jetty at Patrician Island. We'd done it loads of times before. That morning, Brett makes this big show and dives off like he was Tarzan or something.' His hands were trembling as he clutched the mug and stared into the liquid. 'He didn't come up again and it seemed like ages. After a while, I jumped in and the water was really shallow. He just kind of floated up on his face and he wasn't breathing. Some nurse was there and gave him mouth-to-mouth and he woke up but couldn't move. The helicopter came and he went to hospital for months.'

He slurped some of his drink. 'At least the bastards who own the resort paid up. They owed him and didn't want any bad publicity.'

'When was the last time you had contact with him?'

Dobbie sat up straight, almost spilling his coffee. 'What the hell are you asking? Let me guess. It's persecute a cripple week so you're trying to go him for drugs as well? They don't do him much good now so you can piss off.'

Kate noticed a slight slump in Dobbie's posture, as though he was ashamed, or even guilty about something. From where she stood, she could see perspiration seeping through the back of his shirt. He was no genius and he was worried. Being street smart enough to take the pictures without being caught in them wasn't necessarily enough to escape drug and possible homicide charges.

She thought about Candice Penfold and the other unknown women who were drugged, molested and subjected to God knows what indecent acts in this very house, while Dobbie looked on and took happy snaps to show around. She felt bile rise in her throat. Someone had to protect society from evils like this, but some smarmy lawyer would probably get him off, despite his guilt. She thought of how the media had portrayed Lilly Stavos as a party girl, a euphemism for loose, easy and anything but innocent. No wonder the Penfolds wanted to keep their daughter's name out of the paper if the alternative meant they'd have to endure the same treatment.

'Brett sent an email the other night, rambling about how he found God or something. It didn't make much sense. I didn't bother answering back. I reckon he's losing it big time.'

Kate moved forward and placed one hand on the table, leaning into Dobbie's personal space. 'Is there something you want to get off your chest about Brett? Something you're having trouble living with?'

'What do you reckon?' Dobbie locked eyes with Kate. His anger was palpable as he clutched the mug tighter and his fingertips blanched. 'It could have been any one of us that day.'

Oliver sat forward and spoke slowly. 'Seems Brett was under the impression that bad things happen to bad people. That's why he wanted to change.'

Dobbie continued to stare at Kate and moved his face even closer to hers. She could smell the coffee and last night's alcohol, seeping through his pores. The stench of his body odour strengthened. She was smelling fear.

'Sometimes,' he snarled, 'for some people, shit just happens.'

'Is that why you killed him and set fire to the place, to make sure he couldn't find God and drop you in it to save his soul?'

He pulled back and his eyes darted across the table. Kate wondered if he was thinking about doing a runner, but as he was still only wearing a towel around his waist, he wouldn't get far. In the end he just sat there and tried to act calm, finishing off his drink. Sweat formed rivulets on his forehead, giving away how scared he was right now. This guy was guilty and couldn't hide it. After a prolonged silence, he spoke quietly.

'I want my lawyer. I'm not saying anything else until my lawyer's here.'

Maloney re-entered the room holding the sealed evidence collected from the wardrobe.

'Fine,' Kate said, refusing to back off. 'But you're wrong about something. Shit never just happens. It's always created by an arsehole. You better check – you might have just crapped yourself again.'

28

Kate arrived early at the office to prepare for a meeting with Gareth Russo but, as usual, her partner had beaten her to it. Oliver was kneeling on the floor, looking for something in Fiskar's desk drawer.

'What are you doing?' she asked, swinging her coat onto her chair.

Oliver stood up and moved to another desk. 'Doesn't anyone have pens around here? There aren't any in the supply cupboard. Aha. Finally.' He held a blue pen up to the ceiling, like a victory trophy. He clicked the point in and out. It looked like a promotional pen.

'You'd think they'd buy us stationery,' he said. 'It's ridiculous having to scavenge for everything. No wonder so many police have other jobs on the side.'

Kate had heard that record numbers of police were moonlighting, thanks to the introduction of twelve-hour shifts in some areas. In three days, officers could clock up a week's worth of hours. The intention was to give them more time with their families but, instead, many were supplementing their incomes with second and third jobs. Private businesses, nightclubs and pubs paid well for security and there was no shortage of police taking up the offers. The problem was that sometimes the line between ethical and dodgy became blurred. Free meals, drinks and cash payments had the anti-corruption vigilantes going wild.

As far as Kate knew, no one in her office had a second job, although she probably wouldn't be the first to know if they did. She thought about Russo implying that they were all under scrutiny. Maybe some individual in their office was the target of an investigation, not the whole unit. She tried to think who had been behaving suspiciously. Then again, the saying went that it was the greedy police scammers who got caught. The others, the ones who took small amounts in kickbacks, were harder to detect but over a career could accumulate a nifty addition to their superannuation. Luckily, she had never worked with anyone corrupt – or at least, known anyone who was caught. She wondered if the investigations were warranted, or whether politicians were simply on witch-hunts to restore the public's faith that bad seeds were being weeded out.

Kate felt in her jacket pocket for a pen, but it wasn't there. Unlocking her own desk drawer, she reached in to her private collection, bought from charity spruikers outside the nearby supermarket. She grabbed a Children's Hospital ballpoint with a bandaged bear on top. At the back of the drawer, something caught her eye. Wedged under a note-pad was an envelope. Kate glanced around the office. She always locked the drawer and no one else had a key.

Russo had just arrived and called out, 'Five minutes in my office for the Penfold review, people.'

Other detectives filed in, absorbed in banter and chatter. Oliver had his head down in his notes, making fast work of the stolen pen. Kate jiggled the drawer, as if it wasn't moving properly. She slid the envelope forward and opened it, making sure it remained out of sight.

Oh my God! She straightened up and closed the drawer, her heart hammering. When she was sure no one else was paying attention, she opened it again and this time had a closer look at the contents. There were nineteen, no, twenty brand new hundred dollar bills. A post-it note read, 'Your share, as promised'.

She closed then locked the drawer and scanned the faces of everyone in the room. One of them had to have put it there. It could have been meant for someone else, except that her drawer was always locked. Someone had to have set her up to look like she was on the take. There was an internal inves-tigation going on and somebody was feeling threa-tened. But who?

'Are you all right?'

Kate started.

'You look as though you're about to face a death squad.' Oliver had suddenly wheeled his chair beside hers.

She tried to read his face, but had no idea whether he was being sarcastic, clever or innocent. The money in the envelope had changed everything. 'What's that supposed to mean?'

He laughed. 'Just that I have more reason to be nervous considering the way I seem to press Russo's buttons about proper procedure.'

Kate barely heard what Oliver said. She rubbed her forehead and felt nauseated. None of this made sense.

'Now, people!' the inspector called.

Kate made sure her drawer was firmly locked and headed into the meeting. Any one of these people, including Oliver, could be the corrupt one. Worse, the culprit was prepared to set her up for the fall.

Gareth Russo sat at his desk with Kate's report in his hands.

'So this guy, Dobbie, is tied to your homicide victim and had what you think is a reasonable motive for killing Spender. He has no alibi and this accelerant-detecting dog positively identified some clothes from his wardrobe, even though they'd been washed or dry-cleaned.' Russo leant back in his chair. 'Is that going to hold up in court?'

Oliver mentioned the lab's delay in confirming what specific accelerant was found on the clothing. Kate half listened and glanced outside into the main office area. A data clerk sat at a computer terminal while Fiskars and Rench chatted on their phones. Within moments, her security in the place and comfort in its familiarity had vanished. She considered what she really knew about her colleagues. The answer was, very little, despite having shared office space and cases for years. They had probably spent more time working together than they had with their spouses, and yet she had no idea what they did in their spare time.

Her colleagues often chatted about what was going on in their lives outside work, but usually she switched off, treating these conversations like white-noise in the background. She always had something more important to focus on. Now, looking around the office, she tried to imagine any of these people being corrupt. Fiskars was an arsehole, but had a good arrest record. His network of informants didn't seem to let him down. He was lazy but still got results. She remembered him mentioning a club once, where wealthy singles went.

Kate thought about how something highly suspicious could in reality be completely innocent. One of her easiest investigations involved the 'black widow', a woman who had married three times; each husband had died within months of the wedding. But instead of being a killer, the woman had married men with terminal illnesses. She had met them at a cancer support group after the death of her first husband from a brain tumour.

It was plausible that Fiskars could have joined an exclusive club to meet wealthy socialites, which is what all his wives were. As for Rench, he rarely spoke outside of his partner's earshot. She assumed he was divorced, judging by the derogatory comments he made about marriage.

Liz Gould had always been conscientious and efficient and had happily helped Kate with a couple of cases. She now preferred not to chat and rushed off as soon as possible to collect her son from daycare. Kate couldn't imagine Liz having either the time or energy to be corrupt.

Laurie Sheehan saved money by doing his own renovations. Then again, he seemed to take pride in the improvements and treated it like a hobby. The other detectives worked hard and seemed decent enough, though Kate's social contact with them was minimal. As far as she knew, or had assumed, everyone in homicide was financially stable and wouldn't need to supplement their income by illegal means. But how would she know if someone had drug, gambling or other debts?

'Farrer, are you with us?'

Kate's attention returned to the update. 'Of course.'

'Maybe something in the debris has been overlooked. I want you to go over the forensic findings with Fiskars. May as well review the Moat Place evidence as well. They're both fires, afer all, and it looks like Dobbie's got his fingers in more than one pie.' He put his elbows on the table and pinched the bridge of his nose. 'We should have the manpower to form a bloody taskforce, but that's the best I can do for you now.'

Kate knew she should notify someone about the money, but wanted to think it through before deciding what to do. She approached Fiskars, who quickly ended his phone call.

'What can I do you for?' Under the circumstances, the innocent attempt at humour wasn't remotely amusing.

'Russo wants us to join forces and go over the two fire deaths.'

Fiskars grinned. 'Fine with me.' He handed her two large files.

Kate noted that the Moat Place file was much larger. 'Have you had any luck finding the owners of the house yet?'

'The doctor and his wife are still away and out of contact. They paid someone to do the lawns once a month, but the guy knew nothing about who was living in the place. We've been chasing up leads from the police phone line, but so far most of the calls have been cranks, which I'm still sifting through. There's one from the local newsagent which could be something, but so far it's been a bloody waste of time. If you ask me, the baby didn't survive. They don't just disappear without someone noticing.'

His phone rang and Kate took the opportunity to return to her desk with the list of callers. Maybe they were on a wild goose chase. The victim had endured a pregnancy and a fluid clot in her lungs, but the baby had definitely been born alive. The milk stains on the cloth nappy proved it. And they still had no idea where the mother had been killed. All they had were the remains of the house in which her childless body had been torched.

'If you want, we'll go see the newsagent.'

'Suits me,' Fiskars answered. 'I'll get up to speed on Mark Dobbie and make some calls. See if one of my contacts knows him.'

She grabbed her jacket and Fiskars' file. Oliver picked up his jacket and she saw his silver pen fall out of the top pocket.

29

Oliver drove while Kate went through the file, but she could not stop thinking about Oliver's silver pen. When she had walked in on him earlier, he was searching through desk drawers. He had lied about the pen, knowing full well he had one in his pocket. He took it everywhere with him and it had been the only one she'd seen him use in his notebook.

Maybe she was not alone in being set up with a wad of money. This morning, Oliver had looked like he was hiding something. Then he had lied to her without batting an eyelid. He was good at it. She had thought him honest but was now unsure.

She decided to mention the money to Oliver while no one else was around and see how he reacted. The sinking feeling of being let down was rapidly evolving into anger. Police needed to know whether or not they could rely on their partners, if the situation ever arose where their lives depended on it. The question of trust wasn't a luxury. It was a necessity.

'I have to talk to you about something. It's private and it can't go any further.'

Oliver flicked her a glance then concentrated on the road again. 'OK.'

'Someone planted money in my desk.'

He didn't react.

'A substantial amount, two thousand dollars.'

This time he looked at her. 'That's a reasonable amount of cash. What do you mean, planted?'

'As in, placed in an envelope with the words "Your share as promised" written on it.'

He checked the rear-vision mirror more than once, and fiddled with the side-mirror as they drove along. He seemed almost nervous.

'What are you going to do with it?'

'I don't know. That's why I'm talking to you.'

They braked behind a school bus and the children in the back seat waved and pulled faces at them. Neither was in the mood to respond. Kate wanted to hear what he suggested. If he encouraged her to keep the money, he was not the honest man she had judged him to be. On the other hand, insisting that she turn it in immediately, as per protocol, would go a long way to convincing her he was aboveboard.

'You've got a couple of choices,' he began, checking the mirrors again. 'You could sit on it and see if someone stakes a claim, or you hand it in, which will trigger a full-on investigation into homicide. If you do that, everyone will know it's you who contacted the anti-corruption unit and you could bring yourself a fair bit of grief. It'll also stuff everyone around and take them away from their work.'

Kate felt her stomach lurch. She didn't want to hear this from him. 'But if I don't report it and there's an investigation anyway, I'll be in deep trouble. My prints are already all over the envelope. I don't see that I have a choice.'

'I can't make the decision for you, but how do you know you'll be believed? Don't you think it's a bit suspicious that you just happened to "find" this money in your desk? I mean, was it broken into?'

'No, but we both know that locks are only for honest people.'

A car sped past them, and Oliver ignored it. Kate began to wonder where corruption started. Was it turning a blind eye to someone speeding when it was inconvenient to book the offender? They had all done it over the years, and she was complicit right now.

'Think carefully before you decide,' he said. 'If no one claims it, the money could end up being yours. You've worked a lot of unpaid overtime this last week. And is anyone getting hurt?'

Bile rose to the back of her mouth and she swallowed hard. 'That's not the point. What if I'm being tested for honesty?'

'Then the fact that you didn't report it immediately means you already have some serious explaining to do if you eventually decide to notify internal investigators.'

Oliver had a point, but she could explain the delay as a result of meetings and work commitments. He was encouraging her not to report the money. Kate had just lost faith in her partner. More than that, she felt an ache in her stomach, as though she had lost a friend. It wasn't just Oliver she could no longer trust, it was her own judgement. She decided to request a change of partner at the first opportunity.

Oliver stopped at a petrol station not far from the Moat Place house. While he went inside for a bottle of water, Kate made the call to the anti-corruption unit. After giving her details and agreeing to wait for further instruction, she hung up and took a deep breath. There was no going back now.

She watched an oil tanker deposit its load into one of the underground storage containers while the driver squatted by the hosepipe. Oliver was not visible inside. Had he gone to the toilet or disappeared for a moment to make a call? Damn him. Now she would have to watch every move he made.

At the newsagent inside the Queensgate shopping village, a short queue of people waited to check their tickets for a win in last night's Powerball game. Once again, Oliver's attention was drawn to a large television screen suspended from the ceiling, rotating ads for phone cards and holidays. That thing with men and TVs was really beginning to grate on her.

The shop itself was compact, and full of school supplies.

While they waited for the staff to serve the customers, they gravitated to the magazine racks.

Curious to see what Oliver chose, she moved around behind him once he'd perused the options. Computing and digital photography were his choice. She realised how little she knew him. She was sure he would have gone for a periodical on something feel-good and domestic, like growing organic vegetables. But after finding the money in her drawer and seeing him rifling through the office, she was sure there was more to him than met the eye.

Kate picked up a copy of the *Trading Post* then decided to people-watch instead. She could always tell a lot about an area that way. All she had to do was sit in a shopping centre for a few minutes and she'd have a good grasp on the demographic and average income in the surrounding suburbs.

Queensgate was an affluent area but many locals had probably taken on a huge debt to afford the location. Some of the women were dressed for the gym, though instead of designer gear, they wore Target-type outfits – cheap but presentable. The suits chosen by the newsagency's women customers were neither designer label nor tailor-made. One woman had on full make-up, blouse, tight black skirt and stockings, but the matching jacket was too large across the back. These people were working hard and obviously had financial priorities other than expensive clothes.

Oliver seemed to be studying the clientele as well. He moved forward as soon as the shop was empty of customers, approaching the older worker who was presumably the owner.

'What can I help you with today?' The man smiled as he spoke.

'Are you Mike White?' Oliver asked.

The man nodded just as the phone rang. The female assistant took her time to answer, waiting to find out what Oliver had to say. The older man flashed her a look and she backed away to the phone on the wall. Oliver introduced himself and Kate, and asked if they could have a quiet conversation with him about his call to Crime Stoppers. Without hesitating, the newsagent agreed and signalled to the girl on the phone that he'd be gone for a few minutes. She was busy explaining that the papers had been delivered late because they had arrived late that morning. No wonder she hesitated to answer the phone, Kate thought. It was quicker and easier to abuse someone over the phone than come down and do it in person.

'We could grab a coffee and chat, if you don't mind. I haven't had breakfast yet,' White said. He looked weary, face drawn, with deep lines taking the focus from his clear grey eyes. He cheerfully stepped outside his shop into the compact, friendly mall containing a bakery, independent supermarket, butcher, video shop and takeaway; the hub of a local community.

Mike waved at or greeted all the shop staff he saw, and some customers as well, and they all responded. This really was a tight, friendly community and Mike White understood that. He would definitely know what was going on in the neighbourhood, Kate thought.

As they approached the bakery, the smell of fresh bread rolls made her stomach gurgle. Oliver and Mike ordered coffees, and she bought some warm cheese rolls. They chose a plastic table just back from the electronic doors and Kate tore open the paper bag, turning it into a makeshift plate. 'Help yourself.'

Mike didn't need to be asked twice. 'Thanks kindly,' he said, and tucked in.

'Have you been in the area long?' she asked, tearing open a packet of sugar and dumping the contents into her ceramic mug.

'About three years. I come from a corporate background but always wanted to run a news-agency. Don't know whether that was so smart or not now. People just don't appreciate the hours, or what you put up with.'

Schoolchildren began to appear in the mall, with tidy hair and clean uniforms, some accompanied by parents. Within minutes the mall was buzzing with activity. Kate checked her watch. Eight thirty meant a school must be close by.

Exhausted mothers were already returning in packs and stopping for a caffeine fix after dropping their kids off. A boy around ten slurped on a soft drink carried in one hand; the other hand held a half-eaten custard tart.

'Hell of a way to start the day,' Oliver said, nodding at the boy.

244

'You don't see it that much around here.' Mike watched the boy meander past. 'Most kids will get a proper breakfast, but with million dollar mortgages, there are a lot of families where both parents work. I guess sometimes the kids suffer.'

Kate sipped her coffee and felt it warm her throat. It was great coffee. She'd have to remember the place. 'Tell us what you know about the house-fire in Moat Place.'

Mike nodded and curled his fingers around his mug. 'I've been waiting for you to come and ask about that.'

'What do you know about the owners?' she enquired.

Mike waited until a family group had passed. 'They don't live around here. Respectable doctor and his wife, apparently. But nothing much respectable goes on in that place.'

'Meaning?'

'It's no great secret to us. I mean, my wife and I were approached to join them.'

Kate frowned. 'Them? Who are they?'

'You look around and you're probably thinking, nice neighbourhood, happy families, but there's a very active group out here. They thrive in boring suburbia. Hell, they distribute newsletters through PO boxes in the centre.' He stared at the detectives as though he had spelt it all out for them.

A child who looked too young to be in uniform skipped past, followed by her mother and an uncooperative toddler. When they had gone, Mike whispered, 'That was a well-known swingers' house.'

Kate sat back. It was hardly surprising that infidelity became a game when debt, stress and boredom crept into relationships. Swingers swapped partners for new and different sexual experiences on a casual basis. And it might help to explain why the young mother had been murdered. Infidelity and jealousy were behind most murders.

'Did you see anything suspicious before the fire started?'

'I was doing my morning deliveries. It was about five-thirty, still dark. I saw Belinda Mercuro's car parked out front. Her husband is a landscape gardener and she does events planning – conferences and courses.'

Oliver wanted to know how sure the newsagent was. 'That's pretty observant for someone who throws papers out of his van in the dark. How can you be absolutely certain?'

Mike smiled and finished off another roll. 'I could see the car clear enough. I get to know the regulars and can tell who shouldn't be outside someone else's house.' He leant forward and spoke very quietly. 'Don't look around, but there's a bloke with a tie on coming along now with two kids. They're not his. Saw his car parked outside their house this morning. Mind you, his wife brought their own kids to school earlier on.'

Oliver seemed shocked. 'They're that brazen?'

'Not deliberately, but if your wife thinks you're away on business and you're off with another woman, the price you pay is helping out by taking your mistress's kids to school the next morning.'

'What if the parents run into each other, or the kids talk?' Kate asked. 'It's a pretty big gamble when they go to the same school.'

'Like I said, it's a small community, but not everyone realises how small until they get caught.'

Kate watched some of the children being pulled along by a parent – or, from her new perspective, a parent's lover – and wondered what happened to them in the long term. They did not deserve to be made to comply with their parents' emotional deceit. Dysfunction was not the domain of the impoverished. With more money came more opportunity for infidelity and selfishness. Did the swingers ever stop to consider their children? If the newsagent knew about Moat Place and its swingers' club, how many others knew?

Then someone, she thought, had to know who the dead young mother was, and who had killed her. Swapping sexual partners might have sounded like a good idea, but could have invoked jealousy in the murdered woman's partner, especially if she enjoyed the illicit trysts. He had to be top of their list of suspects, if they could only identify who 'he' was.

30

A call to Belinda Mercuro's assistant informed Kate that the woman they wanted to interview was attending a conference at an eco-lodge in the Blue Mountains, just over an hour away. Kate decided to interview Mrs Mercuro at work, which would give her the option of embarrassing her in front of clients if she proved uncooperative.

She and Oliver headed up the M7 motorway and along the M4 west. The drive took them from the base of the mountains, through Wentworth Falls, and up higher to picturesque Katoomba, one of Kate's favourite places. A nearby pub in Blackheath served the biggest and best meat pies she had ever tasted. The last time she had been there was with a group of bushwalkers in freezing, wet conditions and the fireplace in the pub was a welcome relief from the weather. The pie's flaky pastry had covered a bowl with a rim the size of a dinner plate. The stewed lamb and gravy inside were tender, rich and piping hot. Everyone deserved the experience at least once.

She glanced at Oliver. There would be no friendly lunch after this morning's strange events.

She would rather go hungry than sit with someone whose honesty was in doubt. Russo had hinted that the unit was being investigated and she was beginning to wonder if Oliver was the target. His behaviour this morning had been suspicious. One thing she was sure of: she would now have to keep her guard up with him at all times.

They meandered along, intermittently slowed by roadworks. The old railway stations adjacent to the road were a constant reminder of an older, more glorious era. Through her open window Kate breathed in the crisp mountain air.

Past Katoomba, Oliver checked the map and told Kate to turn off to the right where the sign indicated Evans Road lookout. After the turn they followed a narrow road past country-style cafés with wooden verandahs, and a mix of holiday cottages and permanent homes. Bushwalkers with backpacks traipsed along the verge, on the pilgrimage to the lookout at the end of the long, tortuous road.

Kate almost missed the driveway of the Jemby Rinjah Eco-Lodge, which was camouflaged by a forest of gum trees discreetly interrupted by the narrow road. The place had a peaceful ambience and Kate appreciated the attempt to blend into the environment. Arriving at the reception building, it became obvious why Mike White was so confident he had seen Belinda Mercuro's car in Moat Place the morning of the fire. Parked across two spaces in the visitors' section was a pink Mazda 626 convertible, with personalised plates: BLINDA.

They entered the wooden building and found, sitting unobtrusively behind a counter inside the doorway, a middle-aged man wearing a khaki shirt with the lodge's name embroidered on the pocket. Like the place itself, he almost blended into the surroundings.

'Welcome,' he said, remaining seated and smiling almost shyly. 'May I help you?'

Oliver leant on the counter and glanced around. Beside them, a sunken lounge area surrounded a circular wood fire. On the same level, a restaurant with benches instead of chairs gave the place a rustic feel. Each place was set for lunch. The absence of tablecloths enhanced the impression that the outdoors had been brought inside. Fairy lights hung from exposed beams in the raised ceiling. Glass doors to a balcony looked out onto a panorama of bushland.

'This place is amazing. It's so . . .'

The man smiled at Oliver. 'Natural? We plan to keep it that way. Our motto is "leave only footprints, take only photographs".'

'Looks like it's working.'

The doors to reception opened and a group of elderly people with cameras ploughed through and milled around the fire. A woman with a Canadian accent declared that she couldn't believe she had seen a quoll, and the others chattered like children who had just opened their Christmas presents. 'That blue-tongue lizard nearly scared me to death,' one of them said, causing her companions

250

to erupt into laughter. 'Why didn't you tell me it was there? The thing could have taken my toe off.' More laughter ensued. Kate had to smile at the exaggeration. Seeing unbridled enthusiasm for life was rare. It seemed pure. Right now, she envied the man behind the desk his job.

'Tourists come from all over the world to experience what we aim to preserve. These folks came up from Sydney just for the day,' he said, again with that smile.

Waitresses brought out glasses of wine on trays, and the group didn't hesitate to indulge.

'We put on a barbecue lunch and they have a ball.'

'Half their luck,' Kate said. 'We were told that we could find Belinda Mercuro here.'

'She's probably in the conference centre. I'll just check.' He handed Oliver a pamphlet about the place. 'Won't be a minute,' he said. 'This will explain what we do here.' Instead of dialling an extension, the man left his station in search of Belinda Mercuro.

Keen to breathe in some more fresh air, Kate stepped outside onto the balcony. The first thing that struck her was the quiet. No traffic, no machinery, and no irritating phones; just the sounds of birds communicating and flapping their wings as they passed overhead. Oliver excused himself to visit the composting toilets and she was grateful for the moment alone. A crimson rosella landed on the railing, quickly followed by more. They're used to being fed, she thought, almost sorry for not having seed.

Oliver returned, absorbed in the pamphlet. 'Did you know the Blue Mountains are over ninety million years old? The entire area used to be coastal plains, but rivers and creeks eroded the landscape to form the valleys and escarpments. That's some serious erosion.'

Kate had walked along some of the tracks that showcased incredible cliff walls and waterfalls and had often heard of the legends behind the landmarks. Her favourite involved the three monoliths, aptly called the Three Sisters. The story was that three Aboriginal sisters were in love with men they were forbidden to marry. They were turned to stone to protect them during the war of the tribes, but the man who turned them to stone died in one of the battles, so they remained in stone for eternity.

Kate had also helped search for walkers who had wandered off the tourist trails, completely underestimating conditions. More than once the mountains had trapped people in stony graves.

Clomping on the decking drew their attention away from their private thoughts.

'We wanted those floral arrangements here for a client two hours ago. How hard can it possibly be to put together bouquets of flowers native to this area?' The woman didn't bother introducing herself. She stood, one hand on the hip of her tight white trousers, her top half covered by an off the shoulder gold-threaded piece. She tapped one of her leopard-skin-patterned shoes. Her dark hair was dragged into a long ponytail and her heavily made-up face was unusual. A broad forehead and prominent cheekbones framed large, wide-set, cat-like eyes. Or so the make-up made them appear. It was the sort of face that could have peered out from a magazine in the 1980s. The birds scattered as soon as she appeared.

'Detective Sergeant Farrer, and this is Detective Constable Parke. We're investigating the fire at a house in Moat Place, Castle Hill.'

The woman's expression froze and her manner suddenly seemed less confident. 'I don't know anything about it.'

'Your car,' Kate said, 'was positively identified as being outside the house right before it burnt down.'

The woman looked around to make sure no one was listening. 'Look, I don't know anything about the fire, or what the papers said about the body. I hooked up with someone the night before then left first thing in the morning. Everything was fine when I drove off.'

'Why didn't you come forward when we appealed for information?' Kate demanded. This woman had to be ridiculously naive to think that such a gaudy car would go unnoticed in the neighbourhood.

She fiddled with a gold bracelet on her right hand. 'My husband does landscapes all over the state. He travels a lot and I get lonely, but I can't afford for him to find out. Not yet.'

Kate said, hands on her hips, 'We know about the swingers' club. We can always have this conversation at the police station or with your husband present.'

Belinda Mercuro's bottom lip began to quiver. 'None of this can get out, or my business, my marriage and my life will be over.'

Kate was quickly losing patience. 'That didn't occur to you before you both became swingers?'

Oliver intervened. 'We need to know about the body found in the house. What can you tell us about her?'

The woman began to cry crocodile tears. 'I swear she wasn't there at the time. Look, all I know is that very few of us have keys to the place. My business partner and her husband own it, and they only invite reputable couples to the parties there. But my husband and I agreed not to have affairs outside of that. If you get attached to someone, the marriage is over. I broke the rule.'

Oliver shifted his weight. 'You were having an affair there behind your husband's back?'

She sniffed and stared out at the view. 'Yes. It wasn't really an affair, it was just . . . physical.'

'Does he have a key?'

She shook her head. 'He left a note on my car suggesting we meet there because he wanted me. I let him in, but he didn't need a key to leave. He just had to snib the lock as he left.'

'What time did you go?'

She looked up at the sky then briefly closed her eyes. 'I had a breakfast meeting in the city, so I was gone by six-thirty. I swear to God, there was no other woman there – alive or dead. You can't let my husband find out.'

'What's the name of your lover?' Kate said, trying not to sound sarcastic. It didn't sound much like love had anything to do with it.

'He's my personal trainer. His name is Mark. Mark Dobbie.'

31

Inside the police headquarters laboratory, which dealt with everything from blood and bodily fluids to explosives and toxins, John Zimmer sat in his overalls sipping a takeaway coffee at a computer. Near him, a machine whirred through its cycle. It seemed as though Zimmer practically lived there lately. Then Kate saw the reason – a petite new lab technician.

'I hope you're not harassing the staff,' Kate said, and the technician blushed. Zimmer rolled his eyes and mouthed, 'Thanks,' behind her back. Kate couldn't believe how obvious he was. If the woman was bright enough to have a degree or higher in forensic science, she would see through John Zimmer's intentions pretty fast.

'Anything on the clothes we got on the Dobbie search? Have you identified the accelerant yet?'

The technician checked her chart. 'Petrol. The clothes had been washed, but there was definitely petrol on the trouser legs. From the distribution, it looks like he wiped his hands after spilling it on them.'

Petrol! That was the accelerant used at Moat

Place. Kate realised with a sense of foreboding that Mark Dobbie was now linked to both the house-fire and Candice Penfold's disappearance.

'Hey,' Zimmer piped up, a big grin on his juvenile face. 'The quadriplegic murder scene, the one you almost cooked in. I've got something.'

Kate hoped it incriminated Dobbie. The guy was more dangerous than anyone had realised.

Zimmer slid off the stool and moved towards a see-through cabinet. Inside was the melted smoke detector. He snapped on some gloves and pulled it from the cabinet.

'Look here,' he said, pointing to an impression in the plastic. 'We got lucky. It's a perfect fingerprint.'

'Anyone in the system? Our suspect's name is Mark Dobbie.' She flipped open her notebook and gave his date of birth, address and the date he was fingerprinted for the drugs charges.

Zimmer put a gloved hand on her forearm, then removed it, leaving a powdery residue on her sleeve. 'I know you're pretty keen to nail this bastard, we all are. Hell, I was there when you came out of that fire. As big a pain in the arse as you are, even I wouldn't want you to go that way.' He grinned again.

Kate remembered the camaraderie that morning with Oliver and Zimmer, and felt a little guilty about her comment when she had arrived. Another machine whirred to a stop and the technician pressed some buttons, setting it off again.

'Yeah well, I'm going to hang around to solve this, on my own if I have to.'

'Kate, you've gotta give the rest of us some credit for trying. I'm running the print through the database now. It's going to take a couple of hours, and I can't go far. Some of us are on your side too, you know.'

Kate didn't know what to say, but was grateful when the technician interrupted: 'Detective, I have an update for you on the blood found on,' she checked the file, 'the car belonging to Candice Penfold. It was weird, so I checked it twice and got a supervisor to review it as well. There were two different types of blood on the seat.'

Two? Maybe she had fought her attacker and drawn his blood. They had a chance of finding her killer after all.

'The first one was identified as belonging to Candice Penfold, because it shared the pattern of DNA found in her hair. She is blood group AO negative. The other blood pattern looked similar so I double-checked it, in case it was a close relative.'

Kate held her breath, then remembered that Robert Penfold was Candice's adopted father. The blood cannot have been his. With the sister overseas, that just left Janine Penfold.

'There wasn't that much blood to test but we managed to determine that it was O negative,' the technician continued nervously. 'We also found traces of matter on the seat which pathology has confirmed to be human epithelial cells and foetal squames. In the seams we located foetal haemoglobin.'

Kate had to be sure what she was hearing. 'Hang on, did you say foetal blood and squames?' Peter Latham had mentioned squames in connection to the Moat Place case.

'Yes. We think that Candice Penfold must have given birth in the back seat of her car.'

'Why didn't it come up before in the DNA database?' Oliver asked, leaning back in his seat. Though Kate had filled him in on Dobbie's connection to both cases, they were still reeling from the knowledge that the charred body from Moat Place was Candice.

'There's a delay in processing DNA at the moment, and we didn't collect the samples from Candice's room until after the car was found. Besides, we narrowed the search with the physical description and were looking for matches with missing women who we knew had given birth recently.'

Kate thought about all the time they had wasted, not to mention putting the Lamberts through the trauma of thinking their daughter was dead. The pieces fitted together now – Candice must have found Audrey Lambert's credit card and decided to use it during her planned disappearance. Somewhere along the way, things had gone horribly wrong. And Dobbie was the key to it all.

As for the Penfolds, Kate was angry that they had failed to tell them that their missing daughter was pregnant. But her anger dissolved when she realised she'd soon be telling them their daughter was dead.

Peter Latham appeared in the office, dressed in ill-matched jacket and trousers and a vintage Mickey Mouse tie. His hair was combed and his beard trimmed. He was obviously on his way to somewhere special.

'Thanks for the call about the Penfold girl's car. I agree. It was foetal haemoglobin they found. I double-checked by ordering a Beta HCG level on the blood taken from the burnt body. Thanks to the hair you collected from her brush, we can now confirm that the deceased is Candice Penfold.'

Before Kate had a chance to ask, Oliver interjected: 'Beta HCG – isn't that the pregnancy hormone?'

'Exactly. The level was low, but detectable. It was too soon for her to have conceived again after delivering, so we assume the levels were dropping after this pregnancy.'

Inspector Russo returned from a meeting, threw his files on a desk and stood with his arms folded. 'Farrer, I got your message. Could she have had a miscarriage or a backyard abortion?'

Peter turned around. They needed no introduction. 'Judging by the size of her uterus, no. It was too large, especially as it would have been a first-time pregnancy. It's too late for terminations at that stage, but it's possible the foetus died in utero and was delivered stillborn.'

'But there were milk stains on the cloth we found

in the nappy bag.' Kate didn't want to believe the baby hadn't survived.

'If the baby did die,' Oliver said, 'Candice still might have needed to express some milk a few days after the birth. It's also possible the stains were from formula. I'll organise an analysis.'

Kate began to clench her fists. She thought of the obsessive-compulsive mother, and the supposedly loving father. No wonder she had been brought in on the case. Even in this day and age, they wanted to keep the pregnancy a dirty little secret. She should have known they were lying all along. Her bullshit detector didn't usually let her down. Lately it was worse than useless.

'So the parents knew and withheld the information from us.'

Peter sat and rubbed his tidied beard. 'Not necessarily. I went over the case notes. Candice was a yoyo dieter and prone to weight gain. She had cysts on her ovaries, which could mean that her menstrual cycle was irregular.'

'Are you trying to say that no one noticed a woman getting progressively bigger over nine months? That's ridiculous.' Kate was so in tune with her body, she couldn't believe that anyone could 'disguise' a pregnancy from her family, especially when she lived with them.

Oliver spoke next. 'My wife was sixteen weeks pregnant with her first before we knew. She put on some weight and felt crappy, but we thought it was work pressure and her hormones. She had no idea what to expect, it being her first, and she often went months without menstruating.'

Suddenly, Oliver's ability to get in touch with his 'female side' went from admirable to inappropriate. 'Too much information,' Kate warned.

'I'm just saying that if two educated people can't tell, what hope does a naive young woman with a learning disability have?'

Peter nodded. 'I can list a litany of cases where women, or girls, experience stomach pains and then get the shock of their lives when they deliver a baby in the toilet, or in a car. That's the first they or their families know about the pregnancy. Either they're ignorant, or in complete denial.'

Kate thought of the photographs of Candice Penfold underneath Brett Spender, naked and probably unconscious.

Oliver obviously had exactly the same notion. 'If Dobbie drugged her with Rohypnol, GHB or God knows what else, she may have had complete amnesia about the episode. And I bet they didn't bother to use condoms.'

Peter scratched his beard again. The new trim must have felt itchy. 'My mother used to say that it was the good girls who got caught. She said the ones who had regular premarital sex planned it and got away with it. It was the good girls who had sex once who got caught. Maybe she was right.'

Russo adjusted his already rolled-up sleeves. 'It still happens. I've interviewed an underage teen-ager who ran away because she had sat in the back of a car with a boy. That's all she did, sit, but her mother had told her that she'd get pregnant if she ever got in the back of a car with a fellow. I'm assuming that's how the girl was conceived and the mum was afraid history would repeat itself.' He refolded his arms. 'The poor kid was convinced she was pregnant and panicked. We like to think society's enlightened, but there really is a lot of ignorance out there. It's the first rule of communication. Make sure the interviewee understands the question and fully comprehends their answer. Speaking of which, where are Fiskars and Rench? They ought to be here.'

Kate and Oliver suddenly found some paperwork to check.

'I saw them on their way out when I came up,' said John Zimmer, who'd just appeared. 'My guess is they're gone for the day.' He winked for Kate's benefit. This time she didn't mind, given he had just let the boss know how lazy those two bastards could be. She couldn't help the feeling, though, that she was about to owe Zimmer a favour.

'Good news,' he went on. 'I've just finished the check on the fingerprint we got from the damaged smoke detector in the Spender homicide case. It matches one we found on one of the glass shards from the broken window Kate used to get into the house. Anyways, thought you'd want to know. It doesn't match anyone on our database.'

Kate leant forward. 'Did you run it against Mark Dobbie?'

Zimmer lowered his chin and raised both eyebrows. 'Of course, but it's a completely different pattern. Your guy might have had motive, but my guess is, someone else topped Spender and set fire to the place.'

'Or,' Kate said, 'he's working with an accomplice.'

Zimmer grinned again. 'Then why did he leave his prints in the freezer at the Moat Place fire?'

'What?' Kate couldn't believe the luck.

'The freezer from Moat Place was pulled apart,' Zimmer explained. 'It had partly melted but I managed to lift fingerprints on the inside that are a match for Mark Dobbie. Nothing came up when I first ran the check but I just did another search and bingo. He wasn't in our system until you booked him the other day. And we can confirm that the body in the house was definitely in the freezer at some point. The freezer contained traces of dirt and fibres that matched the shirt Peter sampled on the bent inside elbow. We also found hairs and skin cells in it that also belonged to the victim.'

'Thanks, John,' Kate said. She felt like punching the air. Zimmer had just given them the breakthrough they desperately needed. That Dobbie's prints were inside the freezer where Candice Penfold's body had been kept was incredibly damning. She wanted to bring him in, now.

'We're not going to rush this,' Russo instructed, looking directly at Kate. 'Put him under surveillance and tap his phone. He may just lead us to his mate or let slip what he did with the baby.'

'But we know he was at the house where Candice Penfold was burnt, he had motive to kill her and the opportunity. For God's sake, he even had petrol on his clothes,' she argued.

Oliver consulted his notebook. 'Belinda Mercuro's alibi checks out for the time the fire started. She was miles away with a client. All I have to do is get her to confirm that the petrol-stained clothes were the ones Dobbie had on that day. Otherwise, don't we risk him fleeing?'

Russo paused a moment, rocking slightly on his heels. 'I know this guy is bad news, but if he doesn't know we have evidence linking him to the scene, he probably thinks he got away with it. If someone else is involved, it may be our only chance to nail whoever's in it with him and locate the child, or what remains of the child.'

Kate considered Russo's idea, but something unnerved her. 'What if Mrs Mercuro has already told him we paid her a visit?'

'If he's under surveillance, he can't go far. Get on to it straight away.' Russo pulled his glasses over his nose and collected his files. 'Let's just hope that he hasn't already disappeared.'

32

Kate stood outside the Penfolds' home with Oliver, neither of them wanting to press the doorbell. She thought of Robert Penfold and felt a twinge of guilt. He obviously loved his stepdaughters very much. With biological children who refused to see him, it made sense now that he was protective of Candice and Lesley.

The only consolation was that the family could now begin to grieve. Candice could receive a proper burial while the family obtained some form of closure, whatever that meant. Oliver made no move towards the bell and they stood there in silence, bracing themselves for the unpleasant task.

Kate shuddered as she recalled the local policeman arriving at her father's property. She was out in the paddock on her motorbike, checking the fences. Or that's what she had told her father. The truth was that she was angry with Billy for speeding off after their stupid argument. They both had foul tempers, but always made up straight away. It was like an unwritten rule and both were supposed to abide by it.

266

She had never forgiven Billy for breaking their rule. Not even now, after all these years. Remembering her reaction to being told Billy had died brought tears to her eyes; the reaction was automatic and Kate had no control over it. It was another reason she was still angry with him. He hadn't just left her that day. He had taken away her emotional control.

Kate took a deep breath and rang the bell. It didn't take long before Janine Penfold's face peered through the stained-glass panel next to the door. She tentatively unlocked the chain and deadlock, and invited them in. It was as though she already knew why they had come, although an unexpected visit by police late at night would be any parent's idea of a nightmare.

Janine Penfold seemed so rattled that she forgot that Kate and Oliver still had their shoes on. They had forgotten too. They entered the home with solemn faces, convinced Janine Penfold understood exactly why they were there. Even so, it didn't make the job any easier.

Kate cleared her dry throat. 'Are your husband and Lesley home?'

Mrs Penfold avoided eye contact and led them into the kitchen. 'They're due back any minute. Robert took Lesley to see some friends. With Candice . . .' Her voice trailed away. 'Well, we just wanted to make sure she is safe.'

She pulled out a brand new sponge from a collection under the sink, wet it with an orange-smelling spray and wiped the bench.

Kate decided to wait until the other two were back before telling them the horrific news. She suspected that Janine would need her family for physical and emotional support.

Oliver began an inane conversation about the quality of household cleaners compared to twenty years ago, and Janine Penfold chatted away, seemingly grateful for the distraction. When he'd exhausted all possible cleaning topics, Oliver reverted to asking questions about the fish in the fish-tank, but Janine denied knowing much about them.

As an awkward silence continued, Kate checked her watch. They had been in the house only six minutes, but it felt like hours. Her mouth was still dry. She would rather talk in front of a thousand people than break bad news to a family. No matter how hard you tried, it was impossible to do it well. Instead, there was a high chance of doing an appalling job and making the situation even worse.

The sound of the garage door opening and the purr of a well-serviced engine did not alleviate the tension. Kate felt perspiration spreading under her arms and wiped her hands on her trousers. Car doors clunked and Lesley and her father came rushing through from the next room. Lesley had a hopeful look on her face, which was instantly dashed when she saw Kate and Oliver standing uncomfortably in the kitchen. Robert Penfold seemed inches shorter, a man braced for the worst thing anyone could hear.

Kate decided not to postpone the agony. 'I'm sorry we are here so late, but we wanted to speak to you all in person.'

Oliver had the priest-look again, hands clasped in front, head down. He had moved towards Janine. For that gesture, Kate was grateful. He would comfort Mrs Penfold, leaving her to explain the facts.

'We should probably go somewhere where we can all sit down,' Kate suggested.

'Where's Candy?' Lesley demanded. 'You've either found her, or . . .'

Robert Penfold moved forward. Kate noticed his hands trembling despite the grip he had on his daughter's shoulders.

'I'm so sorry,' Kate swallowed, 'but Candice has been killed. We've positively identified her body and I'm afraid there's no doubt it's her.'

Janine Penfold dropped to her knees, buried her face in her hands and sobbed. Oliver bent down and placed an arm around her back. Lesley covered her face with her hands and seemed to be holding her breath. Robert stared ahead, immobile.

'The body was found in a house-fire,' Kate continued, 'but we were unable to identify Candice until today.'

'What happened?' Lesley asked in between sobs. 'What house? Where was she?'

'We found her on a bed in a house at Castle Hill, but we believe she had been murdered and that someone then set fire to the house.'

'Who would have killed our Candy?' Robert asked, and then his face seemed to engorge, the veins above his collar distending. 'My God, if Mark Dobbie had anything to do with it, I swear—'

'Stop right there,' Kate said, putting out her hand. She didn't want to hear him threaten to murder Dobbie, just in case he or anyone else actually followed through. 'Look, obviously this is a shock and you're very upset. We understand that, but making threats isn't going to bring Candy back.'

'What does she look like?' Janine Penfold whispered, looking up with a childlike expression. 'Can we see her?'

Kate swallowed hard. 'We had to use DNA to confirm it was her. You see the fire . . . the fire made her face difficult to recognise. We won't need you to formally identify Candy, if that's what you're wondering about.' Kate knew how inadequately she had answered the question, but she imagined that viewing Candice's body would cause even more distress to the family. At least now, they could give her a proper burial, and the formerly nameless body would no longer have to remain unclaimed as a mere number in the morgue.

Janine wailed from the floor and slumped into Oliver's arms. Robert stayed by Lesley's side and led her into the lounge room. Kate followed and sat on the other side of the glass coffee table. Oliver remained in the kitchen with the inconsolable Janine.

'There is some more news that may come as a shock.' Kate wanted to gauge their reactions to see if they knew about the pregnancy. 'We think that Candy gave birth in her car. There were two different bloodstains on the seats. It was her blood and the DNA profile tells us the other, a small amount, belonged to a newborn baby that had to have been hers.'

The blood seemed to drain from Robert's face. 'That's impossible,' he muttered. 'There's no way she was pregnant.'

Lesley shook her long blonde hair. 'No, she would have told me. There's no way she would have kept that a secret from me. We shared everything.'

Kate rubbed her hands along her thighs. 'It is possible that Candy may not have known she was pregnant.'

Robert Penfold began to pace. 'This doesn't make any sense. Maybe you have the wrong body. Maybe it isn't Candy at all.'

Denial was understandable, especially if the family didn't know about the pregnancy.

'What happened to the baby?' Lesley asked, her eyes swollen and face devoid of expression.

'We don't know, but we're checking hospitals and doctors, and after the fire there was a public appeal for information. If the baby's alive . . .' Kate felt their torment increase. 'We'll find him or her. You need to know that we can't prove the baby was even born alive, but Candy had a nappy bag with her at the house, and there were milk stains on a cloth nappy we found inside it, so we're not giving up.'

In a few minutes, the family had lost their daughter, discovered she had been murdered, and learnt about her pregnancy. In the one breath, Robert had discovered that he and Janine might be grandparents, but any joy was quickly crushed by the notion that the baby, too, could be dead.

Completely exhausted, Kate and Oliver finally left the house. They had been there an hour in total. While Oliver consoled Janine Penfold, Kate had answered Robert Penfold's questions as best she could without implicating Mark Dobbie. Better than anyone, Kate knew that the next stage of grieving involved anger. The last thing they wanted was for an enraged father to seek revenge before they could arrest Dobbie. The family needed Robert Penfold to be there for them, not under arrest for a vigilante attack.

As she drove away from the house with Oliver, she was grateful that Inspector Russo had ordered Dobbie to be placed under surveillance. If the drug-rapist could lead them to Candice's baby, the Penfolds would have a living reminder of their daughter – a grandchild to love and nurture. If he had killed the child as well, they could at least bury the remains with their daughter.

Kate wanted above all to find the baby. Maybe Dobbie had spared it, but if he had any brains, he would have disposed of the tiny body by now. For once, she hoped she had overestimated a suspect.

33

Kate showered, still nursing the headache she had climbed into bed with. A couple of paracetamol tablets were the best she could muster before the shops opened. She threw on a pair of yoga pants and a pink breast cancer T-shirt she had bought on sale. Into a shopping bag she loaded her MP3 player, a change of clothes and three different hats, two pairs of sweatbands and her gun. Not quite the average jogger or shopper, but she would pass for either one.

She also threw in some apples, bananas and grapes she had left in the fridge. The apples looked dodgy, but would do if she got hungry enough. After refilling a couple of bottles of water, she drove away to relieve the surveillance officer and was surprised to find Adam Rench in the car. She opened the passenger door and moved a pizza box, along with multiple bags of crisps and chocolate bars, empty plastic bottles and a cold thermos, onto the backseat.

'You've been here eight hours, not a week,' she said, amazed by the amount he had consumed. 'Where's Fiskars?'

Rench chewed on gum, his eyes covered by reflective sunglasses. 'Sick leave. The man came down with one hell of an ulcer yesterday.'

'Ulcer? Did the drink get to him?'

Rench turned his head. 'It's stress.'

'Bullshit,' Kate said. 'He's never done enough work to get stressed.'

Rench clenched his jaw. 'You'd better be careful who you go talking to like that. It's on the record. He has one of the highest arrest rates.'

'Yeah, for catching the world's most stupid criminals. Like when that moron escaped from custody and went back to the crime scene – under his watch, if I remember – and then turned up the next morning at the local station because he was cold and hungry.'

'It's still a good result. Johnno nailed that armed robber and murderer.'

'Only because the same moron confessed to both crimes. That's how he got into custody in the first place. Your team had three months of chasing your tails before the guilt got to him.'

'At least we make arrests. You take months off, leaving us with the extra work, and now you're prancing around with the new guy, your sex-crazed little boyfriend. From the way "Drover" trots around, you'll be getting stretch marks before you know it.'

Kate dug her fingernails into her palms. She was used to his childish insults, but being disgusting about her and Oliver made her blood pressure rise to seething. And given he was saying it to her face, no doubt he'd blabbed it all over the station by now. She hoped Oliver's pregnant wife didn't hear that sort of garbage.

Her phone rang and she flipped it open. It was her partner. She left the car, slamming the door on Rench's perverted laughter. Oliver had arrived and was relieving the second car, parked in view of the back of Dobbie's home. If he left by either exit, they would know.

'Sounds as though they had a quiet night. Let's hope he does something this morning.'

'Just make sure we don't stuff this up,' Kate snapped, unsure why she was suddenly annoyed with him. She was tired and wanted Dobbie put away for Candice's murder. That way he wouldn't hurt any more women. She also wanted to know where the baby was. She was now doubtful that watching him would lead them anywhere.

'You OK?' Oliver asked.

She tugged on the back of her hair. 'Fine. We're all tired. Rench is here itching to hand over.'

'Don't tell me he's stressed,' Oliver said.

'Just worry about Dobbie. Let me know if he makes a move.'

Kate hung up, wondering why he had chosen the word 'stressed' to describe his fellow detective. If he knew about Fiskars, how had he found out since last night? Russo must have called him. Then again, it could be common knowledge by now.

Rench wound down the passenger window. 'Can I get out of here? Some of us got called back in and have been working all night.'

She bent down to hear what he had to say.

'Not much happened. When he went to the local pub, the dog squad put the bugs inside the house. He came home alone and it was quiet until about six thirty this morning, when he appeared in his underpants and pinched the neighbour's paper. So far we can get him for grand larceny.'

Wit was not one of Rench's strengths – not that he knew it. He chuckled and handed over the long-lens camera in a black bag, and the receiver for the listening device. Despite his bravado, Rench looked worried about something. It was possible that Fiskars really was sick after all.

Kate returned to the silver hatchback she had borrowed from the unmarked car pool. Silver cars were noticed less than other colours and made the best choice for surveillance. She chose a parking spot away from Dobbie's house, so as not to be noticeable, under shade and near enough to a corner store to look like she was waiting for a customer, and settled in for a long day.

A tap on her window startled her. She knew the face of the officer, but couldn't recall his name. 'Oliver Parke wanted me to give you this,' he said, handing over a walkie-talkie. 'Wish I'd thought of it, although it would have been a waste of time with Rench in the other car. Have a good one.'

Kate examined what looked like a piece of military equipment, only this had a superhero sticker on it. Her partner had brought one of the kids' toys. She pressed the speak button, not expecting it to have good enough range: 'Testing, one two three.'

Oliver's voice came through loudly. 'Now we can chat without racking up phone bills,' he said, 'over.'

This was a childlike side to her partner she hadn't seen before. She wished she could trust him completely and that he hadn't suggested she keep the money she had found in her drawer. She wasn't sure whether to confront him with her suspicions about his involvement, or get this job done first. She wanted Dobbie nailed, she decided, so everything else could wait. For now, they were streets away from each other, preparing for one of the most boring of police jobs.

Dobbie's house stayed quiet for a couple of hours. The temperature slowly rose and Kate began to feel uncomfortable, even with the window open. Perspiration made her yoga pants stick to the leather seat. She looked at the walkie-talkie and decided to find out if Oliver was in a better position.

'Wise One to New Boy, over.'

A moment passed before he answered. Static alerted her to his call.

'Yes, Wise One, over.'

'Shouldn't you be home with your family on a weekend?'

'They have gone to the devil-in-laws.'

It was the first time Oliver had maligned someone. She tried to imagine what sort of mother wouldn't be be happy to have him as a son-in-law. Hell, he even changed the kids' nappies.

'Don't you have someone more interesting to be with, O Wise One? Over.'

The question took her aback. It hadn't occurred to her that Oliver might wonder whether or not she was in a relationship. She was so used to functioning on her own, she took it for granted that people around her knew that, even if it was none of their business.

She focused on Dobbie's house. 'Hey, more interesting than playing with kids' toys and pretending to be invisible to catch a baddie? You've got to be kidding. Any movement at the back of the house?'

'Nothing. What's a five letter word for deceit that ends in u-d?'

He was doing the crossword. Kate had had him pegged as more of a Sudoku type.

'Fraud,' she answered.

'Hey, it fits. It was right there all the time, only I didn't see it. Funny how things are so obvious once you know the answer.'

She wondered what he was playing at. Suddenly Dobbie's neighbour caught her notice. He headed out with a walking stick and a fluffy dog that could have fitted in his jacket pocket. Judging by the size of its legs, walking to the letterbox and back would have been a workout. The man they had spoken to the first time they met Dobbie wrote down the numberplate of a car parked on the road outside his house. She shook her head. The old curmudgeon had a real thing about that piece of asphalt.

Just then, a white Sigma arrived, parking behind the offending vehicle. A young woman stepped out and pulled down her short skirt before checking herself again in the side-mirror. She minced off along Dobbie's driveway and disappeared.

Kate grabbed the walkie-talkie. 'Oliver, we may have a problem. A young woman has just gone inside.'

'All right. We can't touch him until he does something. Unless you think she's underage?'

'No, but we're not going to hear him if he drugs her and takes photos.'

Kate began to feel her pulse race and her breathing quicken. What if he was expecting them to burst in and he had a gun? What if he was more unstable than they realised? She took a sip of water and tried to calm herself down, breathing in and out, counting two, three, four. Trying not to let her mind race and imagine the worst case scenario.

Fearing a panic attack, she recited her calming mantra: *I'm a survivor, not a victim* . Feeling more in control, she checked her weapon, which she kept beneath a magazine on the passenger seat. Any hint of distress from the woman inside and Kate would have to intervene. She reminded herself that she wasn't alone. Oliver was less than a minute away. Dobbie didn't even know they were there.

'Kate, are you OK? Kate?' Oliver's voice sounded concerned. 'You'd better not be planning to go in.'

She pressed the speak button: 'I'm OK, just dropped the gadget for a moment,' she lied.

'Don't do it again. Listen, we're partners and partners watch each other's backs. I'm here to protect you as well. We can't afford to lose contact.'

Kate tried to convince herself that was true.

Oliver's voice crackled through the walkie-talkie. 'If this woman came here of her own volition, we can't just smash into the place. We can listen in to what's going on, and act only if it sounds like she's in danger. Remember, we're trying to find the baby. This could be our only chance.'

Oliver was right, but the thought of being outside while a sexual assault might be taking place inside Dobbie's house was almost too much to think about. She turned up the volume on the bug in his house. The pair chatted about exercise routines and training. It sounded as though Dobbie was showing her how to lift weights and she giggled in a flirty, adoring way.

Thankfully, within minutes the woman had made a date with Dobbie and left the house, alone. Kate took some deep breaths and relaxed. She was about to call Oliver when Dobbie appeared, exiting his driveway.

'He's on the move,' she said, 'in his car, headed south along Manning Road.'

'You follow first. I'll tag in the Territory.'

Kate started the engine and slowly pulled out into the traffic, careful not to look conspicuous. She headed along Manning Road, keeping three cars between Dobbie and herself. Dobbie's car was also silver. She wondered if that was the reason the newsagent hadn't noticed it parked in Moat Place the morning of the fire.

In the rear-vision mirror, she spotted Oliver, four cars back. The plan was to take turns following Dobbie so he didn't get suspicious.

They passed through the first sets of lights without problems, then he turned left into Bayleaf Street, where a large shopping mall was located. If he went in there, they might blow their cover, or lose him.

Kate gripped the steering wheel and kept calm. He wasn't carrying any luggage or bag, and he was dressed very casually in jeans and a T-shirt. Someone as vain as Dobbie would surely take some other belongings if he was about to flee. Past the shopping centre, she spotted him six cars ahead. She pulled into the left lane and had a good view as they went down a hill.

Dobbie was headed somewhere else.

The time was 1.15 pm and weekend crowds were filling up cafés and all the car parks. Dobbie turned into a sidestreet and Kate followed. He reverse parallel parked about 50 metres ahead.

She turned into an alleyway on the right, out of his sight, and watched Oliver drive past at normal speed. She was sure that Dobbie hadn't seen them as he locked his car and sauntered into the corner pub, tossing his keys in his hand as he went. She drove around the block and parked on the opposite side of the road, within view of his vehicle.

With a floppy hat covering her hair, large sunglasses on her face and shopping bags in hand, Kate strolled along the street, looking in shop windows. Pausing to look at the lunch menu outside the door of the pub, she saw Dobbie sitting at the bar holding a menu. The beer in front of him also suggested this was where he would eat. The bartender chatted to his customers, including Dobbie.

Kate returned to Oliver's car and filled him in. They would be there a while if he wasn't ordering takeaway. Inside the car, Oliver had an esky and offered her an iced tea. She could see the condensation on it and couldn't refuse the cold drink.

'Don't suppose you were ever a boy scout,' she said, unscrewing the lid and watching for Dobbie's return.

Oliver laughed, a hearty, rich laugh. 'Am I that obvious?'

No, Kate thought. She had no idea what he had done before joining homicide. He seemed to be the proverbial jack-of-all-trades, not to mention part-time priest and personality change artist.

'Why are you here?' she asked.

'Because we need to watch this mongrel and find the baby.'

'No,' she said, wiping some moisture from her chin. 'Here in this job?'

'Oh.' Oliver tapped the steering wheel as if playing a piano. 'I guess we all want to make a difference, for the better. Same reason you're here.'

Kate stopped drinking and raised one eyebrow. 'The money, the glamour, the perks.'

Oliver laughed again, and Kate wondered how many perks he had managed.

When he stopped, he frowned. 'You really care about the victims. Last night wasn't easy, but you handled it as well as anyone could. It made a difference because you cared. And the Penfolds know that, even if they don't thank you for it.'

Kate shifted from the seat and stepped out of the car. 'Let's hope Dobbie does us a favour this afternoon and stuffs up.'

She returned to her car a few minutes before Dobbie left the pub, checking his watch. His pace suggested he had somewhere else to be. Within a minute they were back on the main road, headed for Kellyville. The traffic was lighter than on a weekday so they had no trouble following, alternating positions closest to Dobbie. He still drove as if he had no idea he was being dogged.

Off Windsor Road, Dobbie turned down Showground Road then into Victoria Avenue. He appeared to be heading for a large shopping complex with an outdoor car park. This was in the midst of suburbia, where traffic was thinner. Kate stayed out of sight behind a slow four-wheel drive, then let Oliver take over as they approached the shops.

Dobbie entered via an exit, narrowly avoiding a family sedan. The car tooted and he responded by giving them the finger. Kate swung around to the signposted entrance and pulled in an aisle away. Oliver did the same and this time, wearing a football cap, he parked in an aisle that placed Dobbie between them, separated by a scattering of other cars.

From the lack of fumes coming out of his exhaust, it seemed Dobbie had turned off the engine.

They waited, curious to see what he was doing. It didn't take long for a pale blue BMW convertible to drive up and down the aisles before pulling in next to Dobbie, driver's window to driver's window. Kate could see the BMW owner waving his hands around and she grabbed the camera. Through the windscreen she snapped photos of him retrieving a plastic shopping bag from the floor and handing it across to Dobbie. There was a moment when she thought the BMW driver would get out, but Dobbie handed over a smaller bag and the transaction appeared complete.

'It's a drug deal. I'm going in.' Kate dropped the walkietalkie on the passenger seat.

'No! You'll ruin everything,' Oliver yelled into the handset. 'Don't go in! I repeat, do not go in.'

Kate revved the engine and floored the accelerator as she swung the car into the aisle, then slammed on the brakes as she spun the steering wheel to place the car into position, blocking the BMW and Dobbie's rear end. Before Dobbie had a chance to get into first gear, a screech of tyres came from the other side and Oliver's car was positioned to block the forward exit. Kate pulled her gun and announced they were police.

'Hand the bag over,' Kate yelled into Dobbie's window, 'and keep your hands on the windscreen.' She looked inside the bag and saw that it contained smaller plastic bags of pills.

With a gun aimed at his face, Dobbie made no attempt to escape. Not even a smartarse comment. Kate was pleased that they now spoke the same language.

'Thanks, Mark,' she said. 'We'll take you to the station but your help has been invaluable.'

'You fucking arsehole, you set me up!' the other man yelled. 'Dobbie, you little fucker, your life is over.'

'She's lying! She's the crazy cop who's been harassing me. I'm the one who is being set up.' Kate handcuffed her captive.

The dealer turned to Oliver. 'You're going to regret this. You fucking betrayed me.'

Oliver glared at Kate. 'Do you know what you've just done?'

'Arrested the parties in a drug deal, that's all.' Kate called for back-up and uniformed officers arrived in record time. As they put the dealer into the back of the paddy wagon, she escorted Dobbie to the marked police car.

When the wagon and car drove away, Oliver's temper seethed. 'So much for protecting each other's backs.' He stood close, finger jabbing the air near his partner's chest. 'I thought the idea was to exercise restraint and keep him under surveillance, not lock the dopey bastard up.'

Kate stood defiant, hands on hips. 'I made a call. A suspected crime was taking place, a drug deal, and I couldn't stand by and watch it happen.'

'But why the hell did you thank Dobbie for his help? You've just made him a marked man with the drug syndicate. And you've just made us targets, too.'

'Back off.' Kate felt her face flush. She could not fathom Oliver's anger, and didn't like being challenged on a decision she had made as the senior officer. 'You're wrong. I just gave Dobbie a very good reason to tell us what he did with Candice Penfold's baby.'

'Jesus! We don't even know if the baby ever took a breath. If she gave birth to the child in her car, there was no help and no care if the baby had trouble breathing. It could have been ill, for Christ's sake. Did that occur to you? Babies can die bloody quickly if they can't get medical attention in an emergency.'

Kate took a step back and ran a hand through her hair. Oliver might be right. Maybe the nappy bag was full of samples, and that was why there weren't any clothes in it. All that stuff could have been bought before Candice gave birth. The baby could have died of natural causes. She accepted that she had taken a risk and should have discussed it with him first.

He walked away then turned back. 'You said you're not a gambler but you just took one hell of a chance.' He was shaking with rage. 'Don't ever gamble with my life again!'

'You're paranoid,' she blurted, shocked by Oliver's reaction but not having anything smarter to say.

'Maybe I have good reason to be,' he said, pacing the hot asphalt.

Kate put her hands on her hips again. 'OK, I should have run it by you, but when I saw the drugs I just reacted.'

'*If* they really are drugs. So far we have suspicions and nothing else.'

'You're wrong,' Kate retorted, sure of one thing. 'If he thinks his life is worth bargaining for, he might just tell us what he did with the baby. I made the call to arrest him because this could be our only chance to ever know what happened to that child. That's the risk I took.'

34

Mark Dobbie's lawyer conferred with his client then told Kate and Oliver that he was ready for the interview to commence. Dobbie understood his rights and was prepared to make a statement.

Kate and Oliver entered the interrogation room with pens and notepads. Oliver ensured the video camera was recording.

'This is an interview with Mark Dobbie on the fifteenth of March, 3.40 pm. Also present are Detective Sergeant Kate Farrer, Detective Constable Oliver Parke and counsel for Mr Dobbie, Mr Arnold Siegel.'

Dobbie leant back and stared at the ceiling. There was no sign of the arrogance or ego they had witnessed at his home. He was in serious trouble, and he knew it. With a new drugs charge while out on bail, the only place he was going from this room was prison.

Kate opened the now substantial file and took her time. With each passing minute, Dobbie's bravado lessened even further.

'Is there anything you would like to tell us before we start?' She joined her hands over the file contents, obscuring the pages.

Dobbie shook his head.

'For the record, please?' she prompted.

'No,' Dobbie responded, like a petulant child.

'We would like to talk about a house in Moat Place, Castle Hill.'

Kate stared at Dobbie, and noticed his pupils constrict. The muscles in his hands tightened against the desk.

'Have you ever been there?'

'I could have been, I go to lots of places. Don't remember them all.'

Kate leant forward and slapped the table. Dobbie started, like a schoolboy caught by a teacher reading a magazine in class.

'We're not here to play games. I asked if you've ever been to 32 Moat Place in Castle Hill?'

He deferred to his lawyer, who nodded. 'Now I recall. I went there once to meet a friend.'

Finally, they were getting somewhere. Maybe Dobbie's lawyer was a good influence on his client.

'Did you arrange the meeting?'

'Hell, no. This friend, Belinda Mercuro, left a message on my car suggesting we hook up there.'

Kate took notes. Even when being charged with serious crimes, he boasted about his attractiveness to women. Belinda Mercuro had already been interviewed again, this time by Rench, and had identified the petrol-stained clothes as belonging to Dobbie. She had also said Dobbie put the note on her car. One of them had to be lying.

289

'A witness has placed you at the scene prior to a fire commencing at the residence you admit you attended.'

Dobbie said nothing, a sour expression on his face.

Kate continued. 'We have confirmed that the clothes you were wearing that day have traces of petrol on them, the same accelerant used to light the fire. We also have video surveillance footage of you filling a small tin with petrol at a station less than a kilometre from the house, which you paid for with cash.'

Kate turned some pages and handed across a black and white photo of Dobbie paying at the petrol station cash register at 7.15 am on 3 March, less than an hour before the house was set alight. Fiskars had come through in the end, locating the image before being struck down by the ulcer.

'You can't pin that on me,' he said. 'Sure, I was at the house and met someone there. But then I left.' He folded both arms and glanced at his lawyer. 'The petrol got on my clothes when I filled up the jerry can. End of story.'

'Not quite,' Kate continued. 'Most of the house burnt, but by some sheer stroke of luck, the garage was spared. In that garage was a large freezer, which forensics have confirmed contained the body of Candice Penfold.'

Dobbie began to perspire, just above his top lip. Kate's heart raced. She knew she had him and she was still to reveal the most incriminating evidence.

'We found fingerprints on the freezer. Not just on the outside, but the inside as well. Do you have any idea who those prints might belong to?'

Dobbie's breathing became more shallow and rapid. His lawyer placed a hand on Dobbie's sleeve and whispered something to him that neither the tape nor the senior detective could pick up.

Dobbie stared at Kate with a look of pure hatred. He ran his hands through his waxed hair and placed them on the table, as if he was laying out cards.

'All right. I lit the fire, but I didn't kill that Penfold bitch.'

'Who killed her then?' Kate shot back.

'How the fuck should I know? She was stone fucking cold when I found her.' Dobbie leant over the table towards Kate. 'I'm telling you, I've been set up. You should be arresting that sick fucker Robert Penfold.'

'So you expect us to believe that you just happened to find Candice Penfold's body?' Kate sat back in disbelief.

'Let's accept for the moment,' Oliver said in an even voice, 'that you were having a snoop around when you stumbled upon the body. What did you do next?'

'I knew you guys would think I had something to do with it, because of me and Lesley. So I did the only smart thing and set the place on fire.'

'How did the body get onto the bed?' Again, Oliver's voice sounded completely neutral.

Dobbie shook his head, as if the answer was obvious. 'I put her there. She was never going to burn in a heavy-duty freezer, was she?'

Kate was silent and Dobbie looked increasingly uncomfortable. The lawyer wrote something down.

'OK,' Kate spoke at last. 'Exactly how did you start the fire?'

'I grabbed some tissues and lit a candle to get them to burn next to the bed, but they just kept going out. That's when I went to get petrol. I panicked and didn't know what else to do.'

Kate found it difficult to believe how moronic Dobbie was. Or were they being played for fools?

'Just to confirm,' she said, 'you admit to setting fire to the house and Candice Penfold's body?'

'Yes. I mean, I lit the fire, but I didn't burn that bitch.'

Kate didn't follow. 'How does that work? You've just admitted you started the fire.'

'I poured petrol around the house but not on her.'

For some reason, Dobbie seemed to think that made him innocent of a crime. He sat back, almost looking relaxed.

The lawyer whispered to his client again. Dobbie nodded.

'You want to know everything that happened? Me and Belinda made love on the bed, and I didn't

use a condom so my stuff was . . . well, on the bed.'
He looked at Oliver. 'It's not as if she's gonna get
pregnant. I mean, she's too old. Besides, sex is just
like eating. You get good meals and bad ones, but
you don't cover your tongue with Glad Wrap
before having a taste. Know what I mean?'

Kate held her breath. This man had no concept
of decency or respect for anyone. It either failed to
occur to him that as he satisfied his 'hunger' he
could have been spreading sexually acquired in-
fections, or he just didn't care. He didn't even
notice Kate's reaction.

'Belinda had to go to some meeting, but I felt like
a shower and had a wank while I was at it. So you
see, I'd left evidence of me all over the place.'

The lawyer interjected. 'Please bear in mind,
Detectives, Mark is not being charged with pro-
miscuity, sexual intercourse or masturbation.'

In other words, Kate knew, he was trying to
argue that being a Lothario didn't make Dobbie a
murderer. Killing Candice Penfold did that.

Oliver watched intently. 'Fair enough. What
happened next?'

'I got cleaned up, fixed my hair and by then it
was getting light. I felt like a feed but there was
bugger-all in the house. The fridge had some
mouldy bread and that was it. I poked around
in the garage and there was this huge freezer.' He
held his arms to their widest span. 'One of those
long, rectangular ones, like a tuckerbox, only
bigger.'

His hands returned to his lap. 'Anyway, the lid was stuck, like someone had jammed it or something, which was kind of weird because there wasn't a lock on it. I grabbed a screwdriver from a shelf and jemmied it open.'

Kate kept her focus on the suspect's face, looking for signs that he was lying.

'What time would that have been?'

'You know so much, you tell me. All I know is it was dark inside the garage and I had to find the light switch.'

Dobbie glanced at his lawyer, who nodded.

'When I opened the lid, there she was, staring at me.'

Oliver pushed across a glass of water. After a few gulps Dobbie added, 'You know the rest.'

'Did you really believe a frozen body would vanish without a trace in a fire?' Kate asked, still finding the story hard to believe.

Dobbie tapped the tabletop. 'Ice melts, doesn't it?' I figured the petrol would make the bed burn fast and hot enough to destroy the body.'

Kate was stunned by his stupidity and not entirely satisfied with his explanation. 'If you knew the freezer wouldn't burn, why did you leave fingerprints all over it?'

'Guess I didn't think about it at the time.' Dobbie turned his hands palms up. 'For fuck's sake, what did you expect? You guys would have nailed me for murder. Like I said, I panicked. Once I had the petrol, I forgot about the fucking freezer.'

Siegel confirmed the admission. 'As my client has stated, he discovered the body inside the freezer. The woman was already dead and frozen solid when he found her.'

35

Back in the office, Kate flicked her notepad across her desk. She felt like kicking something. That bastard Dobbie was trying to squirm his way out of Candice's murder by claiming that he had nothing to do with her death.

'If we can't tie Dobbie to Candice's time of death, which we can't establish due to the fact that she was deep frozen, that bastard's going to get away with it.' She tugged the back of her hair with increasing aggression and paced the carpet. 'Because he cooperated, the charges will probably be watered down to some bullshit like "unlawful disposal of a body".'

Oliver stood with arms folded. 'We just have to find out where he killed her then. He's no genius. It has to be somewhere he normally goes. Maybe we've missed something.'

'The only thing we've missed is getting justice for the Penfolds and all the women that bastard has drug-raped.'

'What about the freezer in the garage? Wasn't there dirt that may have transferred from the murder scene to the body? It's a long shot, but anything there could help us work out where she was killed, or at least tie Dobbie to the murder.'

As usual, Oliver had made a good point. She needed to check with Zimmer about the exact type of dirt found.

Inspector Russo appeared from his office in jeans and a striped casual shirt, sleeves still rolled immaculately. 'I know you've had a setback but I might have a positive lead for you. A community worker called not long ago claiming that someone she knows is trying to hide a baby. Apparently the child appeared in the house some time in the last month, between the carer's visits. The caller sounds genuine to me. I told her you would be coming, even though it's the weekend.' He handed Oliver a piece of paper with the details scrawled on it. 'She'll be at this address for the rest of the day. After you check the story out, you might as well both go home.'

Kate glanced at her watch. By the time they interviewed the woman, it would be dark anyway. Some early mark, when they weren't even supposed to be working this weekend.

Oliver folded the note and grabbed his jacket from the back of his chair. 'Any sign of Rench? Shouldn't he be on call, given it's his case . . . ?'

Russo turned around. 'Rench is on leave as of this morning, if you weren't already aware.'

Kate shrugged her shoulders. How were they supposed to know? He'd seemed under pressure at the stakeout, but they all were. Having been on overnight, he should have been home asleep, not organising time off. Then again, Fiskars and Rench did everything together, both at work and outside it, from the way they carried on. Maybe Rench was off keeping Fiskars company. It was just like them to dump work on someone else. The department wouldn't replace them so it would mean extra hours for everyone.

Oliver just stood there staring, even after Russo had returned to his office, then he hung his head. His mobile phone rang. He checked the caller and let it ring out.

'You all right?' Kate asked.

'Yeah. It's been a long few days, that's all. I need to go to the bathroom. Can we meet downstairs at the car?'

'Sure.' Kate headed for the kitchenette and pulled a couple of slices of raisin bread from a loaf in the fridge. On the way downstairs she stopped at a vending machine and bought the highest caffeine soft drink it contained. She thought about the dealer they had arrested and how he had accused Dobbie of setting him up. No doubt he would have made the same claim when interviewed by the drug squad. In prison, Dobbie would be marked as a snitch and suffer the consequences. If he became an informant, he would be placed in a separate section for his own protection.

The dealer was pretty pissed off, but not just with Dobbie. His reaction to Oliver was more telling. He had said the detective betrayed him.

Was that Oliver's game? Turning a blind eye to drug deals for payment, or even taking a cut of the deals? It would be very expensive to feed and clothe a family of six – soon to be seven. Given the way Oliver always checked the computers, maybe he was looking for alerts by the drug squad about pending raids. It would be easy for the homicide office to request alerts about certain criminals, by arguing that they were of interest to a murder case. That would also explain the internal investigation. Oliver had started at the unit while she was on leave and Russo had said that things had changed in her absence. It was beginning to make sense.

Ten minutes later Oliver appeared at the car. Kate had just finished her makeshift lunch and was already in the driver's seat of her undercover four-wheel drive. On the road, her partner seemed quiet and preoccupied.

'With two men down, we'll be expected to pull more hours.' Kate tapped on the steering wheel at the traffic lights. 'How's your wife going to take it?'

'She copes with anything. It could always be worse. What sort of men are Fiskars and Rench anyway?'

Kate accelerated at the green light. The question surprised her. 'Fiskars has a good arrest record, but it's usually luck or some informant that comes through for him. Rench is like a mini version without the resourcefulness. They've been partners since I started in homicide. As much as I don't like their bullshit, they have good contacts and chase leads, I guess.'

'What about in themselves? Do they have families? What do they do outside work?'

'You're asking me?'

Oliver rolled his eyes. 'Good point. Don't you think it's odd that they're both on stress leave at exactly the same time?'

Kate thought about the answer. Russo had only mentioned leave in reference to Rench, he hadn't said anything about stress. Even so, it was strange that they were both away from work at the same time.

'They go to the races with the social club once a year. They also have dinners and get-togethers. Usually I try not to know.'

'Would you trust them?'

Kate hadn't really thought about their trustworthiness and, coming from Oliver, after what the dealer had said, she found that an odd question. They were colleagues, detectives. Surely that went without saying. Or did it? She had trusted Oliver in the beginning.

'I wouldn't want either of them as a partner, if that's what you're getting at.' She sneaked a glance at Oliver to try to understand what he was fishing for. He was concentrating on the traffic ahead.

'Do they do things by the book or do they cut corners to get results? I mean, they don't seem to have done much on the Moat Place investigation.'

Kate slowed behind a bus. 'It's hard to be sure what they did and didn't do. Fiskars got the video footage of Dobbie at the petrol station, but the file notes are pretty sketchy. And they did have other cases.'

Oliver was silent the rest of the way. Kate wondered what Fiskars and Rench were staying away from. She wouldn't have been surprised if her partner knew the answer. Were the three of them involved in some way? Was Oliver worried about himself and whether they'd turn informants? Right now, she didn't want to know, or even discuss it.

They arrived at an office in Northmead. A tall, broad-shouldered woman met them at the front and opened the glass door with a key.

'Thanks for coming,' she said. 'I'm Vivien Bastick, a senior case officer. I hoped you would take my call seriously.' She had recently put on bright lipstick that had bled beyond her lips, into the creases that smokers get over time.

Inside the small entry, chairs were lined up next to each other, with little room to walk between them. Past the reception counter, cluttered desks with papers piled a foot high butted against each other.

'You'll have to excuse the mess. We're funded by the government and this one doesn't really support the disabled.'

'What specifically do you do here?' Oliver enquired.

'We organise respite for parents of disabled children, and help those who can cope integrate into society in community housing. Often the families we wish to support are the ones who continually support us by volunteering or raising money.'

'Can you tell us more about the reason for your call?'

Vivien lifted two chairs from the waiting area and lodged them in the only spare space available. She sat at what appeared to be her own desk, which was the messiest, but only just.

'One of our clients is aged thirty and lives independently with special support. She was a change-of-life baby, an only child, and both parents are now deceased. They cared for her full-time until the father died and the mother became ill.'

'Can you give us her name?'

'I hope this isn't a breach of confidentiality.' The woman seemed to be having second thoughts.

Kate became frustrated. 'You have a duty of care to society as well, to prevent harm from coming to your clients and their families. If you know of a baby who may be in danger—'

'Polly Pringle,' the woman blurted, as if she needed to say it quickly to avoid the guilt.

'Is that her real name? It sounds—' Oliver began.

'Like a character in a story? She was named Pollyanna because her mother loved the book.'

Neither detective acknowledged familiarity with the name but Kate had a feeling she'd heard it before.

Vivien Bastick's shoulders dropped. 'The classic children's story by Eleanor H Porter – do you know it?'

Kate shook her head. She had never been a big reader. Books were a luxury her father could not afford. Without a local library, the only books she saw were the mind-numbing old English novels that passed for school texts; they usually had pages torn out but didn't make sense to her anyway.

Oliver tried to lean back but almost knocked over a pile of papers. 'How disabled is Polly?'

'She has a number of physical problems, including epilepsy, a heart defect and she has marked developmental delay. She was pretty much cloistered by her mother and only exposed to doctors when necessary. Her emotional age is estimated at . . .' she looked through the file, 'that of a ten-year-old. Her IQ is around seventy-five to eighty.'

Kate was surprised that Polly would be allowed to live on her own and care for herself. Ten-year-olds were incapable of coping without a parent or guardian, especially in relation to making financial or life decisions. With sub-normal intelligence, life would be extremely difficult for this woman. No child should be left to live alone with a carer visiting only once a month.

'Why isn't she being cared for? Surely she's very vulnerable in the community, especially to assault, sexual abuse, robbery, manipulation. Isn't there another family member who could help her?'

'There's no one. The mother lost three children in infancy, probably due to heart abnormalities. Polly was the only survivor.'

Vivien put her elbows on the desk and looked over the mounds of paperwork awaiting her attention.

'Do you see these files? Each one represents someone who should be looked after, but there are no care facilities anymore. It's cheaper for society to leave the most vulnerable to fend for themselves. That's why our homeless rate is so high. How many of them have untreated mental illness or below average intelligence, or are just plain illiterate and can't apply for welfare support? Polly's one of the lucky ones. Her parents provided for her. But she is scared of the world and pretty much stays inside because her mother told her never to open the door to strangers.'

'She must go out sometimes, for groceries, clothes?'

'Not necessarily. Groceries are all delivered. She has a standing order on the internet, which she at least knows how to update if she needs anything extra. Utilities are paid by direct debit. Otherwise, she phones us. If she needs clothes, I take her out once every few months and drive her to the doctor and dentist. She doesn't want much. Her television and PlayStation games are her world. With the inheritance, there's no need for a pension cheque either.'

For some disabled people, being placed alone in the community wasn't liberating, it was more like imprisonment, Kate thought.

'You said on the phone that you think Polly is hiding a baby?'

Vivien pursed her lips. 'I knocked on the door for our last visit yesterday and Polly wouldn't take the chain off the door. She said she was busy and I heard a baby crying from inside. From what I could see, the place was a mess. It's normally kept pretty clean and neat.'

Oliver was taking notes. 'Could she have had a visitor, like a neighbour, or been babysitting?'

'I called out, but no one answered. I tried again a couple of hours later and ran into the delivery-man. He had tins of baby formula and packs of nappies in with the weekly groceries. The rest was Polly's normal order. No more, no less.'

Which probably ruled out anyone staying with the woman, Kate thought.

'What concerned me,' Vivien added, 'was her refusal to open the door. Polly is a simple soul, never deceitful or secretive. If I didn't know better, I would swear that she was terrified of opening that door, or of anyone discovering that there was a baby inside.'

In that instant, Kate remembered. A birthday card on Candice Penfold's noticeboard had been inscribed with the childish handwriting of someone called Polly.

36

Kate and Oliver followed Vivien Bastick by car up Windsor Road and arrived ten minutes later in a quiet suburban street. New-looking apartment buildings filled the block. Banners hung from balconies advertising apartments still for sale for the bargain price of half a million dollars. In classic real-estate jargon, traditionally cheap accommodation without land was now classified as executive housing for the time-poor, so could cost more than a house, only without a garden, garage or privacy. Kate preferred the inner city.

'That's Polly's unit, three from the left, second storey.' The carer pointed to a balcony that differed from the others in that the window behind it was the only one with drawn curtains. They headed through a vine arbour and up the stairs to the door of number nine. Vivien Bastick buzzed on the doorbell-intercom and announced herself.

The door opened a fraction and a female voice told them to come back another time.

'Polly, it's important that I see you.'

'Go away. I don't need you anymore.'

Kate rolled her hand in a circle, to encourage Vivien to keep talking.

'I have something for you. A present.'

The carer bit her lip after the words came out. She wasn't used to lying to clients, it seemed.

'I like presents.' The voice inside hesitated. 'If I take it will you go away?'

'You'll need to open the door for this one, Polly. It's too big to fit through right now.'

The door clunked shut. Kate and Oliver stood ready to break the chain if necessary. They didn't have to. The door opened to reveal Polly, who stood about five feet tall and had long mousy-brown hair tucked behind her prominent and low-slung ears. Eyes closed and her hands held out palms upward, she was like a child ready for her present. Vivien guided her into the apartment and she kept her eyes closed.

'I've brought two very special people to meet you,' she said.

Polly opened her eyes and looked around. 'You tricked me. I don't want to see anyone. I'm not supposed to let anyone in.'

Oliver stepped forward to shake hands. 'It's OK to let us in. I'm Oliver and I really like playing games. I hear you're good at them.'

Amidst the mess, the stench of faeces and vomit filled the unit. A plastic bin overflowed with disposable nappies, all used. Furnishings were sparse, but there was an old wooden cabinet with glass doors and a miniature china collection inside. Dirty plates were stacked on the small kitchen bench, enough for a few days' worth of meals.

Polly's eyes flicked to the bedroom and back.

'This is my friend Kate and she wants to meet you as well.'

'Hello,' Kate said. 'You have a lovely home.'

'My mum always told me cleaning means you don't get sick, but sometimes I forget.'

Judging by the degree of mess and the number of dirty nappies, the place hadn't been cleaned in days, or perhaps weeks. A pile of PlayStation games lay scattered on the floor.

'What's your favourite?' Oliver asked, sitting on a clean patch of carpet.

Polly's eyes flicked to the bedroom again. 'Dora the Explorer. You have to go now. It's cleaning time.'

Vivien put her arm around Polly's shoulders. 'It's all right. You can do all that later and we can even help.'

Kate took the opportunity to move closer to the bedroom. Inside she saw a baby on the bed, surrounded by pillows. She was unable to see its face.

'Is this your baby?' Kate asked.

Polly rushed to the doorway and blocked the detective from the room.

'You, you have to go now.' Her voice became higher pitched. 'You have to go now.'

'Polly, it's all right. Calm down, we're here to help you.'

The young woman clenched her fists and her

face reddened. 'You have to go. You're not allowed to be here!'

Kate tried to step into the room, but Polly shoved her hard in the chest. She fell backwards and landed on the floor. Oliver swiftly crossed the room and grabbed the woman by her arms. Like a child having a tantrum, she kicked at him and thrashed her body, screaming to be let go.

'They're trying to take my baby!' she squealed. 'Help!'

'We are police officers and we need to look at the baby,' Oliver said, struggling to hold her arms by her sides with a bear-type hug.

Kate managed to get past them and the baby woke with the noise. It began crying. Kate picked it up and tried to calm it against her chest. The piercing noises it made sent a shudder through her. At least there was no doubt he was alive.

'Put him back,' Polly screamed. 'You can't touch him.' She began to cry. 'I promised I'd look after him.'

Oliver steered the woman over to the lounge and pushed her gently into a seat. 'We need to find out where the baby came from. And who the mother is,' he said, pressing firmly on her shoulders.

She sobbed for a while. Vivien sat beside her and pulled a tissue from her pocket. 'You've been doing a wonderful job taking care of him. What's his name?'

Polly looked up at Oliver. 'Jesus. It's the baby Jesus.'

Kate felt nausea rising. No one had told them the girl was violent or delusional. It was a miracle the child had remained alive in her care. They needed to get it to hospital and make sure it really was all right. If this was Candice Penfold's child, the family needed to be told. She hoped this baby was the one they'd been searching for; that might help ease some of the family's grief. With her spare hand, she dialled for an ambulance and police back-up. If the woman became violent, she would have to be properly restrained.

Kate carried the crying child back into the bedroom. On the floor lay a handbag, a wallet protruding from it. With one hand she picked it up, careful not to upset the baby. He had stopped crying and was closing his eyes. Inside the wallet was a driver's licence. She checked the photo ID and Candice Penfold stared back at her. On a shelf in the room stood a photo of Lesley and her sister, smiling at the camera.

Kate dialled her mobile again, this time for crime scene. The whole apartment needed to be cordoned off. If Mark Dobbie was telling the truth about finding Candice's body already frozen, someone else had to have been the killer. Could Polly Pringle have been involved somehow?

Carrying the baby into the lounge room, Kate passed the bag over to Oliver. 'My prints are on it, so be careful, but it's Candice Penfold's. I think we just found our missing child.'

Polly remained seated and her carer placed an

arm around the distressed woman's shoulders again as Oliver backed away to check the baby.

Kate was relieved to hand him over.

'Put Jesus back or you'll be in trouble.' Polly sounded frightened.

'Why?' Vivien asked.

'Because Candy said not to let anyone take him away. She had to go but she's coming back. I promised not to let anyone in. If you put him back, I won't tell her.' Polly stood up, her voice becoming shrill again. 'Don't take him, Candy's coming back.'

'Stay calm, Polly, it's all right. Who do you think wants to take him away?' Kate asked. 'Did Candy say who might come?'

'Bad people. If they find out who Jesus is, they'll take him away.'

An ambulance siren whirred its arrival outside. Kate nodded at Oliver, who slipped out the door which she then locked. Polly turned around and made a run for him but was too late. As Polly punched, spat at and kicked the detective as hard as she could, Vivien stood out of the way.

Kate defended her face but took the blows to her legs. She pushed into Polly's chest, trying to knock her to the floor, getting in close to stop the blows. The strength of the woman belied her size. Kate felt a finger gouge her right eye and she pushed hard. With a swift move, she swung one leg around, hitting the hysterical woman behind the knee. With that, the angry woman's weight buckled and Kate ined her to the floor, quickly pushing her over onto her stomach and pulling both arms behind her back. She applied pressure with her knee to mini-mise the chance of further harm being done to either of them.

'Was that necessary?' Vivien Bastick commented once Kate had gained control. Beneath her, Polly bucked and tried to spit in between screaming for help.

Kate panted for breath and glared at the carer through a swelling eyelid. 'It was for her protection as much as mine. Can you unlock the door?'

Two uniformed police burst through and sur-veyed the scene. Oliver quickly followed and told them to cuff the woman on the floor.

He noticed Kate's eye and took her by the wrist. 'The ambos can check out your eye while they're here.'

She didn't have the strength to argue. The rush of adrenalin had worn off and now she felt sore in the legs and face. At least they had found the missing child – alive.

37

The ringtone jolted Kate from a dream about riding a motorbike across the countryside. In this dream, she was free and could feel the wind in her face. She ignored the interruption and rolled over, desperate to recapture the peaceful moment.

The sound broke the quiet again, and she willed it away. After yesterday, surely she had earned a sleep-in. Another ring and she fumbled for the damn thing on the floor.

As she pressed the answer button, she heard Inspector Russo's unmistakable voice: 'Farrer, we have a media problem.'

Kate blinked and tried to read the time on her bedside clock. Five thirty. He had to be kidding.

'I've just found out the lead bloody article in today's *Daily Mail* is about police assaulting a tiny mentally disabled woman and carting her off in handcuffs, with phrases like "excessive force", "police brutality", and a picture of some sad-looking woman-child with a bruised face.'

Kate sat up and ran her hand through her hair, tugging hard on a piece at the back of her neck.

'That's not what happened. The woman became violent and I had to restrain her in the safest and most effective way. I stopped her doing more harm to herself.'

'That's not what some woman from the carers' network is saying. She says she saw the whole thing and your reaction was way over the top.'

Vivien Bastick's guilt about revealing Polly's details and what had happened as a result had probably gotten the better of her. And some human rights lawyer had probably jumped on the bandwagon. The public failed to appreciate that women were just as capable of violence and killing as men were, and having a low IQ didn't make a difference. Most of the men in prison had a mental illness or low intelligence, or had damaged parts of their brain through substance abuse. That didn't stop juries convicting them. Women in prison were no different.

'That woman-child is a person of interest in the Penfold murder investigation, and she had Candice's baby in her flat. She became violent and I defended myself, without using any weapon. I subdued her with minimal force. I've got bruises and a gouged eye as proof.'

'The lawyer says you barged into her home without a warrant and took a child she was entrusted with babysitting. He claims she was trying to protect the child and didn't understand you were police. This is a bloody PR fiasco.'

Kate shook her head. 'We can't prove anything until the DNA they took at the hospital comes back. Candice's belongings were in the apartment.'

'Well, the results are back and the baby is a Penfold. I'm supposed to give the Commissioner a statement for the media in half an hour and he has a press conference at noon. Let's hope there are no leaks before then.'

Kate assumed he had finished the conversation and was about to hang up. He asked one more question. 'Did anyone notify the Penfolds last night?'

'We thought it better to wait until we had confirmation of the child's identity.' She had asked the lab to rush analysis of the mouth swab to see if it fit with the foetal blood from Candice Penfold's car. Obviously, it had been pushed through thanks to pressure from Russo.

'You'd better get over there before the press or there'll be even more hell to pay. Shit will fly if they find out about the grandchild from some slimy reporter. No one deserves that, Farrer.' With that, he hung up.

Before showering, Kate tried to get hold of Oliver but there was no answer on his mobile or on the home number he had given her. Damn. He might as well have buggered off on stress leave too.

She washed and changed into her only skirt, a grey below-knee pencil style. For this job, a skirt seemed somehow appropriate, or maybe it was just that she thought the Penfolds deserved her best effort.

After unsuccessfully trying Oliver again, she grabbed her keys and headed out, feeling faintly relieved to be without him.

Propped against the step and front door of the Penfolds' home were scores of bouquets, some of them expensive florist's arrangements delivered as requested, but left abandoned outside. Glancing down at the cards, Kate saw that some had been written by younger people, with love hearts and circles on top of 'i's. For someone who didn't have friends, Candice was suddenly popular in death. It always amazed Kate how people voluntarily attached themselves to tragedy, regardless of how little they had known the deceased. She wrote down the names on the cards, out of habit but also in case the killer was amongst the supposed mourners – even though Polly Pringle had been held for questioning, they still couldn't rule anything out.

Having been exposed to Polly's violent outburst, Kate believed the disabled woman was capable of killing. The rage in her face had seemed like decades of anger and frustration let loose without any sense of rational thought or self-control. What she couldn't understand was how a woman with no car, who was unable to drive, moved Candice's body if she had killed her in the apartment. How could she have got to Moat Place and back? The young woman's strength could have enabled her to lift the body into the freezer, but no other fingerprints were found apart from Dobbie's. If he was telling the truth, whoever put the body there had the presence of mind to wipe the whole thing clean. That involved rational thinking and planning. Perhaps everyone had underestimated Polly. Or perhaps someone was trying to protect her.

One card in particular caught Kate's attention. Belinda, Ian and the Mercuro family. What connection did the two families have? There were still more questions than answers, which made Kate nervous. None of this made sense, although murder rarely did. Without knowing where Candice was murdered, the case for homicide against Polly was thin. And Mark Dobbie just happening upon the body after meeting Belinda Mercuro was impossible to believe. If, as he claimed, he was set up, it would have taken significant forward planning and manipulation. With Polly's developmental age, it was doubtful she could have done it. Although she was well aware of scores of examples of child-killers, they typically preyed on children even younger than themselves. But the look on Polly's face when she described the baby as being 'Jesus' haunted Kate. Who knew what someone with delusions might be capable of?

After writing down the final name, she stood and straightened her skirt. It occurred to her that the family might have gone away for some time together. If that was the case, she had no way of preventing them from hearing about the child through the media. Instead she hoped that they had given up opening the door, preferring to close out the world that had taken their child and sister.

She pressed the doorbell and was relieved to hear footsteps inside. The only one who wore shoes in the house was Janine.

'Just leave whatever it is at the door,' the female voice called.

'Mrs Penfold, it's Kate Farrer. I need to speak with you.'

Keys turned, deadlocks were unbolted. Janine opened the door. For the first time, her face was make-up free and her hair was combed flat against her head. She wore a dressing gown that made her appear smaller, swamped by its size. The effect added years to her.

'I'm sorry to disturb you so early, but it's very important that we talk.'

'Hasn't it all been said?'

Kate felt her stomach lurch. 'No, I have some news you should hear.' She stepped inside and slipped off her shoes out of respect. 'Are the others awake?'

'Robert's in the garden. He likes it out there. And Lesley's upstairs. I'll put the kettle on and bring her down. Come through.'

In the kitchen, the tidy surfaces were covered in more bouquets. Some were boxed arrangements of brightly coloured gerberas, others the sorts of extravagant displays that are given to opera singers or ballet stars on opening night. Lilies and orchids dominated the cut glass vases.

'I'm sorry you had to see that mess out the front, but we ran out of vases. Most are from complete strangers. And to think I used to love flowers.' She clicked the kettle on and retied her dressing gown. 'Have a seat, I'll be back in a moment.'

Kate thanked her and wandered towards the open glass door that led onto the wooden deck. Robert Penfold was hunched over, digging something out of the garden with a spade. No iPod, radio or distractions apart from the bird sounds. He was wearing wooden clogs and a full apron.

She glanced at the trees and bushes, which all looked the same to her. Passion for gardening was something she didn't relate to. No sooner did you mow a lawn than it grew back. A pulled-out weed just multiplied. It seemed to her that gardening was akin to constantly trying to push a stream uphill with a stick. Where was the satisfaction in it? Even so, the idea of a magnificent garden like this one, private and secluded, did have its appeal. She just wouldn't want to maintain it.

She saw Robert turn to his wife and put down his tools before removing a pair of gardening gloves. A minute later, he entered through the back door and was washing his hands in what was probably the laundry sink. When he appeared, the apron and clogs were absent. Lesley came downstairs and into the kitchen, dressed in a tracksuit. With puffy eyes, she finger-combed her blonde hair and sat at the table without a word.

Robert joined her, and Kate sat opposite them. Mrs Penfold hovered, as if waiting for an order in a restaurant. The other two obviously noticed Kate's black eye for the first time.

'Again, I apologise for coming so early. I understand what an incredibly difficult time this is for you, but you need to know that there's been a development in the case.'

'Have you arrested whoever did it?' Lesley wiped her eyes with a tissue from her pocket.

'No, but we have found Candice's baby. Alive.'

Robert straightened. 'How? Where is – is it a boy or a girl? This is unbelievable.'

'It's a baby boy, a few weeks old. He's fine, but he's in hospital, just so he can be checked out thoroughly. We needed to run some tests, including one for DNA.'

'Why a DNA test?' Robert was frowning.

'To confirm that he is Candice's. A swab was taken from inside his mouth. It's a completely painless procedure.'

Janine Penfold was fighting back tears. She covered her mouth with her hands and slid into a chair.

'Oh my God, Mum, you're a grandmother, and I'm an auntie.' Lesley smiled through her tears. 'Can we see him? I mean, does he look like Candy?' She dabbed her nose. 'This is a miracle.'

'I don't believe it.' Janine Penfold stared at the table. 'This is all too much. The other night it sounded as if you thought he was dead. Now he's turned up? None of this can possibly be real. Do you have any idea who the father is?' She turned to her husband.

'Let the detective speak,' Robert said gently.

Kate felt more drained than ever. They listened while she described Dobbie denying the murder but admitting that he set fire to the house her body was found in, and how Polly Pringle had been minding the baby, whom she had called Jesus. She also explained that it could take a while to come up with a DNA match for the father. After finishing, she was unsure whether she had clarified things or confused them.

'Polly Pringle,' Robert said. 'I know that name from somewhere.'

'Mrs Pringle was the housekeeper we had years ago,' Lesley offered, 'the one with the disabled daughter.'

'That's right,' Janine said. 'Sometimes she would bring the girl with her. You'd play together, but she was a few years older than you. She had some kind of syndrome that made her appear odd.'

'Did Candy and Polly have much contact lately apart from the birthday card she had pinned up in her room?' It appeared that Candice had gone there voluntarily, knowing she could hide and that Polly would keep quiet about the baby.

'We got Christmas cards but last I heard, the parents had both died.'

Lesley went upstairs and returned with the card.

'May I borrow that?' Kate asked.

Lesley handed it over. Any evidence connecting the women was important.

'When can we see the little boy?' Robert asked, his hands shaking again.

'The nurses have been told not to let anyone in until the morning. I know it's hard, but you won't have to wait much longer.'

Kate stood to depart and left the three family members sitting in silence at the table. She showed herself out after collecting her shoes and headed into the office.

38

That evening, despite her exhaustion, Kate found it difficult to fall asleep. She had gone to bed early only to be kept awake by montages flashing through her drifting mind. Each image was haunting – Candice's burnt body in the begging position, pleading for justice. The photos of her naked, being raped by Brett Spender, then the body of the pathetic man who had finally discovered what he thought was good karma, only to be burnt alive.

She saw images of Robert Penfold pulling out the smallest of weeds in his garden, while his wife scrubbed the dirt with sponges. Then Oliver reached out for money but what she gave him was not enough. Polly Pringle scratched at her while the baby lay there in silence. As she floated off to sleep, she heard Billy's motorbike. He was coming back to her.

Suddenly, she heard knocking. At first she thought it was part of her dream and opened the door that had appeared in her mind. The knocking continued and she returned to consciousness. Someone really was at the door. Nine o'clock at night was a hell of a time for a social call.

Cautiously, she demanded to know who was there.

'It's Oliver. We need to talk.'

'Go home,' she said through the closed door. She thought again of the drug dealer accusing Oliver of betraying him. 'I've nothing to say to you outside work.'

'You don't understand, Kate. I'm not who you think I am.'

Kate rested her forehead against the door. She was too tired and frustrated to talk about it. At this moment, she was beyond caring.

That didn't stop Oliver from talking through the door. 'I had a visit from the internal boys. I know you handed in the money.'

'You screwed up there. It's gone for good. Did you think you could set me up?'

Kate heard Oliver's mobile phone ring, and then the sound of him answering it. She strained to hear what he was saying. Had he come to threaten her? Was he working with someone else? Her chest began to tighten, and she tried to slow her breathing, cupping her hands over her mouth and nose to rebreathe the expired air. While Oliver talked on his phone, her thoracic muscles slowly relaxed.

Oliver went quiet as Kate's mobile rang. She rushed to it, ready to warn whoever was on the phone that she could be in danger. It was a nurse from the hospital.

'Detective, I didn't know what to do. I've called the police and we've started a search. Security's here and have locked the major entrances and exits. The other nurses are beside themselves.'

'Slow down,' Kate said. 'I have no idea what you're—'

'The baby! The one we're minding for community services, the one whose mother was murdered? He's missing.'

Kate let a slow, forced breath out. 'What do you mean, missing? How can you misplace a baby?'

'You don't understand. Someone has kidnapped him. They've taken the baby.'

'I'll be right there.'

Kate had almost forgotten about Oliver until he spoke through the door. 'The baby's missing. We have to go.'

That must have been what the call he had just taken was about. He wasn't speaking to his co-conspirator. What was she thinking? Kate threw on jeans and a T-shirt, slipped her feet into runners and grabbed her gun. When she opened the door, Oliver was already in the car with the engine running and the flashing blue light on top. He was as eager to get to the hospital as she was.

Once in the car, she phoned for back-up. Polly Pringle had been released and could have gone to the hospital to take back the baby Jesus. This poor infant had lived such a short while, yet had already endured enough trauma for a lifetime.

She and Oliver didn't speak until they arrived at the hospital entrance. Two marked cars were there already. The detectives flashed their IDs and were shown through to the security office by one of the hospital administrators, who introduced them to the head of security. He unlocked the door and led them into the monitor room, where six televisions showed rotating views of entrances and exits.

'We record for twenty-four hours. Then we . . . what we do is we wipe the tapes. Well, if there are no reported incidents, that is. I've been reviewing, well, going over the vision for the last two hours.' He spoke in a staccato fashion, probably reflecting his sense of urgency. 'It could have been a while before they noticed the kid missing. So far, no one's walked out with a baby or pram.'

Kate wouldn't have expected that anyone would be leaving the hospital this late at night with a newborn. The only children coming and going at this hour would have been through casualty.

'Can you check the emergency department as well?' Oliver said. 'A child is less likely to be noticed going out through there.'

They studied a few tapes. So far, no one recognisable had been picked up. She thought about the publicity the case had brought. Any disturbed person could have walked in and taken the child, or someone wanting a ransom from the Penfolds. *Shit. Anyone could have done it.*

'What time's shift change?'

The administrator checked his watch. 'In about half an hour. All the evening nurses, path workers, technicians, kitchen staff go home at the same time.'

If someone had the child, it would make sense to wait until the greatest number of people were on the move.

Oliver clenched his jaw. 'What about the doctors?'

'They either go until the morning, or finish at midnight.'

An image on the screen caught Kate's attention. 'That one, there.'

The guard paused the image and homed in. 'She's got a scarf and a raincoat on.' There hadn't been rain for days, and none forecast for the next week.

'We get a lot of old people coming through here with coats on in all sorts of weather.'

'Can you run it forward?'

They watched the female figure walk briskly into the hospital, looking to both sides. They couldn't make out a face, but the posture was straight and the figure average sized. That was not an old lady's gait.

'The shape doesn't fit Polly Pringle,' she thought out loud.

Oliver stared at the screen. 'But it could be her carer, Vivien Bastick. If there's no vision of her leaving, she and the baby could still be in the building.'

The administrator fiddled with a set of keys. 'I've got our head of nursing and two guards searching the wards. It's a thousand-bed hospital, so the area's large.' He sounded almost apologetic about his lack of control of the situation.

'Why not more people searching?'

He rattled the keys. 'We felt it wise not to alarm the staff and patients at this stage.'

Kate suspected that his priority was keeping a lid on this. If the child was found quickly, no one in the wider community would need to know. So much for a caring professional, she thought, and dialled Russo. She suggested sending a patrol car to locate Polly Pringle, and to see if Vivien Bastick was with her or at her home. Vivien's defence of Polly was completely irresponsible. Maybe she had known all along what Polly had done and was still involved somehow. She hoped, for the baby's sake, that it wasn't an unknown kidnapper.

Phones rang in the security office. One of the ward staff had lost her keys to the drug cupboard. The administrator offered to sort it out and quickly vanished.

Kate told the guard to phone her immediately if anything turned up on the surveillance tape. If the baby was still in the hospital, they didn't have long to find him before the change of shift.

'I want all exits blocked and every staff member's ID and bags checked before anyone leaves. I don't care how long it takes.'

The guard grabbed his walkie-talkie and called in his guards.

Oliver grabbed Kate's arm. 'I know where the kids' ward is.' He led the way to the stairwell and they ran up the six flights. The place was like a maze, with colour-coded footsteps leading down different corridors. The kids' section was bright yellow. Inside the heavy double doors was a different world. Murals of cartoon characters and fairies lined the walls, and paintings covered windows into the rooms. They met the ward sister at the desk, crying and apologising to another nurse. The place was dark apart from corridor lights and the nurse's station desk lamps. A mother stood in an adjacent room, clutching the hand of her sleeping child, looking clearly disturbed by the staff 's distress.

'Did anyone see anything? Anything that could help us find the baby?'

The nurse shook her head. 'The grandmother came, sat with him for a while and then left when he was asleep. I know there weren't supposed to be visitors, but she was so desperate to see him. I came back half an hour later and he was gone. None of the other nurses saw or heard a thing.'

Oliver had checked the ward's whiteboard and located the Penfold baby's room.

'How did you know it was the grandmother?' Kate asked.

'Because she told me.' The nurse burst into tears, realising the mistake she had made. The woman claiming to be the baby's grandmother could have been anyone.

'What was she wearing?'

The nurse wiped her eyes with a handkerchief. 'God, it was a dark scarf and a plastic raincoat.

That I do remember because she said she didn't want reporters to recognise her.'

Shit. How could a nurse be so thoughtless? The kidnapper had covered her head and was unlikely to have left forensic evidence. The abduction had been planned, not a spontaneous act. That did not augur well for finding the child. Kate's chest tightened again.

'Anything about her face or hair colour?'

'She was wearing sunglasses because she had been crying, she said, and didn't want to upset her grandson. She said she just wanted to see him, that's all.' The other nurse put her arms around her colleague.

Kate knew they would be no more help right now. 'We need statements from everyone on the ward, relatives and any child old enough to give one. No one leaves the ward until I say so.'

The nurses nodded. Kate followed Oliver as he headed towards the room the baby had been in. He stopped at the toilets to help a young boy in pyjamas with his drip-stand.

'Hey, champ. Don't suppose you saw a lady with sunglasses and a raincoat?'

The boy nodded.

'It's really important that we find her. Do you know which way she went?'

The boy pointed to the end of the ward furthest from the nurse's station.

Oliver knelt down. 'This is really important police business. Do you know if she was carrying anything or had anyone with her?'

The boy tugged on his Spiderman pyjama shirt and nodded.

Oliver said, 'You'd be a real life hero if you can tell me.'

The little boy showed him the Spiderman image on the material. 'She had a bubba. My mum's growing a bubba in her tummy.'

'Thanks, champ. You're going to be a great big brother.' Oliver patted him on the shoulder.

Kate called down to the security office. 'The woman wearing the raincoat's got the child. She took the fire exit in the north wing of the kids' ward. Where does it lead?'

'Upstairs is surgical then medical wards. Below are orthopaedic and cancer.'

Kate followed Oliver, who was already heading towards the back of the ward. He pushed through the fire exit door and looked above and below the handrail.

'You go up, I'll go down,' she ordered. 'And call me if you find anything. Don't try and go it alone. This woman's dangerous.'

39

Oliver pulled open the fire door on the floor above the kids' ward and took the gun out from under his denim jacket. In a treatment room off the corridor, something colourful poked out beneath a white sheet in an oversized laundry bin. He clutched his weapon and slowly approached. With his left hand, he ripped off the sheet and pointed the gun, ready to fire if necessary.

'Police,' he said. 'Come out, we know you're there.' His heart was pounding up to his neck.

Edging closer, he peered into the hamper, finger poised on the trigger. There was no sign of the baby, but he had just found the discarded scarf and coat.

He searched the next room, opening all the cupboards, then found his way to the nurses' station. After flashing his badge, a nurse escorted him through each room. He thanked her and told her to seal the laundry room. No one was to enter or touch anything inside. She obliged. He dialled Kate but her phone immediately went to voicemail. He told her of the find and that he was headed up to the next floor.

On the upper ward, the layout was exactly the same. He repeated the order of the search, first with the laundry room and hall cupboards. He headed for the nurses' station, but the area was empty. The only sign of activity was a board that lit up when buzzers were pressed. This was a much busier ward, with seriously ill patients.

He tried a room with a curtain pulled around a bed and the light on, but the stench of someone on a bedpan made him retreat. On the other side of the corridor, he pushed the treatment room door but it wouldn't open. Through a round window in the door he could see syringe medications lined up in green plastic dishes alongside charts on the bench. Two of the medicine cupboard doors above them were open.

Oliver noticed a second entrance to the room on the other side and followed the corridor around to it. He looked in but it was still empty. More buzzers were sounding and he could hear someone calling for assistance. He almost gagged when a nurse scurried past with a vomit bowl filled with blood.

'Bloody warfarin, ought to be banned,' she muttered. 'The tissues are right next to your bed, Mrs Palmer,' she called to whoever continued to buzz.

Oliver entered the medication room and his eyes automatically focused on the linen trolley pushed against the opposite exit. Someone had shoved a broom through the handles, locking them. He hesitated before slowly stepping forward, gun propped in his sweaty hand. A short cry rang out from the trolley.

Thank God. With his left hand he peeled off the top crumpled sheet and the wail let loose.

'You're OK, little one,' he said, putting the gun on the floor and reaching in. With the baby safe in his arms, he pulled out his mobile. Before he could press redial, he saw a flash of movement in his peripheral vision. Turning his back to protect the child, he felt a sting, then pain in the back of his thigh. Reaching down with one hand, he yanked out an empty syringe.

Kate was with the security guard when his phone rang. A nurse had heard a baby cry on the medical ward, he reported to Kate, but she was unable to get into the medication room to check it out.

Kate asked to speak to the nurse. 'Is a detective on the ward?'

'We haven't seen one,' the voice answered. 'All the medications are out ready to give to patients, but we can't get in. Someone's wedged the doors closed on both entrances, and they've thrown sheets over the windows. We can't see inside.'

Kate asked her to hold for one moment. She dialled Oliver's number on her mobile and could hear his phone ring through the landline phone she held against her ear.

'A phone's ringing in the treatment room, but no one's answering it,' the nurse confirmed.

'Stay away from the doors,' Kate ordered, then she heard the gunshot. The line went dead.

Oliver had to be in the treatment room, locked in with the baby. Someone had fired a gun. Kate's pulse drilled and she took the deepest breath possible. If the baby's kidnapper had his phone he might already be hurt, or worse. She had to think fast. By the time the tactical response team arrived, it might be too late for Oliver.

'Clear the ward of as many people as possible,' she told the security guard, 'quickly and quietly. I'm going up there.'

'But you don't understand,' the director of nursing implored. 'That's a medical ward. Most of the patients are elderly and many are immobile. It's where we keep some of our rehabilitation people as well, after their strokes or heart attacks.'

Shit.

The guard led the way. 'I'll show you the short-cut.'

The pair ran down the corridor, as fast as they could.

Oliver held the baby to his chest. He refused to hand him over.

Janine Penfold waved the gun at him again, careful not to get too close. 'I don't want to do it, but I'll shoot. Give him to me.'

'I can't do that. He's just a tiny baby.'

Janine's eyes filled with tears. 'It doesn't matter. I just injected you with a bottle of insulin. In a few

335

minutes you'll be unconscious.' She sniffed. 'I didn't want to hurt you, but there was no other way.'

Phones rang outside on the ward and Oliver could hear movement. He hoped the nurses were getting as many people out as possible and that back-up was on the way.

'Why do you want to hurt your own grandson?' he asked, trying to buy time and keep her from going outside with the gun.

'Don't call him that.' She reached for a syringe on the bench. The substance it contained was orange. 'He has to be taken away before any more harm is done. I've been trying to work out what to do. Now I don't have a choice.'

Oliver didn't understand. Was the woman psychotic? She sounded like Polly Pringle. What wasn't he grasping? He struggled to think clearly enough to calm her down.

'Why? He hasn't hurt anyone. He's how Candice, your daughter, is living on.'

Oliver felt cold, then hot and began to perspire.

The woman looked at the baby, who appeared to have understood how important it was to be calm. He had stopped crying.

'You don't understand,' she said, steadying the gun. 'He isn't just Candice's. He's Robert's child as well.'

336

40

Within minutes, Kate had arrived on the ward. It had the same layout as the one she had searched three floors below. Two nurses were struggling to wheel beds out of rooms and Kate whispered for them to stop. The noise might upset whoever was inside that room.

They spoke quietly down one end of the corridor.

'Is there another way in?' Kate asked.

The security guard, still puffing, put his hands on his belt. 'Only way is through the space between the floors. It's tight but a small person could fit in there.'

Kate looked at the square cork tiles on the ceiling.

'You'd have to remove one from next door then climb through. All you have to do is slide one from above, lower yourself down and you're in.'

'Are you sure that's the only way?'

'Absolutely. We had a psych patient disappear and found him when he fell through into the next room, which happened to be another patient's toilet and that guy was on it at the time.'

337

Kate stared at the ceiling. A small, dark, tight place. It was the only way to get in quickly to save the baby. No one would expect the police to enter from the ceiling, or at least that's what she hoped.

Her heart pounded inside her chest. She couldn't do it, couldn't go back inside such a tiny hole. She would freeze and make the situation worse. There had to be another option.

One of the nurses crawled along the floor, obviously trying to avoid getting shot.

'I'm in charge tonight. What can I do to help?'

'What's in the room?'

'As far as I could tell, there are two people in there, a man and a woman. She has a gun. I slid my compact mirror under the door and saw them. I'm pretty sure they didn't see me.'

The nurse could have gotten herself or someone else killed, but the information was helpful. Oliver was being held hostage, and the baby had to be inside there too.

'What medications are laid out?'

The nurse squinted, as if trying to remember the precise order. 'A multi-vitamin injection, a rapid acting insulin, some antibiotics and potassium to be loaded into a bag.'

'Which of those could be fatal if used as a weapon?'

The nurse looked at the guard. 'The insulin, I suppose, and potassium, but they could take a few minutes to work.' She hesitated, then volunteered, 'There are also scalpel blades in there, but you'd

338

have to know how to open a sterile dressing pack and load the blade onto the handle to hold it like a weapon.'

'Has the baby made any more noise?'

The nurse covered her mouth with one hand. 'Oh my God. Nothing since the gunshot.'

Kate knew she had no choice but to go into the roof space. 'I'll need your torch,' she said, and the guard pulled it from his belt. 'Can you give me a hand?'

'Are you sure this is a good idea? What if that crazy woman starts shooting again?' the nurse implored, but she didn't have a better plan.

'If she's hurt that baby, or Oliver, they could be in there dying right now. Get some emergency people on stand-by in case anyone gets shot. They might already need it.'

Kate took some deep breaths. As much as the idea of being in the roof space terrified her, she had to act quickly. *I'm a survivor*, she whispered to herself as she took off her shoes and climbed on top of a stainless steel set of drawers the guard had wheeled in from another room. He steadied it as Kate gently pushed up on a tile and slid it to one side. Dust dropped down on her face and head, and she suppressed a cough. Silently, she put the torch into the roof space and pulled herself up.

'Robert is the father?' Oliver began to feel light-headed, as though he hadn't eaten all day. The insulin had begun to work. He clutched the baby closer.

Janine Penfold was still pointing the gun at his head. She had calmed down and seemed more in control than she had moments before.

'He always had a close relationship with the girls, you know. I was frightened you'd pick that up with all your questions. He spoilt Candice, because she wasn't as pretty or as smart as Lesley. And Candy used their "special bond" to get what she wanted. She lorded it over me.'

Sweat dripped from Oliver's brow. He began to move on the spot, agitated, unable to stand still. His body was reacting to his dropping sugar levels.

'Stop that,' she yelled. 'You move again and I'll have to kill you.'

Oliver stood still. Suddenly, everything made sense. 'You killed Candy, didn't you?' he asked. He didn't know how much longer he could remain standing. 'Dobbie didn't kill her. You did.'

Janine took a step back, colliding with the bench, her face drained of colour. 'I didn't mean to. I mean, that was an accident. I only meant to stop her leaving by frightening her with the spade. She came over to talk and wouldn't tell me where the baby was.' Her eyes glazed over with tears. 'She kept lying, telling me she was a virgin, and Robert couldn't be the father, but I knew the truth.'

'You murdered Candy to protect your husband?'

'No.' Janine Penfold's voice was firm. 'It was an accident. I pleaded with her to give the baby up. No one else had to know. I could have fixed things. The family didn't have to suffer.'

She sniffed and wiped her nose on a sleeve, the gun still pointed at Oliver and the baby. 'But Candy just walked away, she wouldn't listen to reason. I grabbed the spade. That's when I snapped and hit her.'

Oliver dropped to his knees, unable to stay upright any longer. He'd protect the baby until his last moments . . .

Kate tried to breathe but the weight on her chest was much heavier than before. For a moment, she was back with her abductor, helpless and vulnerable. The light from the corridor quickly faded as she inched her way towards the treatment room ceiling, crawling along the beam. Panic filled her, and she struggled to keep going, almost losing balance when a cockroach ran across her hand.

Breathe out, two, three, four, she told herself. Her heart kept hammering. Then she heard the voices. She was stunned by Janine Penfold's confession. Oliver's voice was slurred.

'Candice was drugged . . . and . . . raped. She didn't remember.'

'Liar!' the woman yelled. 'That's what she wanted you to think. She was a tease.'

'The baby isn't your husband's.' Oliver sounded drunk. 'We believe he was fathered by one of the rapists.'

Body shaking, Kate held her breath and slowly moved a tile sideways, giving her a view inside the room.

Oliver sat holding the baby. He looked ill, sweaty and pale. She couldn't tell if the baby was alive, but there was no sign of blood. She could see Janine Penfold's back and her hand holding the gun.

Her partner slumped lower onto the floor and the woman moved closer. The baby began to cry and Oliver placed him on the floor. Janine Penfold grabbed another syringe and knelt down, ready to inject the helpless child. She put the gun on the floor beside her.

Kate tried to move the tile along but her fingers cramped. Shit, not now. Not another attack.

Then it started. First Oliver's legs twitched, followed by his arms. Within seconds he was having an uncontrollable seizure and Kate had no time to think. Her fingers loosened and she pulled her gun. With the woman distracted by Oliver's convulsions, she lowered herself onto the bench. Her foot knocked a bottle, sending it smashing to the floor.

Janine Penfold spun around and lunged at Kate with the syringe. Kate kicked at the hand with her bare foot and made contact, dislodging the weapon. She didn't see the needle in Janine's other hand but felt it land in her calf muscle, orange liquid inside. Pain seared through her leg.

The crazed woman screamed and pushed on the syringe. Kate punched her hard in the face, knocking her backwards onto the floor. She dived at the woman, pinning her arms down and called for help from the guard.

'I've got her pegged, but we need a doctor right now!'

The guard tried to open the doors blocked by the laundry basket. She heard the window break, a sheet protecting them all from shards of glass. The nurse and another woman, this one dressed in a doctor's coat, rushed in and immediately went to Oliver's side.

'What's he been given?' the doctor asked, dropping to her knees.

The nurse checked the items on the bench. Pentamin and Actrapid were missing.

'The orange one's still in my leg,' Kate said as the guard helped her restrain Janine Penfold. She pulled it out with her free hand and lifted the baby off the floor. Two police officers cuffed the killer and escorted her into the corridor. Judging by the noise, half the force must have been out there.

'The whole bottle of Actrapid's empty. He's had three hundred units.'

'Get me a cannula and fifty mils of fifty per cent dextrose.'

'Here's the arrest trolley.' Another nurse pushed along a steel cabinet and pulled out an enormous syringe.

The doctor pushed up Oliver's sleeve. 'If you hold his elbow straight, I'll put it right into the vein.'

A male doctor arrived and grabbed a cannula. He didn't look older than twenty, although he must have been. 'What have we got?'

'He's been injected with three hundred units of rapid acting insulin.'

'That's one hell of a hypo.' The younger medico knelt on the floor. 'We'll need another IV access in case yours tissues.'

Oliver's fitting movements slowed, became twitchy, then stopped. Each doctor inserted drips and taped them in place. One nurse put an oxygen mask on Oliver's face while another pinpricked his finger to take blood sugar readings as the youngest doctor drew blood via the cannula into three glass vials. The nurse asked Kate for his name and date of birth.

'He's my partner, Oliver Parke. I'm sorry, I don't know his date of birth.'

The male doctor looked sideways at the nurse.

'Work partner,' Kate added. 'He's a detective. He's married, with kids, but I can't remember his wife's name.' God, why hadn't she listened to him more carefully? How difficult was it to remember one woman's name? She felt ashamed.

The older doctor leant forward. 'Oliver, can you hear me?'

He moaned and tried to sit up.

'Stay there,' she said. 'You've had a seizure from low blood sugar, but your level's coming back up again. You need to stay lying down for a little while longer.' She turned to the trolley nurse. 'The

344

insulin could take up to twenty-four hours to wear off. It's going to keep leaching out of the muscle so I want ten per cent dextrose at two hundred mils per hour and quarter-hourly blood sugars. If it drops below three, give him another bolus of fifty per cent dextrose.'

Oliver began to twitch again. The nurse crouched beside him announced his blood sugar level was 1.2, just as his legs and arms began to flail again and his back arched.

'OK, we need another bolus. Make sure the drips are secure.'

Kate stood helplessly clutching the baby as her partner had another seizure. She was grateful the female doctor was so calm and in control.

'Put up a potassium infusion as well. We don't want him having any heart arrhythmias on us. And we'll need a cardiac bed in ICU.'

Medical staff drew up injections, put them into the tubes in Oliver's veins and another nurse recorded all the orders. Someone else dialled on the treatment room phone, informing intensive care that a patient was on his way up.

Kate watched Oliver's body start to relax in response to the medication. He had contributed a lot to the case and had almost given his life to save the child. She wanted the staff to know what her partner had done and how he had protected them all.

'He risked his life to save this baby and everyone in the ward.'

The staff paused, listening. Kate's voice wavered. 'Please take good care of him.'

'We will. I promise.' The woman in charge threw her stethoscope around her neck and stood up. She placed a hand on Kate's elbow and stroked the baby's blonde hair.

'We're grateful for what you did, too.' She noticed the syringe on the floor. 'You're lucky you were hit with a vitamin injection, but I should look at the site. You got a fair bit of fluid into the muscle, I'll bet, which is why you're limping.'

Kate hadn't even felt her own pain until now, but her leg was aching. 'I'm fine. You have more important things to do right now.'

A gurney arrived and Kate left the room so it had enough space to enter. In the corridor were uniformed and plainclothes police, and members of the tactical response unit, complete with headgear, bulletproof vests and weapons. There was a respectful silence as the bed carrying their fellow officer was wheeled past with its attachments, drips and monitors.

The enormity of what had happened hit Kate like a kick behind her knees, and she felt as though her legs had turned to jelly. Someone put a chair behind her and she sat, still cradling the baby. A nurse with a smiley face name-badge approached her to take the baby, but Kate refused to let him go. The poor boy had been through so much and had lost his mother, not to mention almost being murdered by his grandmother. She thought back to the

346

scene of the house-fire and that nappy bag, and how she'd known she needed to find this child.

It suddenly occurred to her why Polly Pringle had named her charge Jesus. If Candice Penfold could not recall having had sex, she might have thought she had given birth while still a virgin. In Polly's simple view of the world, that would have made this child the second coming, the Son of God. And the child's grandmother was the evil person who wanted him dead. Maybe Polly wasn't psychotic at all. In a strange way, her logic made sense. And somehow she had managed to get the nappies and supplies to care for the baby, whether it was alone or with Candy's help.

The baby gripped Kate's finger as she stroked his dimpled chin. How could something so perfect be the product of rape? The DNA would prove paternity, provided they had the right suspects. She owed it to Candice to finish what they had started, even if Janine had confessed to her daughter's murder. It would also implicate or exonerate Robert Penfold, the young woman's trusted stepfather. Kate felt an overwhelming urge to protect this child from the horrors of the world.

A nurse knelt down and spoke gently to her. 'We need to get this little fellow checked and fed. By the smell of him, he needs a change as well.'

Kate hadn't noticed. He was still gripping her finger and trying to pull it into his mouth. She nodded and silently handed the child over.

'He's in good hands, now,' the nurse said, as a uniformed officer escorted her back to the ward.

John Zimmer arrived in blue crime-scene overalls, camera around his neck. Kate had to admit that seeing him was a relief.

'Mate, you did well in there. From what I hear, you're either incredibly brave, or unbelievably clumsy. In a hospital full of happy drugs, only you could get jabbed with bloody vitamins.'

He winked but she didn't have the energy to banter. She knew he would work the scene thoroughly and collect every bit of evidence to charge Janine Penfold with causing Oliver grievous injury. No clever lawyer would find a hole in the evidence collection now.

Two hours later, she had given her statement multiple times to investigating officers. She knew there would be an enquiry and Oliver would face more questions, possibly about the anti-corruption case as well. The fact that Janine Penfold had grabbed his gun would go against him. It was a cardinal sin for any police officer to surrender his or her weapon, especially if it was then used to threaten or harm anyone else. He was already doing better in ICU but had to stay a full twenty-four hours. No doubt his wife would be with him, anyway.

Kate left the hospital feeling emotionally wrung out and with her leg aching. But before going home, she needed to see Janine Penfold and find out how Candice had ended up in the freezer for

Dobbie to find. In the taxi, the events of the night repeated in her head like a movie. Could she have done anything more quickly? How had she managed her claustrophobia to crawl through the small dark roof space? It was like watching someone else play out the scenes. When it came down to it, she had done her job and overcome her fears.

At the station, Kate grabbed a coffee and waited to hear when the formal interview would commence. A call from Russo told her to head for the interrogation rooms. Inside number four sat Janine Penfold, her legal counsel, Russo and Liz Gould. The two homicide detectives had their backs to the viewing window and Kate could listen in without being seen. It was past midnight, but she would stay as long as necessary.

Janine Penfold appeared composed and initially refused to answer any questions, deferring each time to her lawyer, who just nodded for her to remain silent. Half an hour passed without one answer. Kate knocked on the door and stood back. The inspector suspended the interview, stopped the tape and followed Liz out before closing the door and switching off the intercom button. Neither party could hear the other.

'She's convinced her husband is the baby's father,' Kate told her colleagues. 'If you suggest he preferred Candy to her, for her company, humour and looks, that might be enough to get her temper up again. She's a vain woman who needs to be in control.'

'Any other thoughts?' Russo asked, keen for more input. He wanted the confession as much as anyone.

Kate went on. 'Candy was the great disappointment. Dumb, not pretty, slovenly, and Robert still preferred her. It went against everything Janine lived her life by. I think you've got more of a chance with that angle rather than accusing her of protecting a paedophile.'

Liz Gould thanked her and took the lead when they returned to the interview room. The vanity angle started to work. Despite the 'no comment' instructions from her lawyer, Janine Penfold began to speak: 'You've got it all wrong. Candy manipulated Robert's good will. She played on his kindness and took advantage of him.' She almost spat the words out. 'He felt sorry for her, that was all, but she turned it into something . . .' she looked away, 'unnatural.'

Liz leant forward. 'That must have really made you angry. You did everything for that girl, even tried to help her with her weight problem, and she still turned on you.' The female detective sounded sincerely indignant. 'And when you were there for her, every day, she was laughing behind your back, hiding the pregnancy under your very roof. No wonder you were upset. You had every right to be.'

The lawyer placed a hand on his client's arm, but Janine pulled away.

'Upset? Damn right. She seduced my husband and got pregnant. It would have ruined him if

350

anyone found out, and our family. Everything we've worked so hard for.'

Kate listened, dumbfounded that a mother would blame her child for sexual abuse. She wasn't just protecting Robert, she wanted to punish Candice.

'When did she rub your face in it about the pregnancy?' Liz asked.

'First I knew of it was after she disappeared. That's when she rang me from the car and said she had terrible stomach cramps and was bleeding. Pretty soon after, she started crying and said there was a head coming out from between her legs.'

'What did you do?'

Janine Penfold sounded matter of fact. 'There was nothing I could do. She had run away and didn't tell me where she was. I called back but the phone battery must have been flat.'

Kate tried to imagine the poor, terrified young woman screaming in pain and asking her mother for help. Childbirth was supposed to be the worst pain anyone could experience, and Candice went through it alone in a car.

Russo's experience showed; he seemed unflappable. 'How do you know that Robert was the one who had a sexual relationship with Candy?'

Janine looked at him quizzically. 'Isn't it obvious? She didn't have a boyfriend. No one else would have wanted her.'

The lawyer began scribbling notes while Liz continued. 'When did you next see Candice?'

351

'A few days later she called and said she wanted to come home and tell me some amazing news. I told her we could talk while Robert was at work. She came without the child and wouldn't tell me where it was. She kept saying it was a little Jesus, given to her by God, and that I just wanted to take him away and control her life. She was emotional and made no sense. Can you believe she tried to pretend that she'd never seduced Robert?'

The lawyer wanted it recorded that he had recommended that his client not answer the questions, but Janine Penfold had repeatedly refused his legal advice.

Liz kept up the momentum. She was close to a confession, and they all knew it.

'Where were you when you had the conversation?'

Janine looked down and checked her cuticles. 'In Robert's garden.'

'Did you fight with her, try to convince her she was wrong?'

'She wouldn't listen and kept saying I'd never take her baby. She turned her back on me and just walked off. She wanted to destroy our family. Robert's first wife did the same thing and I couldn't let him go through that again.' She stared at Liz Gould as though she would understand.

'So you just wanted her to listen to you?' Liz asked. 'And maybe give her a bit of a fright?'

'Exactly,' Janine Penfold replied. 'I picked up the spade and hit her on the back of the head, fairly hard, but not too hard. She was just supposed to stop, to listen to me, but she fell down in the garden bed.'

Kate studied the woman describing such heinous actions with little apparent remorse. She had said that she would do anything to protect her family. The way she spoke about her husband bordered on obsession, which fitted with what Kate had seen already. She was no psychiatrist, but even she could see that Janine Penfold had somehow become detached from reality. Considering the woman's personal vanity and preoccupation with image, she was not so different from Dobbie.

Liz Gould urged Janine on. 'What did you do then?'

'What else could I do? When I realised she wasn't breathing, I put on the gardening gloves, got the wheelbarrow and carried her to the boot of her car. Then I came up with the idea of taking her to that swingers' house Belinda had mentioned.'

'Belinda Mercuro?' Russo looked up from his notepad.

'Bin's an old friend. We used to model together and have lunch every now and then. She talked about this house and the men she slept with there. Even drove me past it last time we caught up, but I wasn't interested in being part of the things that went on there.'

'How did Belinda know Mark Dobbie?'

'She wanted a personal trainer and Lesley had once mentioned he'd set up a business, so I suggested him.' Janine Penfold looked pleased with herself. 'I'd seen his website and I knew he was after money. I thought he'd leave Lesley alone if he had someone with more to offer.'

Liz interrupted. 'When did you put the notes on their cars, about meeting up at the house?'

Janine looked thoughtful. 'That was a couple of days later. I never expected him to burn the place down.'

'What happened once you put Candice in the car?' Liz Gould could have been discussing shopping. There was nothing judgmental in her tone. Even so, she must have found Janine Penfold repulsive.

'I drove over there not knowing how to get in, but the garage door was open so I parked in there. They had some meat in the freezer, which I pulled out and threw away later. I put the gardening gloves back on. It was a struggle, but I finally got her into it. All the time, she just stared back at me. It was quite strange, really. She weighed less than I thought.'

Kate was completely mystified. This woman had no qualms about murdering her daughter and moving the body into a freezer in a strange house. The only thing she found odd was her child's lack of body mass. It was dawning on Kate that Janine Penfold's lawyer would almost certainly plead insanity as their defence.

The interview room fell silent for a moment, everyone digesting this information.

Liz Gould broke the silence. 'What did you do after that?'

Janine looked at her nails again and smiled. 'I cleaned the freezer, of course, then hammered the lid so it would stay down. After that, I drove out, closed the garage door and went home. I put the gloves and spade back for Robert. Oh yes, and I cleaned Candy's car – twice – before I dumped it. It was filthy.'

That was why there was only one set of finger-prints inside and on the freezer – Mark Dobbie's – and why cleaning products were found on the seat of Candice's car.

Kate realised Dobbie had been telling the truth about one thing. He hadn't killed Candice, just set fire to the house with her body in it.

She had heard enough for one day. Outside police headquarters, she hailed a taxi and headed home.

41

Kate heard the knocking and had no idea what time it was. After falling asleep on the couch, she had staggered to her bed sometime before dawn. The room was dim and for a moment she felt disorientated.

The knocking grew louder.

Still in her clothes, she blinked at the alarm clock. The time was 3 pm. She had slept nearly thirteen hours straight.

'I'm coming,' she called, her voice husky from sleeping with her mouth open, which she did when she was overtired.

The knocking continued. This time, whoever it was decided to tap out an annoying tune.

She looked through the peephole and saw Oliver on her doorstep. He was out of hospital and looked well, despite his face being distorted by the wide-angle view.

He had something behind his back but she couldn't make out what. 'What are you doing here?'

'I want to thank you for saving my life.'

She pressed her head on the glass. 'Just a minute.' She found her keys and opened the door.

He swung a large bunch of deep purple irises around to his front and had a contrite look on his face.

Kate took the flowers but had no idea what to say.

'I know it hasn't been easy partnering me, but I need to explain what I've been up to.'

'Stop.' She stepped back. 'Thanks for the flowers but I was just doing my job. I think you'd better go. I don't think we should meet outside work.' Kate had no intention of being compromised by listening to his confession, or worse, being accused of corruption herself. Oliver had no right to place her in this situation.

'Hold on.' He put up both hands as if surrendering. 'I'm not who or what you think.'

'Yeah, I figured that. Look, I don't want to have anything to do with your scams. I want you to leave.' She slammed the door but his foot was wedged in it.

'Please hear me out. I need you to understand that I know the money in the drawer wasn't yours.'

'Because you put it there. You weren't looking for a pen, you were trying to plant evidence. You always carry a damn pen in your pocket. It even fell out right after you lied to me.'

'It wasn't like that. I'm sorry, but I had to know whether or not you could be trusted.'

Kate felt anger rise in her body. 'I don't get involved in anything crooked. Move your foot before I break it.'

'Fine.'

He backed away and she closed the door.

'But I'm not leaving,' he called out. 'There's something you need to see. And it isn't money.'

A bright yellow A4 envelope slid under the door. Kate stared at the unmarked stationery. Part of her wanted to destroy it, the other craved to see what was inside, to know once and for all if her partner was crooked, and if anyone else she knew was involved.

Kate bent down and opened the envelope. Inside was a report on corruption in homicide compiled by Detective Constable Oliver Parke, for the anti-corruption unit. Kate froze and re-read the title.

She stood up and opened the door to find Oliver sitting in a chair on her porch. He looked as though he had no intention of leaving. She ushered him in without speaking. As he stepped into the lounge room, she kicked his shin with all the strength she could muster and cursed when pain shot through her foot.

'Serves you right,' he said, clutching his leg, 'but I guess I probably deserved that.'

'You bastard! You lied and made me think you were rotten. Now you expect to waltz in here with flowers and be forgiven?' Her foot throbbed more than she cared to admit.

'If you're finished, I'll make you a coffee and we can discuss this like adults.' He glanced around at the newspapers and plates on the floor. 'You needn't have bothered tidying up before I came.'

Kate jabbed her foot at his leg again, but he was too quick and side-stepped her.

'What else did you lie about?' she asked. 'Let me guess. You're not married and don't have any children?'

'No, that part is mostly true. I've actually got two kids and another on the way. Lucy's taken them away on a holiday for a while, for their own protection. Threats from drug dealers have to be taken seriously. Unfortunately, that's a big down-side to my work sometimes. The other is that I don't make many friends once people find out what I do.'

Kate understood. She had never been kind about internal investigators. Despite the fact that they were doing honest police a favour by weeding out the bad ones, they were still perceived as the enemy. It couldn't have been an easy job. Kate cleared a space on the lounge and begrudgingly offered him a seat.

She returned from the kitchen with two opened beers. 'It's not organic, but obviously I didn't know you were coming.'

'Thanks,' he said. 'I really am sorry for invading your privacy. I think I understand what this means for you.'

He was right. It didn't look like much, but it was home and privacy was important, like the most comforting blanket in the cold. It occurred to Kate that this was the first time she had been alone in her home with a man since her abduction. So far, she felt OK. Her breathing and heart-rate were normal and she seemed in no danger of having a panic attack. Oliver crossed the room and bent down to look at some CDs in a pile on the floor.

'Powderfinger, John Butler Trio, Silverchair. They all fit, but what about the Michael Bublé? Didn't pick you as a fan of crooners.'

'Yeah, well, we're all full of little surprises.'

Kate grabbed the disc from his hands. It had been given to her as a Kris Kringle gift and the truth was, it had become one of her favourite albums. It was the type of music her mother had loved, apparently, and now Kate understood why. She had since bought albums by Frank Sinatra, Perry Como and Dean Martin, but preferred Bublé's voice.

She put the CD in the player and sat on the lounge, cross-legged, after collecting the envelope from the floor. She turned over the title page of the report as Oliver spoke.

'This is why I moved to homicide,' he explained. 'There's a leak in the drug squad and someone in your unit is accessing that information via the intranet. News about drug raids or arrests is passed on so that when the drug squad gets there, the house is clean or there's no target in sight. Dobbie's dealer was one of my informants.'

That was why the dealer had accused Oliver of betraying him, she realised.

Further into the report there were two photographs, one of Rench, the other of Fiskars.

'They've complained to the Police Association about being part of an internal investigation. Seems your colleagues think they're being investigated for sexual harassment of female staff, which in my opinion they should be. Anyhow, the Association advised them to take some time off. Both of them now have doctors' certificates citing the need for stress-leave, so they're on full pay. They're milking the system, but they aren't the focus of the investigation.'

'It's someone else?' Suddenly, Russo came to mind. She hoped it was anyone but the inspector.

'Check the financial statements for Laurie Sheehan.'

Glancing down the numbers, nothing seemed out of place. The salary went into his account fortnightly and small amounts were regularly withdrawn. 'I don't get it. It could be any one of our accounts.'

'Exactly, except that Sheehan has renovated four homes over the last three years. Each one has made a profit at resale of up to $200,000.'

She had to admit that it was a decent amount of money, but it wasn't necessarily expensive to renovate a house. There were plenty of television programs that showed how a quick and superficial makeover could raise a property's value by up to $50,000. Structural improvements would surely increase the value by even more than that?

'So he buys dumps and does them up himself,' Kate said finally. 'Real estate prices have rocketed in that time. It makes sense to me.'

Oliver shook his head. 'Renovating isn't cheap. A bathroom costs thousands just for the materials, and have you ever seen him with paint on his hands or plaster under his nails?'

Kate had to admit that Laurie had never complained of a sore back, knees, arms or any other body part from a weekend of hard labour.

'There are no purchases from hardware shops, tiling places or bathroom suppliers on his credit cards, either.'

Kate checked the accounts again. 'Maybe he pays cash.'

Oliver took a swig of beer. 'He doesn't pay at all. In exchange for tip-offs, guys like Dobbie's supplier send their mates around to do the renovations in lieu of payment. It's a tidy little addition to your superannuation if you make a profit on each house.'

'And you can prove it?' Kate still found it difficult to believe that quiet, polite Laurie, the father-figure of the office, was corrupt.

'We've had his phones tapped for a while and he's clever. Instead of asking for payments, he complains about the cost of things. Just recently he was talking to a dealer's brother and whinged about the cost of private school education for his grandkids. Within a week they were both enrolled in an exclusive school with fees of $50,000 a year. There's been a scholarship set up for these kids, paid by multiple small anonymous donations. Sheehan and the parents aren't paying a cent.'

Kate was stunned by the audacity of it. She wondered how Oliver had managed to track the money trail. That had to be why he was always in the office so early and stayed so late at night. The homicide cases were just a sideline for him. Despite Kate's anger about his deceit, she acknowledged that Oliver made a very good investigator. She sipped her beer.

'This probably sounds crazy, but I actually feel sorry for the old bloke. He's been in the service all his working life,' she said.

'That's hardly an excuse for lying and cheating.'

'Yeah, well, that's pretty rich coming from you.' Kate bit her lip, regretting the comment. Her partner didn't seem comfortable with having to be dishonest, and she understood that when you're dealing with criminal behaviour, sometimes you have to bend rules.

She suddenly saw Oliver in another light. He was not only a logical thinker, he was calculating too. By setting himself up as a father with a large family, he had an instant bond with Liz Gould because he could discuss any aspect of parenting with her. It also gave him a good opening to talk to Laurie Sheehan about the cost of a good education. What parent didn't worry about where to send their kids to school? And if there was a tribe of them, advice about fees became even more important. She thought of Sheehan happily volunteering information to Oliver, oblivious to the harm he was doing himself. And

Oliver could even whinge to Fiskars and Rench about being under the thumb. They would have listened willingly and contributed their own brand of advice, making their misogynist views plain. Oliver had managed to elicit personal information from just about everyone in the department.

'Don't feel sorry for Sheehan,' he said. 'When rumours started that the unit was under investigation, he set you up to take the blame.'

Kate's fingers tightened around her drink.

'A few weeks ago we installed closed circuit cameras in the office. We have footage of him putting that money in your drawer. And he used your computer to access the drug squad info as well. If it weren't for the cameras, you would have had a lot of explaining to do.'

Kate tried to absorb the seriousness of what she had just been told. 'Sorry I kicked you,' she managed.

'No hard feelings. Now, we're still officially partners until tomorrow afternoon and we have one more job to do. Russo wants us to go and see Robert Penfold.'

Kate checked her mobile phone, which had fallen down the side of the lounge. The battery was flat.

'Russo tried to call you with the DNA results,' Oliver explained, 'but your home number was disconnected and your mobile didn't answer. I volunteered to come into the lion's den.'

She had forgotten that she changed her phone number after the abduction. It suited her that no one at work knew it. Even so, she had fallen asleep without even thinking about recharging the mobile battery.

'You were stalling for time when you told Janine Penfold about Dobbie or one of his mates being the baby's father. So is Robert the real father?'

'No. And thanks to Dobbie rolling over, we know who it is. The guy was a mate of his and Spender's who worked as a barman at the resorts they went to. That's why they chose those places to holiday, so they had someone on the inside spiking the girls' drinks. In between jobs, he'd come down and stay with Dobbie. He was with them the night they raped Candice Penfold, although Dobbie swears blind it was Spender and Brown who raped her.'

'What's his name?'

'Calls himself Elvis, but his real name's Aaron Brown. He was on the DNA database because of a previous assault conviction.'

The name was familiar. He had been on the list of people Brett Spender had emailed with his epiphany about karma, just before his death.

'Can you tie him to the Spender murder?'

'That's the good thing. His fingerprint matches the whopping great print they found on the melted smoke detector. Like Dobbie, he's got more brawn than brains and assumed the fire would destroy his fingerprints. He's pleading guilty to try to cut a deal with the prosecutor. Oh, and the hair sample you collected from Candice's brush has been analysed. Hair grows at about a centimetre a month so the lab tested it in sections. The section from around ten months ago contained GHB, the date-rape drug. With Dobbie's evidence, Brown is pleading guilty to raping Candy to get a shorter sentence.'

The cold beer warmed Kate's veins, along with the knowledge that Spender's killer and another of Candy's rapists would be brought to justice.

'Is that what we need to go and tell Robert and Lesley?'

Oliver nodded. 'I thought you might also want to see the little boy. I hear you got quite fond of him. I'll wait outside while you shower and change, if you like.'

Kate felt her cheeks burn. Hospital staff gossiped more than police. At least Robert and Lesley would have closure, if nothing else. She wondered how they had taken the revelation that Janine had killed Candice. And as Oliver had guessed, she was keen to see the little boy again, just to make sure he was being well cared for.

'What's going to happen to Janine Penfold?'

'She's confessed and she's refused a psych assessment so she'll be sentenced in the next few weeks. Don't think she could cope with admitting she'd been wrong about Candy and Robert, and that she'd killed her daughter for nothing, so she's sticking to her story about Candy being a seductress. Now, go get ready. We've got work to do.'

The shower was hot and cleansing and the world felt as right as it could be. When she was dressed and ready to go, Oliver greeted her like a gentleman, opening the car door for her. It was a shame he was leaving homicide, she thought. They made a pretty good team.

42

A removalist truck was parked outside the Penfold house when Oliver and Kate arrived. They entered by the open front door and were greeted by Lesley, who resembled her mother more than ever. It must have been the upswept hairstyle, Kate decided.

'Don't worry about taking off your shoes,' Lesley said, with the air of a woman in charge. 'And be careful with that dresser,' she called to two men on the landing upstairs, 'it's an antique.'

'Are you moving out?' Kate asked.

'No, just making some changes. A lot of this is going into storage and we'll modernise the place a little, get some new furniture, repaint, get rid of the white carpets. They're so impractical.'

This did not seem like the behaviour of a grieving woman.

Oliver looked concerned. 'Are you all right?'

'I wouldn't say that. It's going to take a lot of time to recover after everything that's happened,' she answered softly.

Kate reached out for Lesley's arm. 'We're sorry about what happened with Candice and your mother. You must have been deeply shocked when you found out.'

'I still can't quite believe it. But then, Mum was always hard on Candy. She made it clear she thought Candy spent too much time with Robert.'

Lesley led the way into the kitchen. In a pram lay the little boy, sound asleep. Kate wandered over and had a look at him, careful not to disturb him.

'We've called him Toby.' Lesley paused and stared at the tiny boy with a look of pride. 'He's got Candy's chin and nose, you know.'

Kate stepped quietly away from the pram. 'How's your father doing?'

'He'll be better once the results of the paternal DNA come through.'

'That's why we're here,' Oliver began. 'A friend of Mark Dobbie's, a man called Aaron Brown, has confessed to having non-consensual sex with your sister after drugging her. The results of DNA testing prove he's Toby's father.'

Lesley clasped her hands, her face flooded with relief. The garage door hummed and moments later Robert Penfold emerged from the side door.

Lesley ran towards him and threw herself into his arms.

'The detectives know who raped Candy, the mongrel's confessed. They know he's Toby's father. That means her reputation and yours are still intact.'

Robert glanced at the detectives and tried to break Lesley's hold but she reached up and kissed him firmly on the lips before breaking contact.

'We can get on with our life without any shadows hanging over us,' she explained.

'Maybe now isn't the right time to be discussing that,' Robert said, looking flushed and awkward.

Kate tried to fathom what had just happened. Robert Penfold had been suspected by his wife of having a sexual relationship with one stepdaughter, Candy, but now it appeared he had been having a relationship with his other stepdaughter.

'I've initiated divorce proceedings,' he explained hesitantly. 'Lesley and I only realised how close we were when she moved to New York. It's something neither one of us planned or could control. If you've said all you had to say, we thank you and ask that you leave us in privacy.'

Legally, if Robert Penfold divorced his wife there was nothing to prevent him from marrying Lesley. He had never formally adopted her. Oliver could not hide the just-eaten-grapefruit look on his face.

Lesley stood with her arms around Robert, looking almost defiant.

Kate and Oliver said their goodbyes and left. Neither was able to speak during the car trip home. They had done their jobs and caught both Candice's and Brett Spender's killers. The murders even followed a disturbing kind of logic. Brett Spender was killed so he would remain silent about the drug-rapes, and Janine Penfold had killed her daughter in a rage, suspecting her husband had fathered the little boy. Mark Dobbie's actions seemed tame by comparison.

Justice had technically been done, but nothing could justify the strangeness they had just witnessed.

Kate remembered the way the baby had gripped her finger and she tried to imagine what sort of life he had ahead of him. More than anything, she hoped that he would not be a victim. Like her, she hoped the little boy would continue to be a survivor.

KATHRYN FOX

MALICIOUS INTENT

At a crime scene, blink and you'll miss the truth. Move over Kay Scarpetta – a new forensic pathologist is on the case . . .

When Dr Anya Crichton is asked to look into the seemingly innocent suicide of a teenager, she notices similarities between the girl's death and several other cases she is working on with her friend and colleague, Detective Sergeant Kate Farrer.

All the victims went missing for a period of time, only to be found dead of apparent suicide in most unusual circumstances.

As Anya delves deeper, the pathological findings point to the frightening possibility that the deaths are not only linked, but part of a sinister plot. Nothing can prepare her for the terrifying truth . . .

> '*Malicious Intent* will keep you gripped from start to finish . . . What a compelling new talent!'
> Jeffery Deaver

HODDER

KATHRYN FOX

WITHOUT CONSENT

All of the victims heard the rapist utter the words 'If you can't be hurt, you can't be loved'. They all have a blade-shaped bruise on their chests. And each has been told they will be killed if they go to the police.

Forensic physician Dr Anya Crichton is on the trail of a violent serial rapist. When the attacks start happening more frequently, suspicion immediately falls upon Geoffrey Willard, recently released from twenty years in prison for the brutal rape and murder of a fourteen-year-old girl.

Unravelling the forensic evidence, however, Anya is not so sure they have the right man. And if they don't, then the attacker is still out there.

'Kathryn Fox has created a forensic physician
who readers of Patricia Cornwell will adore'
James Patterson

HODDER